HEADING
for
HOME

HEADING *for* HOME

GREG MCLAUGHLIN

NEW YORK LOS ANGELES

This is a work of fiction. Names, characters, places, and incidents are either products of the author's imagination or, if real, are used fictitiously.

Copyright 2023 by Winding Road Stories

All rights reserved, including the right of reproduction in whole or in part in any form. If you would like permission to use any material from this book other than review purposes, please ask via contact@windingroadstories.com. Thank you for respecting the rights and intellectual property of authors and creatives.

Jacket design by Rejenne Pavon
Jacket Copyright 2023 by Winding Road Stories
Interior book design by A Raven Design
ISBN#: 978-1-960724-06-9 (pbk)
ISBN#: 978-1-960724-07-6 (ebook)

Published by Winding Road Stories
www.windingroadstories.com

Dedicated To my two boys, Casey and Shane McLaughlin, the ballplayers of the family.

And, to my late father, Greg McLaughlin Sr., the best coach, guide, and mentor a boy could ever have had.

1

THE LETTER

Colton Gibson couldn't win.

The University lawyers had statements from players and parents. They had Facebook, Twitter, and Instagram pictures. They had the NCAA and the Patriot League. They had affidavits from a half-dozen coaches on the staff, all looking to cover their tracks.

It didn't help that the team suffered another losing season and the Athletic Department had already decided they needed turnover in the coaching staff. Colt knew the inevitable. He couldn't fight it. He didn't even try.

The notification of his dismissal sat on his dashboard. The logo at the top of the paper, an imposing, brown letter "L," marred the page like a scarlet letter. L for "Loser." L for "Lost." L for "Looking for a Job." The memo flapped in the breeze from the air conditioning vent, then blew off the ledge. Colt watched it flitter past the passenger seat and wedge itself somewhere into a crevice in the spacious back seat of his pick-up truck.

He never felt like a cheater. He hadn't done anything that any other assistant coach across the country hadn't done through the regular course of recruiting. He acted on the direction of the Head Coach. He, himself, had been recruited in the exact same way. But of course, his recruitment had been different because of the identity of the Head Coach and because the team had won the Patriot League three of the previous five seasons.

Colt pondered how a winning coach could get away with the worst infractions. But then, as soon as the team faltered, the tiniest of indiscretions could blossom into unforgivable offenses.

He had been jobless for the past three months, living in his off-campus apartment with nothing to do and no prospects to coach anywhere else. He sent letters to athletic directors and coaches he had opposed through the years. He contacted former players. He even checked job boards for positions at local community colleges and high schools. His severance could get him through another half year or so. But he needed a job. And the one he finally accepted bore no resemblance to what he wanted to do with his life.

On a sunny Friday morning, rather than getting up for early workouts followed by batting practice and his afternoon coaches' meetings, he packed his belongings neatly into the flatbed of his pick-up truck and left the college campus he had called home for the past eight years.

The morning sun flickered like a strobe through the trees, pelting him with short intense blasts of piercing light. The exits along Route 78 grew farther apart and gave way to a winding road through the wooded hills and ridges of central Pennsylvania.

Eight years earlier, he had arrived at Lehigh University as a fresh-faced red-shirt freshman with a long resume of high school accomplishments. He made the varsity baseball team as a sophomore. And after three long years of hard work and dedication, he progressed to second team all-Patriot League—earning the honor twice, once during each of his two senior years.

His clothes fit into two jumbo suitcases, both perched and belted into the condensed back seats of the truck. Out of the corner of his rear-view mirror, they looked like broad-shouldered hitchhikers, silently observing the scenery ahead. The passenger seat beside him contained three paper bags of groceries that he raided from his now former roommate's refrigerator. A six pack of beer sat on the passenger-side floor. And next to the cans of Budweiser, protruding from a black duffel bag full of socks and underwear, his running shoes, topsiders, work boots, and flip flops gave the illusion of an eight-legged passenger stowed away beneath the glove compartment.

His laptop bag, Xbox, and television lay taped in boxes in the back of the flatbed. Beyond the pile of boxes, his bag of baseball gear, brown with a giant letter "L" stared back at him. A glove and several wooden bats bounced with the potholes in the road.

Most distinctively, like the fin of a shark, his five-foot-tall L-screen extended above the roof of the cab, tied down thoroughly to all four corners of the flatbed with strong nylon rope.

He tucked his waves of dirty blond hair under his cap, scratched his three-day old stubble, and sipped his coffee while crunching a bite of a granola bar.

The embankments of the highway temporarily blotted the sun as he took the exit for Springtown, Pennsylvania. He had a few months ahead of him to acclimate to the new residence and then he would start his new job.

Teaching and coaching. If you can do one, you can do the other.

He never expected to put his Physical Education major or teaching certificate to use. He always figured he'd play or coach as a career. He might have had a chance to make a single-A club or walk on to an independent league team. But scouts saw him as a medium-speed lefty with too little power for first base and limited differentiation as an outfielder.

"Can you pitch?" they all asked him, dropping their eyes and twisting their faces at his negative answer.

As Colt wound along Main Street in Springtown—practically the only thoroughfare slicing through the town—his phone rang. The jarring staccato tones broke the trance-like silence and startled him. The smiling face of a middle-aged man in a brown baseball cap popped up on his phone. Coach. Butch. Dad.

Colt paused and took the phone into his hand. His thumb twitched and then recoiled. He flipped the device back into its perch on the dashboard and gazed out the windshield at the passing elm and sycamore trees.

"I don't work for you anymore," he muttered to himself.

The center of Springtown consisted of a railroad crossing at an intersection with a two-pump gas station and a twenty-square-foot post office. A block up from the intersection stood a fire station, a barbershop, a country store, and a town green with a white picket fence surrounding an equally white gazebo. The American flag loomed over a plaque affixed to a large stone next to the gazebo.

Across the green, Colt spied a classic run-down diner pressed up against the train tracks. It occupied an old wooden building that looked like it must have served as the central train station in town during the Second World War.

As he crossed the tracks and passed through the hamlet, he saw the baseball field, set back behind a row of historic houses. It looked well maintained with lush grass and crisp new dirt. A man in his fifties stood next to first base with a long rake and tended to the infield. As Colt's pick-up passed by, the man glanced up from the dirt and observed the silver metal and black netting of his L-screen as it moved out of view.

Colt's phone chirped, informing him that he would reach his destination in one mile. He looked around—seconds after passing the last house—and saw only the green of the trees to his left and the exposed rock of a carved-out ledge to his right.

He almost missed the turn for 166 Main Street. A giant bayberry bush obscured the entrance to the dirt and gravel driveway and hid the mailbox. The sound of pebbles crunched beneath the undercarriage of the truck. Puffs of dust kicked up behind the lift gate as he entered the property where he would live for the next season until he could get back on his feet.

Beyond a row of overgrown cedars, the yard opened to a flat multi-acre patch of yellowish grass. A gray, weathered, two-story farmhouse, that may have once been lily white, squatted at the front edge of the vast property. The meager structure's rickety front porch and dark shutters sagged. Chips of paint clung to the wood like the last leaves of the late autumn. Behind the house, thick woods bordered the wide back yard with a giant glacier-formed hill bordering the far end.

He'd seen a picture of the home in the Lehigh off-campus housing directory. But compared to this, it looked much nicer. In the photo, which Colt quickly determined to be at least twenty years old, the roof appeared brand new, the porch didn't sag, the paint didn't chip and flake, and the gutters were all properly affixed. He looked for the guest house but could only see a detached two-story garage to the right edge of the property, diagonally across the gravel driveway from the main house. He couldn't tell if the red wooden structure was meant to house a car or store grain.

He peered past the oversize barn-like garage, looking for another, nicer, more habitable building. But he quickly realized that the top floor of the garage would likely be the room he had agreed to rent.

As Colt navigated his pickup truck next to the house, he noticed a small boy in the yard by the broad side of the garage. He had a baseball glove and threw a tennis ball against the windowless wall. The ball bounced two or three times. The boy successfully scooped the ball about a third of the time and repeated the drill in total focus, oblivious to the strange man who had just parked in his driveway.

Nice form. Lefty like me.

His instinct as a baseball coach kicked in, and he ran through a mental checklist of observations.

Coordinated. Throws from his ear. Not much arm strength yet. Good potential.

A woman, about his age, appeared at the top step of the porch. She wore a denim mini-skirt and big, fluffy sweater—out of place for the temperate early-April weather. Her medium length brown hair, slightly wavy, with a hint of chestnut framed her face, complimenting her large brown eyes and slender nose. Colt noticed her rubbing the back of her neck as if she had just finished her housework for the day. She smiled tentatively at him and darted her eyes to the boy in the yard as if taking inventory.

Wow. She hardly looks like the old lady I expected.

He exited the truck and removed his cap. As soon as he did, he realized that his hair probably looked terrible, all matted and sweaty. He promptly returned it to his head.

"Gertrude?" he asked, as the woman approached slowly.

"Gertrude was my aunt," she replied. "She passed away a year ago."

Colt instinctively removed and held his hat over his heart. With a slow head nod, he offered condolences. The woman smiled in appreciation. She locked eyes with him, briefly, before shooting another furtive glance to the back yard toward the young boy.

"He's got a good arm for what, like a six-year-old kid," Colt said to her before even getting her name.

"He's eight," she replied flatly.

"Oh. Sorry."

"You're Colt?" she asked, extending her hand. "I'm Ellie Shaw, Gertrude's niece. That's my son, Braden."

Colt noticed Ellie looking at his hat and replaced it on his head before tucking a few errant strands of his hair under the ridge of the brim.

"Come say hello to Mr. Gibson," she called to the boy. "He's going to be our new tenant."

"What's a tenant?" Braden asked once he reached the top of the driveway.

"He's going to rent the apartment above the garage," Ellie clarified.

Braden briefly raised his hand to gesture 'Hello' before returning to his exercise.

"A ballplayer?" Colt asked.

"He loves baseball," she replied taking notice of the L-screen in the back of his truck. "You must be a ballplayer too?"

"I played at Lehigh," Colt replied. He withheld that he had also coached for three seasons after graduating.

"I'm sorry," Ellie's eyes flared. "You won't be able to live here."

"Why not?" Colt asked, shocked at her apparent spot rejection of him. "I thought the campus housing department contacted you."

"Oh, they did," Ellie replied.

"Then what happened?" Colt asked. "Did something fall through with the lease or the security deposit?"

"No, that's all good," Ellie said. "Everything cleared fine. I appreciate the quick Venmo payment. It's not that. I just don't think this'll work out."

"Why not?" Colt asked. "What did I do? Was it something I said?"

"I just think we're going to have too big of a problem getting along." Ellie persisted.

"What problem?"

Ellie didn't respond, other than a shrug of her shoulders.

"Am I missing something here?" Colt continued. "Do you just not like me for some reason?"

"I just don't see this working out."

"Seriously?"

"Nope," she said, with almost a laugh. "No chance."

"What? Why not? What'd I do?" Colt sputtered. "Did I say something or do something wrong?"

Ellie smiled at Colt. *Was she holding back laughter?* He nervously removed his cap, ran his hand through his hair and returned the hat atop his head.

"Is it because I thought your kid was six?"

"It's not that," Ellie said with a shake of her head.

"Honest mistake," Colt stammered. "I'm really not a... I'm a decent... I had three glowing references; one from my history professor, one from the athletic director, and one from the Dean of Student Affairs at Lehigh."

"That's just it," she said, stepping toward Braden and then turning back to grin at Colt. "I went to Lafayette."

As NIGHT FELL, the pervasive din of crickets and cicadas filled the air. The forty-foot trees that lined Ellie's yard created a claustrophobic cocoon around her ten-room farmhouse. She folded Braden's laundry while watching a show about B-list celebrities vying to survive in an exotic jungle. After folding a few items, she moved to the kitchen to put away the dishes while glancing out the window over the sink. Then she folded a few more clothes and watched a minute or two of her show before returning to the kitchen to scrub the frying pan.

Each time she entered the kitchen, she strained to see if the light in the upstairs apartment was still on. She had inherited the home outright from her aunt a year earlier. And while she had no mortgage to pay, she still had a hefty debt from the estate taxes that she owed. The guest apartment provided a steady source of income to defray her costs of living, cover taxes, and pay down her personal debt. But it sat empty for the past six months. The elderly man who had rented from her aunt since the late nineties finally moved out to take residence at a retirement home in Hellertown. His absence left her $750 short of her previous monthly cash flow.

She pushed her financial concerns out of her mind. She could keep herself up all night worrying about money, but tonight, her precarious economics did not cause her edginess. She worried about the strange man whom she had allowed onto her property.

She climbed her creaky cedar stairs to check on Braden. Though his room didn't face the garage apartment, she pulled the window shade up, surveyed the property below, and then slid it back down, flush with the windowsill.

Her phone rang like a shriek in the night. She bolted down the stairs making remarkably little noise and grabbed the phone from its cradle.

"Hey, Ellie," said the cheerful voice on the other line. "How's the new tenant? Is he cute?"

"Jeez, Andrea." Ellie caught her breath, glancing out the kitchen window again. "You scared the crap out of me. I was up in Braden's room tucking him in."

"He's a graduate, so he's probably a little more mature than an undergrad. Does he have a girlfriend? Is he a party animal? What's the deal? Spill."

"I don't know." Ellie pondered answers to Andrea's questions that hadn't crossed her mind until just then. "He seems alright. He paid me first, last, and security. Cash. That's a good sign."

"Is he the snooty, smart type? A rich Ivy brat? Nerdy? Fit? Is he even into women?"

"I don't know. I barely looked at him. He's renting an apartment from me. He's just kind of normal." Ellie paused with a sigh of apprehension. "He's a baseball player."

"Ooh, a trim, sexy ballplayer," Andrea cooed.

"I guess you'd say he's a decent enough looking guy," she admitted slowly, not to give her friend—or herself—too much to get excited about. "Not nerdy. He's definitely, uh, fit."

"Must be in good shape?"

"Sure," Ellie peered out the kitchen window again. "You could say that. He's tall and sort of muscular. He needs a haircut."

Ellie's mind transitioned from viewing Colt as a handsome renter, to a complete stranger, about whom she knew little other than what university he attended.

"Right now, I'm just wishing I hadn't contacted the university," she lamented. "I knew I should've found another senior citizen. This guy could be an axe murderer for all I know."

"I'm sure he's fine." Andrea sobered her tone. "He's a college graduate. He had references. There's no reason to be worried. You want me to come over tonight after my shift at the diner? I could stay over. I'm sure Ed's already asleep in front of the TV."

"No," Ellie replied. "I'll be fine. I need the money and the people I spoke to from the University Housing Office all said he was a great guy."

Andrea teetered, paused, and then blurted, "Seriously, Ell. Is he hot or what?"

At that, a shadow moved across the window above the garage. And then the room went dark. Ellie stared at the blackness. A blue imprint in the back of her eyelid flashed just beyond her peripheral vision—the only reminder of the yellow glow that had just disappeared.

"He's probably just some loser Lehigh frat boy," Ellie replied after a short delay. "I bet he'll be stumbling across my driveway at all hours of the night, parading bimbos in and out."

"I guess—"

"Oh my God." Ellie cut off Andrea, her nerves frayed. Her face reddened like a sudden hot flash. "What's wrong with me? I have a little boy upstairs that I'm supposed to protect. And I just let some strange, attractive guy move into my house—just because I need the rent? Where are my priorities?"

"I'll cut out early..." said Andrea. "... and come right over."

2

THE KITTEN AND THE CHICKEN

The smacking sound was not loud. But it definitely vibrated the walls of his apartment. Colt heard it. It woke him up less from the volume of the noise, and more from the rhythmic persistence of it.

Thwack... Thwack... Thwack...

He pulled the covers over his head and tried to drown it out. But like the drip of a leaky faucet, the pattern drummed into his head.

Thwack... Thwack... Thwack...

Colt threw on a pair of sweatpants. He grabbed a t-shirt from one of the bags that he hadn't yet unpacked and wandered across the unfamiliar bedroom to find his sneakers.

Thwack... Thwack... Thwack...

His stubble had reached four days, and his last shower had taken place in his old apartment, probably on Thursday. Three days of grease clung to his hair, which he stuffed under his cap. The rickety pine staircase buckled and croaked as he headed downstairs but held his weight. He rounded the side of the garage into the morning sun.

Ellie sat at a round wooden table in the cement patio area outside her back door. She wore dark shades with her hair in a ponytail threaded through the back of a pink baseball cap. Light blue and pink flowers dotted her pajama bottoms. Her oversized grey "Lafayette" sweatshirt hid her figure. The pastel colors of her thin pajama bottoms, combined with the pale glow of the morning sunlight, gave her a softer look than Colt recalled from his first feisty yet playful meeting with her the previous day.

She and a tall, medium-build blond woman he assumed to be their age sipped tea and ate doughnuts in the morning sun.

Ellie's sunglasses shielded her brown eyes from him, but she raised her chin and smiled before waving him over. The woman next to her removed her shades and gawked as he ambled their way. Colt put his hand up to wave 'Hi.'

"Good morning," Ellie said. "How was the first night in the apartment?"

"Good, good." Colt repeated the word for lack of any others that came to mind.

"This is my friend, Andrea," Ellie continued.

"Very nice to meet you," said Andrea with her hand extended. "Welcome to Springtown."

Colt awkwardly shook Andrea's hand.

Thwack... Thwack... Thwack...

He registered the sound as Braden's baseball practice drill. The boy stood about twenty feet from the side of the garage. He threw his tennis ball against the wood siding and attempted to field it as it bounced back to him.

"What do you do, Colt?" Andrea asked.

"Teacher," he replied, half watching Braden throw the ball. "I start in September. But I'll be subbing for the next few months until school gets out."

"Springtown Elementary?" Andrea asked. "Ellie and I both went there."

"Were you the only two graduates?" Colt asked with a mischievous grin.

"Practically," Andrea laughed and brushed her hair away from her ears. "My son, Ronnie, and Ellie's Braden are both there now."

"Would you like a muffin?" Ellie asked. "How about some orange juice, or coffee."

"I'm good," Colt replied before turning and walking toward Braden.

Out of the corner of his eye, Colt noticed Andrea shake her head at her friend. With a quick glance over his shoulder, he thought he saw Ellie roll her eyes. Andrea scrunched her lower lip over her upper as if to say, 'Not bad!'

Colt couldn't make out their conversation as he walked away from them toward Braden. But he did catch the phrases, "party-boy" and "frat-brother" as the two women chatted on the patio.

"Hey Colt," Ellie called as he made his way across the lawn. "You were in a fraternity at Lehigh, weren't you?"

"Sure was," he grinned. "TKE all the way."

Braden didn't notice Colt approach him. The young boy threw the ball accurately. It hit the wall and bounced three times. He guided it into the glove on his right hand using his free left hand to secure it. He then took the ball out of his glove with his left hand, cocked it back, stepped and heaved it off target by accident.

"Looking good, big guy," Colt said from enough of a distance to avoid seeming too eager to approach him. He looked back at Ellie. She gave him a smile of approval.

"You need to get your arm back when you throw," Colt addressed Braden.

Braden looked at him blankly. Then he threw the ball at the garage the exact same way. Colt looked back at Ellie again. This time she nodded to him to take a few more steps toward her son. He walked close enough to nearly reach Braden and squatted down to his level.

"Can I see the ball?" he asked.

Braden held it up reluctantly but did not offer it to Colt.

"You have a great arm," Colt started. "But I bet you could throw it even faster if you made one little change."

Braden looked at him, bewildered.

"I can throw forty," he said. "Cordele can throw forty-five. And Mikey Wiltshire throws fifty."

"Fifty?" Colt asked. "Miles an hour? How old is this kid?"

"He's nine."

"Then I'm sure he doesn't throw fifty."

"Yes, he does," Braden insisted. "He does. He throws fifty."

"I see," Colt changed the subject. "Well, I bet you'd like to throw as fast—or even faster—as Mikey Wiltshire, wouldn't you?"

Braden's face lit up. He handed Colt the tennis ball. The boy's enthusiasm reminded him of the many similar mornings in his own childhood backyard with his father. But all that was back at the start of his coaching career; back when he was simply 'Dad' and not the legendary Lehigh institution, 'Coach Butch.'

Ellie and Andrea continued to small talk. Colt could feel Ellie's many glances his way like a recurring blast of sunlight against the back of his neck.

"You want to get your arm back more," Colt guided Braden. He made an L with his arm extending from the top of his shoulder. "If you short-arm the ball by throwing it from your ear, you lose velocity."

Braden held his arm in the position that Colt demonstrated. Just before throwing the ball, his arm angle migrated back to his short-arm technique, and the ball bounced in the grass twice before reaching the wall.

As Colt watched Braden retrieve the ball, he thought of another way to convey his point.

"You ever see a muscle man flex his biceps and chest?" Colt asked then chuckled when Braden gave him a dubious look. "Show me how a body builder makes his muscles."

Braden arched his two arms below his chin and growled.

"I like the growl," said Colt. "But show me how a really strong guy flexes his muscles on either side of his head like this."

Colt extended both arms straight out like a T and then curled his two forearms upward to form what looked like football goal posts with his biceps extended straight out from his shoulder and his forearms pointing to the sky. Braden imitated him but curled his two fists almost into his ears.

Colt moved Braden's two hands outward and then growled as Braden had. Braden growled with him and the two spent the next minute and a half flexing and growling.

"Mama, watch," Braden called to Ellie.

"I see, baby."

Ellie smirked at the sight of Braden and Colt, as they growled and flexed their muscles together. She shook her head and rolled her eyes in what he hoped was mock disapproval. Her reaction injected Colt with an unusual twinge of self-consciousness. *Did she find his impromptu coaching approach too silly or goofy?*

The morning light highlighted the shine of her hair and brightened the brown of her irises. Her wide smile gave away the playfulness of her feigned eyeroll. As she stifled a giggle with the back of her hand, his embarrassment melted away.

Braden stopped flexing and growling. Colt picked up the ball and handed it to his pupil.

"Now, stand sideways to the garage."

Braden complied.

"Bring your arm up and out like the letter L and pretend you're a strong man making that same flexing move."

"Can I growl?" Braden asked.

"Absolutely."

Braden made a high-pitched guttural sound—more like 'Hyah' than a growl. He threw the ball directly into the grass about five feet away. It hopped high in the air and hit the wall on the first bounce. It was a terrible throw, from what Colt saw of his earlier attempts, his worst of the morning.

"That was much better," Colt said. "Did you see how much power you had in that throw?"

"But that was bad."

"That's because you held the ball too tight," Colt observed. The image of a muscle man must've misled Braden into tensing his grip. "This time no growling."

Braden again threw at the correct arm angle. The throw moved through the air a little better, but still landed off-target.

"Now, I want you to move your arm the exact same way," Colt instructed him. "But I want you to hold the ball really gently. Pretend it's an egg. And instead of growling or just being quiet while you throw, I want you to say '*Meow*' like a kitten."

Braden giggled.

"Kittens don't have eggs." He laughed. "Chickens do."

"Right," Colt said, crinkling his brow and rubbing the back of his neck. "Well, maybe the kitten is having a catch with the chicken. You be the kitten and I'll be the chicken."

Colt squatted by the side of the garage like a catcher. "Go ahead, Kitten, grip that egg softly. You don't want to crack it. Get your arm back like the muscle man. But make sure you're gentle like a kitten and say '*Meow*' as you throw the ball to me. I'm a chicken, remember. *Begawk*."

Braden laughed. He cocked his arm back and quietly meowed as he stepped and hurled the tennis ball.

Thwack. It landed right in Colt's outstretched hands. Braden's eyes widened, and his mouth flew open.

"That was awesome," he exclaimed as Colt stood and high-fived the boy's small hand.

"You got yourself an ace here," Colt called back to Ellie who nodded politely and smiled at him.

Braden threw a few more strong, accurate pitches to Colt, following his instructions each time.

"Very coachable," Colt called back to Ellie again.

The sun rose above the tree line. Ellie looked at her watch and told Braden to get into the house to change for his first day of practice. Braden protested that he wanted to field more grounders, and Ellie gave him five more minutes to work with Colt.

Andrea collected her purse and duffel bag and said goodbye to Ellie and Braden.

"Very nice to meet you," she called out to Colt with a noticeable sideways glance at Ellie.

Ellie cleared the table and carried the dirty plates into the kitchen. Colt chatted with Braden about his favorite baseball team and players. As Ellie passed the kitchen window, he caught her casting a quick, furtive glance his way, before disappearing beyond the window frame.

Braden practiced what Colt showed him. His throwing steadily improved.

"You know you should practice catching flies too," Colt said, finally interrupting the boy's rhythm.

"My mom taught me that I should throw the ball on the ground right in front of the garage wall and try to get it to bounce up in the air."

"Your mom's very smart," he said, briefly meeting her eyes as she returned from the kitchen and stood, watching them, across the expanse of her sizeable back yard.

Braden tried to execute what his mother had suggested, but the ball did not bounce well enough to produce a catchable fly ball.

"Let's try a different way," Colt suggested.

Without warning, he suddenly heaved the ball as high as he could. It soared eighty feet in a high arcing motion. Braden put his hand to his forehead to shield the sun and trace the little green orb through the air. The plummeting ball banked off the slanted roof of the garage. And as it bounced into the air and fell toward the ground, Colt moved quickly to catch it. He held it up for Braden to see.

"Whoa," he purred. "D'you see that mommy?"

"Yes, very impressive," Ellie said, a pair of shades obscuring her gaze. "Time to go, baby."

"Now?"

"Now." Ellie raised her voice just enough to prompt the boy to take her seriously.

On Ellie's command, Braden ran into the house. His hat flew off his head about a third of the way across the lawn. His glove dropped out of his hands as he leapt across the patio into the kitchen. Ellie casually picked up after her son.

"Today's Opening day for your town league?" Colt asked.

At mention of the Springtown baseball program, Ellie's body tensed. Her face tightened and her jaw clenched.

"Evaluation day," she replied, with what Colt thought sounded like a hint of sarcasm. "They line them up like cattle, hit balls at them, rate them, and brand them."

"You mean a tryout?" Colt asked, recalling his days of youth baseball. "When I was six, we didn't have tryouts. Everyone made a team. We had ten teams in our league."

"This is a much smaller town. We barely have enough for two or three tee-ball teams."

"Tee-ball?" he asked. "I would think by six..."

"Eight." Ellie interjected.

"Right, eight," he continued. "Eight-year-olds should be playing kid pitch or at least coach pitch by now."

"The All-Star team plays kid pitch against other towns," Ellie explained. "The house league plays tee-ball."

"Most towns have spring league and then pick their All-Stars at the beginning of the summer after the league playoffs. Once the league's wrapped up, the All-Star team goes off to play in the regionals and state playoffs if they make it."

"Not here." Ellie rolled her eyes. "They do what they want here."

Ellie scanned the back door to her house. She turned to check on Braden. Colt caught her attention and flipped her the tennis ball. She reached up with her left hand, while holding Braden's cap in her right. She snared it out of the air like a frog snapping a fly. Her shades flew off her face as she contorted her body to make the catch.

"Nice hands," said Colt, as he retrieved her fallen sunglasses and held them out to her.

Ellie's eyes glinted a mesmerizing brownish-orange in the morning sun. She took the shades from Colt and tucked the ball into the web of her son's mitt.

"Thanks for helping Braden this morning," she said, with a warm, friendly smile. "You ever coach before?"

"Uh, no," Colt deflected the question, the image of his termination letter suddenly flaring across his mind. "Not really."

"You should."

3

THE EVALUATION

The apartment at the top of the stairs consisted of a large living room, a cramped galley kitchen, a decent bathroom, and a bedroom just big enough to fit a bed. The living room had two small windows facing the wooded side of the property and a large bay window looking out over the driveway.

Colt planned to spend much of the day setting up his electronics. The room already had a couch in the middle of the floor. It faced the two small windows and a desk in the far corner. He measured the space between the windows for his forty-two-inch flat screen. Despite the plain, pine walls, which resembled the inside of a coffin from the 1850's, he had considerably more room as a single occupant than he ever had on campus living with two, three, and even four other guys. He set up a small office for himself in the corner. His printer sat on the floor on one side of his feet with his router on the other side. After a short time, he maneuvered all his technology into place. He looked at his handiwork in organizing his living space and beamed with pride at having a place all to himself.

He tried to plug his television into the wall, but his computer and printer took up the only two nearby wall sockets. He painted an image of the downtown area into his mind and recalled the general store. If he couldn't find a power strip there, he'd have to hit the highway up to Hellertown or Bethlehem.

The drive into the center of town took less than two minutes. Along the way, he passed the baseball field and saw a dozen boys spread among three different lines. They took turns fielding grounders and throwing them back to two coaches at each station. For the few seconds he observed as he passed the field, Colt was impressed at the organization and efficiency of the practice. The players all wore crisp red and black uniforms with matching caps and pants. The coaches all had black athletic pants and matching red golf shirts. The squad looked like a pint-sized semi-pro team.

The general store offered little other than a sandy ditch in which to park, and five scant rows containing an eclectic array of goods and supplies. He turned down the first row of canned goods, cookies, chips, and bread. He thought of picking up food for the apartment, but remembered he still had the snacks he stole from his roommate on the counter. The next row offered paper towels, napkins, soaps, and detergents. He couldn't recall if his new bathroom had a roll of toilet paper or not, so he grabbed a single generic brand roll. In the third aisle, he found what he needed, picking up a box of batteries, two power strips, a couple light bulbs, and a pack of coat hangers.

The fourth aisle, which contained automobile supplies, led him to the large freezer cases along the back wall, filled with frozen vegetables, pizzas, and ice cream. It rattled and hummed loudly. He thought of buying a frozen calzone but couldn't remember if his apartment had a microwave and wasn't sure how to heat it up in a conventional oven. The back of the store featured a row of produce and a refrigerated case of milk, eggs, butter, and orange juice. He grabbed an apple, polished it against his cotton shirt and walked his handful of goods toward the front of the store.

Colt grabbed a bottle of water and some Cheez-Its from the

snack aisle. As he approached the checkout counter, a short, elderly man with a semi-circle of grey hair around his bald spot emerged from behind a lunch meat slicer and greeted him.

"New in town?" he asked. "Harley. Vern Harley. I own this place."

"I guess that's why you call it Harley's Market?"

"Huh?" Vern eyed him suspiciously. "You sassing me?"

"Uh, no Sir. Just making small talk."

"Well small talk's for small people," Vern said, still sizing up Colt. "What brings you by the city of Springtown?"

"I'm living down off Main Street."

"Up in the apartment at Gertie Shaw's old place?"

"Yes," Colt lowered his voice reverently. "But she passed away and it's owned by her niece, Ellie, now."

Vern paused, glaring at Colt, as if resisting the urge to roll his eyes at the dated revelation.

"That's right." The clerk scratched the hair above his right ear. "Nice girl. Great kid, little Braden, she's got there. And her Aunt Gertie; she was a sweetheart. Took care of the boy all the while Ellie finished up college. She held out just long enough for her to graduate. You know, it's a small town and we all look out for each other. So, make sure you're a respectful guest, hear? People talk, you know."

"Yes, Sir," Colt replied as he paid for his items and exited the store.

Colt rolled down his window and took in the fresh spring air as he craned his neck to back out of the parking ditch. As he did, a grey-blue Ford Focus zipped around a corner and pulled behind him. For a few seconds, the Ford and his truck froze as the drivers attempted to figure out who would move left and who would move right. Colt pulled forward and made room for the car to ease alongside him. At first, he didn't recognize the car, but as he looked closer, he recognized the deep, brown eyes of his landlord, Ellie Shaw, parked next to him. For a split second, he gathered his thoughts and scanned his mind for a morsel of small talk to cast her way.

"How's tee-ball?" he asked.

"It's tee-ball," she replied. "I forgot to get him a bottle of water and he's thirsty."

"It's hot this morning," Colt said, thrusting his unopened bottle of water toward Ellie. "Take this. It's nice and cold."

Ellie hesitated. She looked furtively over her shoulder toward the field behind the elementary school.

"No. That's yours," she said. "I'll just run in and—"

"Really," Colt interrupted her. "Take it. You should get back there. I'm sure he's thirsty in this sun."

"You sure?" she asked, sheepishly. "You don't mind?"

Colt moved the plastic bottle closer to her and gave it a subtle shake. She took it from his hand with a smile and a "Thanks."

"So, is he on that red and black team?"

"No, that's the 'A-team'," she replied, making air quotes with her fingers.

"They rated all the kids and picked the teams already?"

"Not exactly. We got there right on-time, and the teams were already picked."

"Then what's the point of a tryout?"

"That's a good question." Ellie's face darkened. "And how did they just happen to have uniforms for the A-team already—with their names pre-printed? Basically, it's all the kids from the same neighborhood. They're all from Springtown Hills."

"It seems like they've already practiced together. No team's that well-coordinated on their first day."

"Figures," Ellie said, rolling her eyes. "It's pretty much the same roster as last year's Eight-U team."

"Braden's just as good as any of the kids on that team," said Colt in earnest.

"I know, but we're from Springtown Valley. Apparently, we don't rate."

"I thought you said the other kids were from Springtown too?"

"I said Springtown Hills."

"There's a difference?"

"Welcome to Springtown." Ellie grimaced.

"Well, at least the league has a lot of coaches. They seem well organized," Colt said with as much cheer as he could muster. "Braden'll have a good chance to work his way up to the stronger program."

"Right," Ellie smirked. "There are more coaches for the A-team than players. But the B-team has one guy sipping coffee and placing the ball on the tee, while twenty kids in the field roll around and wrestle to shag them."

At that she thanked him with a sincere smile and drove off to bring Braden his water.

Colt stopped at the manicured baseball field in the center of town on his way back to the apartment. He rested his chin on the fence, watching the red and black team practice running the bases.

The man in his fifties, who Colt had earlier seen raking the field, approached him within a few minutes. "You're the new guy with the pick-up truck? You've got the big L-screen in the back of your flatbed."

"That's me," Colt replied. "Just moved here."

"Welcome. Garrett Kildeer," the man said, limply extending his hand. "I run the Springtown youth baseball program."

Colt shook Garrett's hand and complimented him on his well-organized and talented team.

"You a coach or something?" Garrett asked. "Where'd you get the L-screen?"

"Nah, I just played a lot growing up." Colt found himself getting smoother at glossing over his coaching experience. "I borrowed it from my college."

"You played?"

"Lehigh."

"Alleghany State," said Garrett. "Played my youth ball right here in town on this field, although back before we redesigned it and spruced it up."

"Beautiful park you got here."

"Where'd you play growing up?" Garrett asked. "Local?"

"You mean like Little League?"

"High School."

"Oh, not too far, Allentown."

"Central Catholic?" Garrett asked.

Colt nodded, pausing to watch a wiry shortstop backhand a hard grounder and make a crisp throw to first.

Garrett clapped and shouted encouragement to his talented infielder.

"Nice play." Colt nudged Garrett's rib.

"Hell of a scoop."

They stood in silence for a moment, watching the boy smack his glove and kick the dirt with his cleats.

"Heck of a program over there at Central Catholic," Garrett said. "State champs three or four times in the past twenty years."

Colt nodded, neglecting to correct him that they'd won five, including three during his time at the school.

"My uncle coaches the team," Colt said.

"Always an advantage to play for a family member, right?"

Colt hesitated before muttering, "I guess."

Garrett shifted his attention to the field as one of his outfielders missed a looping fly ball that sailed over his head and tipped off the webbing of his glove.

"Aw come on, Damien," he barked. "You gotta catch those."

Colt stifled his reaction to Garrett's outburst and waited a second or two to comment.

"Tough play," he said, with his back to the fence to avoid being overheard. "The kid could have ranged back first, found the ball in the air and then taken a better route to it. I think he would've had it if he took a better angle."

Colt glanced at the boy. The tall, athletic fielder slumped his shoulders as he chased the rolling ball to the wall and threw it back toward the infield.

"Hit the cut-off man, damn it," Garett snapped, as the ball skipped in the grass and scooted past the second baseman.

The boy nodded and shoved the brim of his cap lower on his brow to hide his eyes. Another coach across the field echoed Garrett's commentary, nearly word-for word, before calling him into the dugout and sending a different player to take his position.

"My twelve-year-old team was the first to play in the states," Garrett continued, his voice suddenly transformed back to the calm, mild-mannered tone from the start of the conversation. "We've been trying to field teams to get back there ever since."

"These guys don't look twelve," said Colt. "You coach another older team too?"

"No," Garrett replied. "*My* twelve-year-old team, from forty years ago, when *I* was twelve."

"Oh, I see," said Colt, holding back the smirk that he felt twitch across his lips. "The squad you've got there in the black and red uniforms looks pretty good for a bunch of six-year-olds."

"They're eight," Garrett corrected him. "And a number of them turned nine just under the cut off for Eight-U, so we're on the older side compared to other teams—kind of a team of veterans. But we're gonna play up an age group at Nine-U, maybe Ten-U to toughen them up."

"Where are the other players?" asked Colt. "The ones that tried out but didn't make it?"

"They play on the rec league field over at Springtown Elementary," Garrett replied, nodding toward the open grass area through the woods behind the drab brick school. "We have a whole league for them. They play a couple games of tee-ball to get acclimated, and then they move on to coach pitch and finally machine pitch. Those boys're not quite ready for real baseball, but they have a good time and we're really focused on their development so that one day, they could play at our level."

"I see," Colt replied, noticing the players on the other field through the woods for the first time.

"If you ever want to help us out, let me know," said Garrett. "We run a strong program here. We're one of the elite All-Star teams in the region. We're gunning for the states, if not this year, then when they're ten or eleven. We start early and pull them together at eight and nine. We want them to play together as a travel team for four or five years until the big twelve-year-old championship. This way, by the time they get there, they're primed to compete for a title and become the second team in town history to win the GPYBA and qualify for states."

"GPYBA?" Colt asked.

"That's the regional league we're in."

"Do the other kids ever get to play on this nice diamond too?"

"You don't need a dirt infield at that level," Garrett replied. "They have a good time. It's just nice to see kids outside, getting a chance to play. Like I said, we run a good program. All the boys in town enjoy it. And if you'd like to help out, let me know. It'd be great to have another college ballplayer, like myself, to inspire our travel boys."

Colt didn't answer at first, instead he fixated on a tall boy throwing with surprisingly fast velocity in the bullpen. "I'll think about it."

ELLIE STOOD by the fence to the Springtown Elementary School, shoulder-to-shoulder with a half-dozen other parents. She watched each ball pop off the tee and roll somewhere near the pitcher's mound where a dozen boys and a few girls clamored over each other to retrieve it. The other dozen players stood around the periphery watching the scrum.

As Ellie had described to Colt, a single coach, in jeans and a blue button-down shirt, placed the ball on the tee between each swing while sipping his coffee and occasionally offering cursory bits of advice like "*watch the ball, now.*"

"Do you want any help?" Ellie called out to the coach.

"Sure, Love," he responded in a thick British accent. "But the league directors told me I'm the only one insured to be on this side of the fence."

"How can we get other coaches insured?"

"You have to speak with the President of the League, Garrett Kildeer," said the coach. "Or you could talk to Jay Smalley. He's the Vice President, and I think he coaches the A-team with Mr. Kildeer. He's on his cell phone on the other side of the right field fence over at Victory Field."

Ellie strode along the chain link enclosure and spotted Smalley standing on a small wood bridge that spanned the stream between the elementary school and the town baseball field. She waited patiently as he conducted his conversation. When he didn't acknowledge her, she moved closer and stared at him until he put up a finger to motion that he would be right with her. Several minutes later, Ellie's stare turned into a glare with her hands on her hips.

"Can I help you with something?" Smalley asked, holding his phone to his shoulder.

"You need more coaches over on this field." Ellie pointed to the patch of uneven grass where the pile of tee-ball players looked like a pack of playful puppies. "This is ridiculous. You've got a hundred coaches over there with ten players. And over here, you've got one guy with twenty kids. Where're the rest of the tee-ball coaches?"

Coach Smalley returned the phone to his ear. "I have to deal with a parent," he said, exhaling in a way that couldn't quite be called a sigh of annoyance. "I'll call you back."

Ellie forced a fake smile to carefully hide her consternation. She peered at the rugged and slightly overweight middle-aged man while awaiting his answer.

"You need to understand," Smalley replied. "Kid pitch requires a much higher-level coach and more staff to cover the finer points of the game. Tee-ball's all about repetition and giving the boys a chance to touch the ball. Mostly it's about having fun."

"It's not just boys. And half of them are either standing around or playing in the grass." Ellie gestured back to the elementary school field. "The others are jumping on top of each other like sumo wrestlers. Someone's going to get hurt. You need more coaches to supervise."

"We get a lot of highly qualified coaching candidates for our A-teams. But it's hard to get people to volunteer for the B and C-teams."

"There are six parents standing around doing nothing," Ellie retorted. "Any one of them could pitch in."

"Listen, this is evaluation week," Smalley said, pursing his lips before continuing. "By this time next week, they'll be divided into the B and C-teams, and they'll start playing their pick-up games. We only have twenty minutes left today I think it'll be OK."

"Let me go out there and help coach," Ellie insisted.

"You can't do that because of insurance reasons. Only designated coaches can be inside the fenced area."

"Fine," Ellie snapped. "Designate me as a coach. I'll have to rearrange my work schedule. But I'll do it if it means the kids'll be safe and maybe even learn something this season."

"Have you ever played?" Smalley asked. "We put our coaches through rigorous background checks and make sure they have an appropriate baseball background."

"I played softball."

"That's not the same." Smalley squinted in the afternoon sun. "The ball's so much bigger. There's no leading. Pitchers don't have to hold runners. We need coaches with more relevant experience."

"What experience does Coach Tremblay have?"

"Believe it or not," Smalley said and looked back at Victory Field as if he needed to leave the conversation to attend to his team. "Cricket's a much more relevant experience and skill set."

"No, it's not," Ellie scoffed.

"Ever feel how hard a cricket ball is?"

Ellie looked at him with a perplexed expression trying to figure out what the feel of a cricket ball had to do with coaching a youth baseball team.

"Trust me," Coach Smalley said, "I've been doing this a long time. I've had two other sons go through the program. I've been to the regional semi-finals. We know what we're doing."

Ellie rolled her eyes and stomped back to the soccer field. She called Braden to bring four friends and a ball with them. They ran out to deep left field where she stood draped over the fence.

"I can't step onto the field for insurance reasons," she said to the three boys and two girls in her group. "But that doesn't mean I can't throw you grounders and flies and have you throw them back to me here on this side of the fence."

Ellie grimaced as she cocked her arm to throw. Braden made several catches. The two girls showed a lot of progress. After about ten minutes and nearly fifty throws, Coach Tremblay called all the players back to the home plate area to discuss the upcoming schedule. Braden made a long accurate throw over the fence into Ellie's waiting hands. As he and his four friends trotted back to rejoin their team, Ellie rubbed her shoulder and walked back to the bleachers to reconnect with the other parents.

On the drive home, Ellie spotted Garrett Kildeer putting away the grounds-keeping tools into the shed by the side of Victory Field. She pulled into the parking lot and waved to speak with him.

"Mrs..." Kildeer started.

"Shaw," Ellie completed his thought. "Ellie Shaw. My son's Braden."

Braden exited the car behind her and started throwing his tennis ball against the side of the concession stand.

"Of course." Kildeer smiled at her. "What can I do for you?"

"I spoke to Jay Smalley about getting more coaches to help

make the tee-ball program better structured. Any chance you can provide more supervision and instruction for those teams?"

"Well, typically, the B and C-teams only get one coach as it's really a one-man job."

"Or woman."

"Of course." Kildeer nodded.

"And that's the other question I have," Ellie continued. "Do we have to call them the A-team, the B-team, and C-team at this age? It's like calling them 'Good', 'Mediocre' and 'Bad'. They're eight years old. It's not right to label them at this age."

"We've always called our All-Stars the 'A's' for short." Kildeer looked quizzically at Ellie. "We could just call them the 'All-Stars'. We've always called the weaker teams by 'B' and 'C'. But I could consider mixing up the naming of the teams this year. How does that sound?"

"Why can't we have even teams, so that they can all play each other and have nice competitive match-ups?"

"The problem with that idea is that the better players wouldn't be challenged," Kildeer responded. "That's not healthy for any program. We don't want to lose them to another league or discourage them from playing baseball altogether. That wouldn't be fair to them."

"And how'd you decide who these 'better' players were?" Ellie felt her voice raise in pitch and volume. She noticed Kildeer edge back a step from her.

"We know the players from last year's tee-ball league."

"Braden didn't play last year," Ellie said. "He broke his finger. Today's practice was supposed to be a tryout."

"Technically, it's an evaluation," Kildeer replied. "But we'll take a second look at Brandon... and give him a shot. We're all about fairness and transparency. We want what's best for every boy in our program."

"And girl?"

"Yes, and the girls, of course."

"And my son is Braden, not Brandon."
"Right."

LATER THAT EVENING, just before dinner, Ellie checked her email. Garret Kildeer had sent out the rosters for the three Peewee League teams.

"Did I make the A-team?" Braden asked.

"No, Honey," Ellie replied, pained and frustrated. "They picked that team in advance."

"What team's Ronnie on?"

"It looks like he's on a team called the "Seadogs.""

"What about Mikey Wiltshire?"

"He's on a team called the 'Athletics'."

"You mean like the Oakland A's? What team am I on? The Phillies? Please be the Phillies."

"It says here you're on a team called the Bees."

"As in like a Bumble Bee?"

"I guess so."

"So, I'm a Bee?"

"Apparently."

4

THE DINER

An empty soda bottle rolled across Colt's floor and settled between his legs beneath the couch. It stared out from its hidden cavern at the flickering hue of the television screen that bathed the room in warm, blue light. Colt munched on Ritz Crackers smeared with peanut butter while he battled the 2009 Philadelphia Phillies with his hand-picked Xbox team of All-Stars.

He took note of the time and paused his game to check the bags of food he had taken from Phil Jones, the roommate he left behind in his off-campus apartment. He swore to himself at the realization that Phil ate crappy food.

For a physical therapy major, you'd think the knucklehead would eat healthier.

The bags contained a dozen packages of Ramen noodles, three boxes of spaghetti, mac and cheese, some English muffins, Oreos, Pop Tarts, Lucky Charms, and a box of frozen French bread pizza.

The pizza looked like the best option for dinner and seemed like the easiest to make. Maybe he should have put it in the freezer rather than leaving it in the bag on the counter all day. He tossed the limp, soggy prepared food into the trash can and grabbed his Lehigh jacket.

As he approached his truck in the driveway, he saw the shadow of Ellie Shaw pass her kitchen window. He noticed her hair sway as she moved.

What home cooked meal might she have served her son tonight, and what leftovers now sit in her refrigerator? He half wished she would come out to her patio again with a fresh casserole or a roast and offer him a bite like she had the other morning.

He shrugged off the hunger-inducing image of a roast pork loin with potatoes and carrots stretched across her kitchen table and started up his engine to find a plate of fast food in this blip of a town.

Colt's pick-up truck rolled across the gravel parking lot of Sandy's Diner, about a mile and a half from Ellie's garage apartment. He recognized Andrea's tall figure passing by the windows as she waited tables.

"Hey stranger," she greeted him at the door. "Come on down and have a seat in the last booth next to Mrs. Parsons over there. I'll be right with you."

Colt nodded to the older lady, alone in her booth, as he slid into his. She flashed a half-smile before returning her eyes to her bowl and loudly sipping her soup.

Of the items on the six-page menu, he decided the pancakes looked best. Along the wall, neatly arranged framed photos of baseball teams, all labeled by year, formed an upper and lower ring around the walls of the diner. The bottom row of pictures closest to his booth included the 1976, 1977, and 1978 Springtown All-Stars. The 1994, 1995, and 1996 All-Stars in brighter color and sharper focus occupied the second row of pictures. He traced the upper row across the two booths in front of him to the most recent picture. The empty space next to the last picture would fit three more frames before they'd have to move up and utilize a third row.

"How's the new place treating you?" Andrea asked with her tiny notepad and pencil perched in hand, ready to scrawl his order.

"The place is nicer than it looks," he replied. "There's a lot of room upstairs. I like it."

"You decided to come to the best place in town for food?" she cracked.

"The only place, I think."

"But still the best," she winked at him.

She tucked her pencil behind her ear and took out a pad of receipts from a pocket in her apron.

"How do you like your landlord?" she asked. "She treating you okay?"

"She's great."

"She's a good friend," Andrea replied, as she ripped off a receipt and laid it on Mrs. Parson's table next to her empty bowl of soup. "And that Braden's a good kid."

"He sure is," Colt said. "She's got a nice property back behind that little farmhouse of hers."

Mrs. Parsons stood from her table. She leaned toward Colt as she clutched her purse to her stomach. "It's not easy for her, you know."

Andrea smirked at Colt and cast him a subtle eyeroll.

"She's got the kid and the three jobs. The poor girl never gets any time to herself."

"Three jobs?" Colt gasped, as Mrs. Parsons left a couple quarters for a tip on the table. "What does she do?"

"She does my taxes," Mrs. Parsons responded before ambling to the register to stuff a half-dozen mints into her purse. "And my neighbor's too."

"Thank you, Mrs. Parsons," Andrea said with a wave. "See you tomorrow night."

Andrea watched the woman exit the diner before turning back to Colt.

"Not that it's really any of your business," Andrea clarified. "Ellie has her CPO degree."

"Her CPA?" Colt asked.

"I don't know," Andrea replied with a smile. "Her C3PO. Whatever you need to do people's taxes for them. She handles half the town."

"Wow, that's a lot."

"It's not easy as a single mom."

"She's not married?" Colt asked, glancing at the menu to confirm his choice of meal.

"Very few *single* moms are."

"Right, I meant as in Braden's Dad, if he was around or anything like that." Colt smiled sheepishly, trying to save face from his absentminded question about Ellie's marital status. "Oh, and how are the pancakes?"

"Nah," Andrea answered his initial question. "Jeffrey never stuck around for her. He tried living at the house with her and Gertie, but that never worked out. Gertie couldn't stand him and made no attempt to welcome him. She blamed him for getting Elles pregnant."

As she spoke, Andrea slid into the opposite side of the booth and placed her elbows on the table. Colt moved back a couple inches to make room as she leaned in toward him. He scanned the restaurant, self-conscious of the dirty looks he expected to receive from the other customers. But instead of angry eyes, he observed a half-dozen elderly patrons slurping soup, reading the paper, scrolling their phones and sipping coffee. Nobody seemed to notice the waitress lounging at his table with him.

"They thought about kicking Mr. Schneider out of the apartment and living there," Andrea explained. "But Gertie's health was failing, and Ellie had to spend all her free time caring for her. Either way I'm not so sure Ellie ever really liked Jeffrey all that much anyway."

"I see," Colt nodded, "Uh, how do the pancakes …"

"I mean, I can't figure out what she saw in him neither," Andrea continued, oblivious to her other customers. "She said she liked him because he was nerdy and smart. But he wasn't half as nerdy as she thought he was—and he was definitely nowhere near as smart as *he* thought he was."

Colt turned the page of the menu and reviewed the choice of sodas. He considered the selection of milkshakes.

"Are the shakes made with real ice cream?" he asked, picturing the vanilla malted milkshake that he wanted to order.

"Yes," Andrea answered before continuing her story without taking a breath. "Jeffrey just took off on her one day. He left Elles with Gertie and Braden, and no child support."

"That's awful." Hunger pangs ate at Colt's stomach. "Uh, how are the home fries? I like them crispy."

"Yes, terrible," Andrea paused. "The home fries are great. The story's terrible. There's more to it and all, but I'll spare you the details. Suffice to say, he left her pretty flat."

"Sounds like a real jerk."

"She's had a couple of them in her life," Andrea concluded. "She doesn't need any more."

The conversation froze. *Did she just throw him a barb?* She buried her face into her notebook and started writing.

"That's a stack of buttermilk pancakes, side of home fries, extra crispy, and our famous vanilla milkshake—with real ice cream, of course. Uh, and malted, I'm guessing. Good choices there, Colt, Darling."

"How'd you know? I didn't say my order."

"Honey, you watch a man's eyes, and they tell you exactly what he wants every time."

Andrea left to place his order, leaving him to study the photos around him of smiling boys in red and black uniforms. A few booths down, he made out the younger, thinner face of Garrett Kildeer posed behind some of the more recent team pictures. After Colt polished off his meal, he settled his bill and left Andrea a generous tip. He figured the good will would go a long way in helping him stay in the positive graces of his new landlord.

He yawned as he left the diner. Not even eleven o'clock he already felt like going to sleep. A part of him bristled at such a change from the pace of his life in the off-campus apartment. As he reached to stretch his seat belt across his lap and return to Ellie's quaint garage apartment, a text pinged across his phone.

> Phil Jones: Frat party in Fountain Hill. Girlz ready to go. Need wingman!!

ELLIE SHAW SPENT the night on her computer. She'd whipped up a western omelet for Braden and packed it full of vegetables including spinach, which he usually refused to eat. Having ground it to small pieces and whipped it into the egg, she managed to sneak it by him this time. She'd read "Green Eggs and Ham" to Braden the night before, and he seemed fascinated or distracted enough by the color of his dinner to give it a try.

"Aw cool," he said, as she served him his plate. "Green eggs!"

After putting him to bed, Ellie searched for the Springtown Peewee Baseball League website to check for any rules or guidelines on how the teams and games would be organized. She had read about the league in a flyer tacked to the bulletin board at the diner. The advertisement contained scant details about the program. It did not offer a website or even an email address. The only contact information provided was the home phone number for Garrett Kildeer. And she had no desire to call him at ten o'clock to question his tactics in running the league.

The email she received from the league seemed to come from a Marketing Automation program and had a "Do Not Reply" return address.

Her Google search failed to find the website for the Springtown Peewee Baseball League—if one even existed. But she found an even more useful page instead. At first, she almost clicked right past it since its only purpose appeared to be to solicit donations. Curious, she clicked the link for 'Home' and read about the Greater Pennsylvania Youth Baseball Association—or GPYBA. As she discovered, the league in town was an affiliate of a larger organization spanning central and eastern Pennsylvania and parts of western New Jersey.

She read the 'Philosophy' page about how the GPYBA believed in equal opportunity for success across all players at all levels in the program. She read about the travel program and how it was designed to provide the more serious and committed players an advanced competitive experience in addition to the robust house leagues that each town was required to manage.

She clicked a page called 'Program Requirements' and gasped at some of the bylaws that she read.

... All players must reside within a common zip code or range of zip codes based on program charter guidelines for each affiliated town ...

... Opportunity for all registrants to play on a team ...

... At least four teams in a structured House League with balanced rosters and a schedule of no less than twelve games between April 15th and May 30th...

... House League play-offs including championship game ...

... Clearly communicated All-Star selection methodology with analytical ranking system and coach voting process to ensure fairness and objectivity ...

... All-Star selection to take place after conclusion of House League season ...

Many of the guidelines had asterisks next to them indicating that they applied to Nine-U age groups and older. For Eight-U, the recommendation called for tee-ball programs with rosters of seven to ten players and no travel program.

... Eight-year-old players are too young for the level of complexity, commitment, and intensity a travel program offers ...

Ellie reviewed the affiliate list. She observed Garrett Kildeer's name as President and Jay Smalley as Vice President for the Springtown franchise. She was surprised to see Oscar Schneider, the elderly tenant that had just moved out of her apartment, listed as the Secretary and two other individuals in town that she didn't know listed as Treasurer and Communications Officer.

She stared at the page for a short while before moving the mouse to the corner to close the window, when another small detail jumped out at her.

... All affiliates required to maintain federal non-profit 501(c3) standards and practices ...

Another hour in and Ellie's eyes ached from viewing her computer monitor, so she decided to take a break and check on her sleeping son. She crept up the stairs, rounded the corner and gazed at the little boy, who, only seven years earlier fit in the fold of her arm.

She tiptoed to the side of his bed, stroked his cheek, and kissed his forehead. He lay curled around his Philadelphia Phillies blanket with the sheet tucked under his chin. His hair flopped over his forehead. She straightened his baseball pajamas and moved his stuffed bear—which also had a baseball hat, glove, and cleats sewn onto its stubby head, hands, and feet.

She paused before turning out his night light. She knew he had a myriad of hopes and dreams floating around in his head, mostly focused on playing baseball. He wanted to be the best player in town. He wanted to make the All-Star team and play in the championship game.

"We could be the first team in town to win the regional championship in like a hundred years or something like that," he told her as she'd tucked him into his bed. "We could have our picture put up in the diner."

In school, he had heard about the older players on the 12-U

teams and their experiences representing Springtown in their black and red uniforms. He wanted to play in high school and college and then score the first pick of the Major League Baseball draft. So much like any kid, he narrated his own success in mock announcer voices with the crowd cheering in the background. It broke her heart to look at his small stature and hopeful eyes and think he may be overlooked by the league directors for a spot to play on the better teams at the higher level of organization and competitiveness.

As Ellie kissed his forehead, Braden opened his eyes a sliver and closed them again. He yawned a high-pitched yelp and rolled toward the wall, pressing his nose against the wood paneling. Ellie backpedaled toward the door. She glanced at her feet, trying to recall the one loose floorboard that she knew creaked the loudest. As she reached the door, she sidestepped a ratty, mud-caked baseball that blocked her walking path.

Ellie clutched the door handle to exit but stood still for a minute watching her boy sleep. She could barely hear him inhale and exhale like he had as an infant. She recalled how she'd check on him a half-dozen times a night, and even more often than that after Jeffrey abandoned them.

She reached for the baseball to wipe off the dirt and place it in a basket on top of his dresser. But as she bent to grab it, the ball rotated out of her grasp. It bounced onto the floor and rolled toward Braden's bed. Ellie lunged for it, but it traversed the loose-fitted floorboard, producing the tiniest of creaking sounds.

Ellie watched in dismay as Braden squirmed, kicked off his covers, opened his eyes to half width and focused on her silhouette, backlit by the yellowy glow of the hallway light.

"Is it morning?" he asked, rubbing his eyes and squinting into the brightness behind his mother's head.

"No, Honey. It's time to go to sleep."

"But I already went to sleep and now I woke up."

"No, you didn't," Ellie bluffed. "You're still asleep."

Braden looked at the ceiling. Uncertainty crinkled his brow. "No. I'm pretty sure I'm awake."

Ellie returned to his side, squatted close to his eyelevel, and moved a lock of hair from his eyes. "You need your sleep so you can grow and be strong on the baseball field."

Braden looked at the ceiling again, seeming to ponder his mother's guidance. "You're right," he said and rolled back toward the wall with the covers pulled to his nose.

Ellie again attempted to pad out of the room. But Braden snapped the blanket away from his face and turned to her with a burning question written across his face.

"What is it, Baby?" Ellie asked.

"How do you do reproduction?"

Ellie froze. She moved forward and heard the pop of two Lego pieces snapping apart under her toes. A jolt of searing pain shot up the length of her body. Her bones screamed beneath her skin, even as she bit her tongue and held back the urge to howl at her top of her lungs. She paused to collect herself, focusing on Braden's surprise question.

"Why do you ask that?" She did her best to keep the panic out of her voice.

"Tonio Maletti told me today in school that he used to play on the A-team last year in the eight-year-old league, but they put him on our team this year instead because he didn't have enough reproduction."

"Oh, Honey." Ellie expelled the tension from her body with an extended sigh. "I think he meant 'production'."

"Well, I told him if he wanted reproduction, he had to hit a home run."

Ellie stifled the urge to chuckle by giving him a long kiss to the forehead.

"That sounds like good advice."

She blew a kiss as she closed Braden's door, leaving it only slightly ajar. She tried to lighten her step as she descended the stairs by clutching both handrails and suspending as much of her weight as she could. As she reached the last of the steps, she heard a creak. The jarring pop bounced up the canyon of the stairwell.

"Momma," the tiny, angelic voice of her boy echoed back down the wooden staircase.

"Yes, Baby," she answered as she returned up the stairs.

"The A-team is going to Hershey Amusement Park to play in a tournament," he said with a strange enthusiasm, as if he could enjoy the other team's good time vicariously. "They're taking a big bus like the pros."

"The pros fly to their games, Honey," Ellie said, peering through the crack in his door. "Where did you hear about that?"

"Mikey Wiltshire told me! They're going to stay in a hotel and everything."

Ellie drew from her son that the A-team would leave on the Saturday before Memorial Day, stay in a hotel for two nights, play five games on Saturday evening and Sunday morning and then spend all day Monday at the amusement park. Braden beamed about it as if he had been selected to attend.

"It's just the A-team?" she asked.

"Yup," he grinned. "But Mikey was going to ask the coach if I could go too."

Ellie's stomach fluttered. Her heart sank. She changed her line of questions. "Do you know what the trip costs?"

"I think a hundred thousand dollars," he answered, with a gaping yawn. "Or maybe just a regular thousand. I forgot."

"Did Mikey explain why his team gets to go and not the others?"

"He just said cause they're the best team."

"He said that?"

"That's what the coaches told them," Braden replied. "Only the All-Stars get to go."

With the conversation still rattling across her mind, she crossed the room, while avoiding the Legos. She re-tucked Braden under covers and told him to go to sleep.

"Ok," he answered, with his eyelids drooping. "This time I will for real."

She returned downstairs to fold laundry, skipping the last step. A cooking show played on the television in the background. After piling Braden's t-shirts next to his shorts and underwear on the couch, Ellie returned to her search of the area baseball leagues and programs. The din of the crickets subsided as she sat on her couch browsing the internet. She quickly found the details of the tournament called The Hershey Bash on a website for the GYPBA. The site indicated that the event offered qualified 9-U teams, not yet eligible for the 10-U district championships, to experience the advanced competition of a playoff setting.

It took a few more searches to find the details around how a team qualified for the Hershey Bash.

Team rosters assembled through GPYBA-approved All-Star selection process.

She read the details to herself while scrolling through the site to find the guidelines.

She maneuvered to the GPYBA site and searched for "All-Star Selection Process," which brought her to a page she had seen previously.

"Regular season league play... evenly constructed teams..." she mumbled to herself as she absorbed the information presented on the page. "Analytical evaluation process at start of season... Second evaluation at end of season before league championship game."

Ellie stared at the screen and pulled her cell phone from her back pocket to text Andrea.

> Ellie: You up?

> Andrea: Sorry, not your type.

> Ellie: Who is? ... Never mind, was there ever a tryout for the All-Star team?

> Andrea: First day of practice.

> Ellie: Who was evaluating them?

> Andrea: Tremblay, I guess.

> Ellie: What about the A-team?

> Andrea: Had their own separate tryout with those other coaches.

> Ellie: Hardly seems fair. Was Tremblay even writing scores down on a piece of paper? And how could they compare the kids on the elementary field to the ones on Victory freakin' Field?

> Andrea: Don't know Elles. Was all I could do just to get Ronnie onto the field. Don't think he even knows there is an A-team.

Ellie stewed on the couch in the dark. The moonlight streamed through her window. Silver light careened off the kitchen counter and illuminated the kitchen table. Ellie pondered her next text to her friend when Andrea beat her to the punch.

> Andrea: He loves practices in your big back yard though. Has fun. That's all that matters.

Ellie slid the phone across the table and bowed her head. Braden's words echoed in her mind.

Cause they're the best team.

Sleepiness finally crept its way into her head. She opened the fridge and grabbed a can of diet soda. She texted *thanx and g'night* to her friend and then returned to her laptop.

In her search engine, she entered "Springtown GPYBA Board." An old site appeared at the top of the results listing Garrett Kildeer as the President, Jay Smalley as the Vice President, and Oscar Schneider as the Secretary.

In need of a brain break, Ellie navigated from her Google search results page to the website for People Magazine to read gossip stories about celebrities. Across her driveway, the door to Colt's apartment clanked open. She glanced at the time on the clock and shot a quick look out the window to see his truck lights flash on. The engine rumbled to a start. In an instant, the wheels kicked dirt and dust into the air against the dim glow of the two lights above the garage door.

I'm winding down my night in my pajamas. And he's just starting his—off to his frat parties or strip clubs.

She kept the lights dim and closed the shades.

"Figures," she said to herself. "Frat Boy's going out partying."

5

THE MISBUTTONED SHIRT

The low morning sun strobed through the trees intermittently blinding Ellie as she peered out the kitchen window into the back yard. Braden stood facing the side of the garage with his glove in one hand and a baseball in the other. As Colt had instructed him, he angled his arm above his head and fired the ball at the wall. Ellie heard him alternate between growling like a lion and meowing like a kitten. She watched him wind up like a pitcher and bounce the ball in the dirt before it reached the distressed wood façade of the barn. The bright green ball careened off the ground, bouncing off the wood paneling and arched back to him at about his eye-level.

Ellie had a sink full of dishes to clean and a pile of mail to sort. Instead, she slipped into her running shoes and slid a sweatshirt over her head and shoulders. She stood on her toes to reach the top shelf in the small mud room between the kitchen and the back yard.

Her hands touched the soft leather catcher's mitt that sat on the top shelf. Tied up like a Christmas present in nylon rope, it glistened in the sun. She wiped the thick layer of dust off the top of the glove and ran her finger along the tight stitching. It bulged in the middle, as if pregnant with a giant, yellow softball that had been tied into the webbing.

The palm of the glove, lighter in color and significantly scuffed, showed off its age. Ellie removed the softball and placed her palm into the webbing, still stiff and relatively well-strung. She untied two leather strands where the netting met the thumb and then retied them even tighter in a double knot.

With a smack of her fist into the palm of the glove, the last shake of dust flew into the air. The popping sound echoed across the tiny mud room.

She found her Lafayette ball cap next to the spot on the shelf outlined by the dust where the glove had sat. Wiping the top of her cap with her hand, she pulled it over her hair and tugged her ponytail through the back. She lowered the brim to shield the harsh morning light, cast open the back door to the patio and ambled toward her son.

As she approached, Braden cocked his head sideways in surprise. *"You're going to throw with me?"*

"Sure," she replied. "Why not?"

"Where's Mr. Colt?"

Well aware the driveway was empty, Ellie ignored the question. Instead, she rubbed her hand into her glove and held it up by her face. With a smack into the webbing, she braced herself to receive a throw from her son.

"You sure about this, Mom?"

"Just throw me a good hard fastball," she replied. "Don't you worry about me."

Braden cocked his arm just as Colt had instructed. He stepped and threw. The ball scooted along the dirt and grass of Ellie's expansive yard. She had to drop to a knee and press her glove low to the ground to field the throw. She scooped it with both her gloved hand and her free hand, which enclosed the ball into the palm of the leather mitt.

"Not bad," she called back to her son.

"I did what he said, but it doesn't always go where I want."

"You have to practice, Honey," Ellie said with a soft, reassuring. "That's all."

Colt's pickup truck appeared from around the corner. It rumbled over the pebbles by the mailbox, disrupting the quiet of the morning. Ellie gave a quick glance and stepped to toss the ball back to her son. Her errant throw bounced twice, much like Braden's had. The young boy had to lower himself to his knee, just as his mother had on his previous throw to her, to reel it into his glove.

Colt emerged from the cabin of his truck. He squinted in the intense light of the sunrise. Ellie observed his wrinkled, misbuttoned flannel shirt. It had distinct finger-shaped buffalo chicken wing stains along the vertical hemline and what looked like a chunk of blue cheese just under the collar.

The dust cloud settled from the dirt driveway. Ellie pulled her cap low on her brow. She shaded her eyes to hide her disappointment at the images in her head of Colt on a love seat in a rundown apartment spilling hot sauce and blue cheese on himself while downing shots with college girls, six or seven years younger than him—and her.

Colt angled his body to fix his misaligned buttons. He didn't turn so far that Ellie couldn't notice how his shirt fell open for a moment. The sun cast shadows in the valleys of his rippled stomach muscles. She found it difficult to look away until he pulled the two sides of the shirt back together.

With a shake of her head, she snapped herself out of her wandering thoughts.

He's a ballplayer and a frat boy, she reminded herself. *Nothing but trouble.*

Braden smacked the ball in his glove and gave a loud sigh of impatience. Worried he might comment on her distraction, Ellie refocused her attention on throwing the ball with him, as Colt finished straightening his button-down shirt.

Braden made another wild throw, this one high over Ellie's head. The ball flew toward the patio behind her. She could feel Colt watching as she sprung across the tufted grass. Instead of letting it fall to the ground, she turned her shoulders and ranged back for it. She hurled her body into the air with her backhand flashing like a leather bird taking off in flight. With impressive athleticism, she snatched the ball out of the air and landed smoothly on her two feet like a gymnast sticking a summersault.

"Wow." Colt clapped. "Nice catch, Willy."

Ellie looked at him perplexed.

"Mays," Colt clarified. "Willy Mays, you know, the leaping over the shoulder catch. You moved like him on that one."

Ellie recalled the iconic video highlight and smiled at his reference. It had been a while since anyone had expressed appreciation for her athletic ability. She thought of thanking him but opted for a nod as if she routinely made similar leaping catches in her back yard while throwing with Braden.

Ellie rubbed her shoulder as she walked toward her son to hand him the ball. A strand of hair twisted from her cap and fell past her ear. It dangled and danced in the breeze, darkened and dampened by sweat in the heat of the summer morning sun. She exhaled and wrapped her left arm around Braden's neck. A squint of pain crossed her face as she shook her right arm by her side.

As Colt traversed the driveway toward his apartment staircase, Ellie witnessed him stumble on a rock and temporarily lose his balance. She stared at him as he awkwardly regained his footing and avoided falling. She tried to wash the disappointment from her expression but found herself shaking her head at him like she did when Braden left Legos all over his bedroom floor. Braden sidestepped her and positioned himself between them.

"Colt," he called out, breaking the wordless standoff between his mother and her guest. "Can you play catch with me and my mom? Mom can't really throw the ball too hard."

Colt stepped toward the back yard, but the sun seemed to irritate his eyes. He squeezed them closed for a few seconds, rubbed the back of his head, and yawned.

"Colt looks a little tired this morning, Honey," Ellie jumped in. "He looks like he could use some coffee and a whole lot of sleep."

"But I thought you drink coffee to wake up?" Braden quipped.

Colt lowered his eyes. The brim of his cap shaded half his face. Ellie wasn't sure if he was hiding from the sun—or shame.

"Sorry Buddy," he muttered.

Braden drooped his shoulders.

"Aww."

"We have to get going to your first practice in a few minutes anyway." Ellie smiled at her son. "We're going to get there nice and early since it's the first day of the season."

Colt swayed by the stairway. He struggled to rebutton his disheveled shirt. Ellie took a few steps toward her car and raised her glove under her chin to give the boy a target. "One more good one right here in my mitt and then you'll be ready to knock 'em dead."

Braden cocked his arm back and fired a solid pitch right to his mother's open glove.

"Nice one, Dude," Colt called out to Braden as he stepped gingerly up the wooden stairs to his apartment. "Good luck in your practice."

As he opened the door to his apartment, Ellie glanced at him, this time, making less effort to hide her disappointment. He nodded politely to her as she coaxed Braden into the car. Ellie watched the door close behind him. His large, athletic body disappeared behind it. She could see his shadow against the shaded front door window, taking off his shirt and disappearing deeper into the gut of the garage apartment.

Ellie cranked the gear shaft into reverse. For a moment, she paused. She gave his closed apartment door one last look, half-expecting it to fling open with Colt pulling a t-shirt over his abs and a cap over his hair with a glove tucked under his arm.

"Of course not, Ellie," she said to herself. "It's not like it's his kid."

She pressed the gas. Her car rumbled over the pebbles in the driveway. The crunching of rocks subsided as her wheels glided over the paved main road into town. The house, the yard and the tenant in her garage apartment all disappeared in her rear-view mirror.

6

THE CHARGE

Exhausted from partying with his old teammates, Colt buried his head into his pillow. Hazy memories of his noisy evening danced across his subconscious as he drifted into his late-morning slumber.

He recalled slinky bodies of scantily clad sorority sisters dancing and wiggling across the floor of the fraternity party room. The pounding of the dance music still reverberated in the back of his eardrums, a relentless reminder of his headache.

Many of his former teammates showed up wearing their Lehigh t-shirts, jackets, and caps. Several of them, not much older than him, had grown significant beer guts and puffy faces compared to their playing days.

When did they transition from having chiseled chins and sharp jawlines to rosy, rounded cheeks? When would he look like that? Did he look like that now and just didn't realize it?

He ran his hand across his unshaven, stubbly chin. Like little daggers, the short, stiff hairs irritated the palm of his hand. He stared at the ceiling and moved his wavy, oily hair out of his face. He wished he had a mirror in his bathroom and reached for his phone on the nightstand to take a picture of himself but thought better of it and put the phone away.

Instead, he dozed, but the sun streaming through his curtains disturbed his sleep and snapped him out of his funk. He felt a minor burst of energy and pushed himself out of bed. With a swig of orange juice and a bite of a Pop-Tart, he checked the clock. Ellie and Braden had only left twenty minutes earlier. He decided to surprise them and show up at the field to watch Braden play.

He splashed his face with water and tried to run his electric shaver over his face. But the battery in the little black gadget had no charge. He dug through his dopp kit and pulled out a razor. He couldn't find any shaving cream and debated whether to pull the blade over his dry four-day stubble or just scrap the idea of shaving altogether. With a shrug, he dragged the dull blade over his lip and worked across his cheeks and chin. With no mirror to show him the spots he missed, he ran his hand along the contours of his face feeling for the remaining bits of stubble. After touching up the last few rough patches, his skin tingled and stung. He felt a few drops of blood and dabbed them with wet toilet paper for a minute or two.

Not wanting to expend the time to take a shower, Colt wet his hair in the sink and dried it with a towel. He grabbed a ball cap and pulled it over his still damp hair, low on his brow to shield his eyes from the sun. He slipped his glove under his arm and bounded down the stairs to his truck. As Ellie had, he backed out the gravelly driveway and sped down the main road.

Once he pulled into the elementary school parking lot, he backed into a spot in the far corner, away from the other cars along the back of the bleachers. He grabbed his glove but hesitated to get out of the truck. Instead, he slid his seat back and watched from his distant parking spot.

From Colt's vantage point, the Seabirds didn't seem to have a coach of their own. Instead, the coach of the Bees, an awkward, gangly forty-something named Mr. Tremblay, handled both sets of boys and girls. He stood in the opening to the dugout with his coffee in one hand and a black garbage bag in the other. Ellie sat with a group of parents on the bleachers by the third base dugout. He rolled down his window, close enough to overhear several parents complain about the coach's late appearance and relaxed approach to teaching the game to the players.

"Ok," Coach Tremblay chirped to the kids, ignoring the grumbling parents. "Which ones are the B's? And, which ones are the C's?"

Half the kids raised their hands while others looked at their parents or gazed back and forth in confusion. A handful of kids sat picking blades of grass, oblivious to the question.

"Are both teams always going to practice at the same time?" Ellie asked from the other side of the fence. "And will we start on time next time?"

"Yes," Tremblay replied over his shoulder as he reached into the garbage bag and handed out blue shirts to the B's and green ones to the C's.

"Are these our uniforms?" Braden asked.

"Yes. These are your game jerseys."

"But they're just plain t-shirts with numbers on the back."

"They're jerseys," Tremblay insisted.

Andrea leaned over the fence to catch the coach's attention. "Are you the coach of both teams?"

"No," Tremblay replied. "I'm the coach of the B's, but the C's..."

"Seabirds," Ellie interrupted.

"Seabirds?" Tremblay repeated with a raised eyebrow. "I was just told they were called B and C."

"It's actually supposed to be the Seabirds and the Bees," she said. "Do you have a roster for each team?"

"Well, no," he replied, scratching his head. "I guess I'll just pass out the shirts now to get that part over with and we can sort it out later."

Once Tremblay arbitrarily reshuffled the teams, he led them in a calisthenics exercise ripped right out of a nineteen-fifties physical education training manual. Tremblay bent stiffly at the hips to touch his toes while the kids flopped on the ground and wrestled each other.

Colt rolled his eyes and shook his head. He fought the impulse to run onto the field and put the buffoon in his place.

He watched Ellie hunch over the fence to the dilapidated elementary school field. A fierce scowl marred the otherwise soft contours of her face, as the coach attempted to explain the rules of the game. Colt made a mental note to himself that he never wanted to find himself on the receiving end of Ellie's angry glare.

"This is the first base," he lectured in his British accent. "This one here is the second base. That one over there is the third base and this one is the home base. We want to head from the first to the second and on to the third. And, if possible, you always want to be heading for home. That is the objective of the game."

"That's a home run," Braden called out.

"That's right," Tremblay replied with a playful enthusiasm that seemed to appeal to most of the kids.

After making sure each player had a glove, which only seventeen of the nineteen had, and checking to see how many had bats, which only seven kids had, he asked the mother of all questions, half to the kids and half to the adults.

"Does anyone have a baseball?"

The twenty parents sitting in the bleachers looked sheepishly back and forth while the kids started running around the field. Ellie turned to Andrea. A look of dread radiated from her eyes, as her face took on a red shade against the green of the grass.

"This coach has no balls?" Andrea whispered loud enough for Colt to overhear from his parking spot.

Braden rummaged through his baseball bag and took out four baseballs that Colt had given him. He clumsily handed them to his coach with a grin.

"I got you covered coach," he said.

Tremblay sent eighteen players out into the infield and set up the tee on top of home plate. He started with Andrea's son, Ronnie Pawlecki, placing the ball on the tee to give him ten swings. An unusually large boy for his age, Ronnie drove each ball past the mound into the area around second base where ten kids stood shoulder to shoulder like a human home run wall.

They all reached out their gloves to make the catches. At one point, one of the kids managed to meet the ball with his glove. But that was the closest anyone came to catching any of Ronnie's hits.

The next few kids struggled to make contact, even off the stationary tee. Braden pounced on each dribbler that came his way. Other kids edged toward the plate to try and get their hands on the ball, but Braden anticipated each hit and reached them all quicker than any of his teammates.

"Good instincts," Colt noted to himself. "He's quick."

At least half the players stood in the base path between second and third base with their backs turned away from the play giggling or sitting on the ground fidgeting in the dirt. Colt wondered if this team would ever win a game once their season started.

Tremblay made an admirable attempt to project a cheerful image and keep some energy in the practice. But teaching one player to hit while eighteen others stood around waiting for their turn proved disastrous. Soon enough, they ran all over the field, throwing their gloves at each other and rolling around like puppies.

Colt could barely contain himself from trotting onto the field and taking over. But he didn't have a child on the team. He didn't know any of the kids, and he hadn't met any of the parents other than Ellie and Andrea.

"Not your place Gibson," he told himself. "Let it ride."

As Andrea and other mothers sat on the swings socializing, Ellie marched to her car on the other side of the parking lot. She retrieved her glove and crossed through the gate onto the field. The women on the swings stopped chatting and watched the confrontation from afar.

"You have any more tees?" she asked Tremblay. "We need to get more kids swinging at a time."

"You can't be out here," Tremblay protested.

"You need help."

"Yes, but you're not supposed to be…"

"Well, I am," she snapped. "We can't have them running around like this. They're here to play baseball."

"They only gave me the one tee," said Tremblay. "They didn't even give me any balls."

Ellie looked around for a minute. She approached the area where the garbage trucks emptied green metal trash bins by the back door to the cafeteria. She grabbed three orange traffic cones, stacked and lugged them back to the field. Colt watched her, trying to figure out what creative idea she had up her sleeve.

"Break them into groups of five," she instructed Tremblay, as she placed an orange cone on top of the first, second and third base plates. "Group one hits on your tee from home plate into the backstop. Group two can hit from first base out into the empty teachers' parking lot. Group three can hit from second base into center field and group four can hit from third base into the playground."

"Now, now, uh wait just a moment, Missy," Tremblay stammered.

Andrea laughed as Ellie spoke over him.

"Round them up and count them off," she ordered him before turning to the swing set area. "Andrea, Dina, we need your help. You just need to place the ball on top of the cone and then let each kid take five swings. The kids who aren't batting have to retrieve the ball. One point for each catch."

Not all the parents seemed to know what instruction to give, including Coach Tremblay who stood at a distance and watched the parents manage the practice on his behalf.

"I'm gonna win," Braden announced as he sprinted to the dugout from center field.

Colt watched Ellie and the other parents, shag balls, place them on the orange parking cones, and instruct the kids on how to watch the ball and level their swings. He considered following her onto the field to help direct the hitting practice. But something held him back.

"It's not your kid," he reminded himself. "And you're not a coach anymore."

Tremblay, having bought into Ellie's practice plan, rounded the kids and explained the logistics to them. With the same enthusiasm he used to start the practice, he rallied the players wanting to win points for catching the ball.

By the end of the practice, Braden had eleven points. Ronnie had four, a stocky boy named Tonio Maletti, tied with an athletic set of twins named Lilly and Lainey Yu with three each. Nobody else made any catches.

In his post-practice address, Tremblay congratulated the team on a productive outing for their first practice. He also announced the first game between the B's and the C's as ten o'clock the next day.

"Practice on Saturdays, games on Sundays," he repeated three times to make sure each kid heard the message. "Great job kids. And thank Mrs. Maletti, Mrs. Pawlecki and Ms. Shaw for all their help. We couldn't have made those twenty-four catches without them!"

After his few platitudes of encouragement, the kids dispersed into the playground adjacent to the field.

Colt turned the key to start the engine. He tossed his glove into the back seat. From the back of the lot, he watched Ellie socialize with the other parents while Braden chased two girls from his team around the swings.

Not feeling like he'd belong among the group of young parents, he engaged the gear shaft, pulled out of the parking lot and returned to his apartment to catch up on the sleep he'd missed.

About an hour later, just as his body relaxed under his covers, he heard Ellie's Ford return to the side of her house. The pebbles of the driveway popped and cracked, and the brakes squeaked as the vehicle came to a stop. When the doors opened, Braden's excited chatter about the practice drifted up Colt's staircase.

Within minutes, the thwacking of his repeated ball-throwing against the wall also commenced. Colt tried to tune it out, but the rhythmic thumping served as an effective wake-up call. He threw off the covers, grabbed his hat and glove and looked out his window. Instead of one eight-year-old throwing the ball, Colt saw two. Braden had a young friend practicing against the wall with him. They both still wore their blue shirts from the practice.

In the kitchen window, he could see Ellie's head bob back and forth. He imagined her frying bacon for BLTs or squeezing lemons for fresh, homemade lemonade. A minute later, she appeared at the patio table with two peanut butter and jelly sandwiches on limp white bread.

The boys dropped their gloves and ran to the table. Ellie disappeared into the kitchen for a moment before returning with a bowl of grapes and a plate full of watermelon slices.

Instead of intruding, Colt decided to stay in. He boiled ramen noodles, reclined on his couch in the dark and played his Xbox for the next hour.

By one o'clock, the nourishment from the ramen noodles wore off and he decided to venture into town for food. He descended the stairs and waved to Braden, who immediately ran over with his friend.

"This is my friend, Steven," Braden said. "Stevie, this is Colt. He's a professional baseball player."

"Really?" Steven asked, eyes wide. "Like from the Phillies?"

"No," Colt laughed. "I played in college. But I didn't make the pros."

A large black Suburban rolled into the driveway. As it roared over the pebbles, Stevie's shoulders drooped.

"My dad's here," he moaned.

Ellie exited the house. The screen door smacked against the frame making a similar thwacking sound to Braden's ball throwing against the garage wall. The sight of Colt standing in the driveway must've caught her by surprise because she blinked before turning her attention to Stevie's father getting out of the SUV.

"Hello Joe." She smiled and handed him a series of manila envelopes. "I balanced the checkbook and wrote all the payroll checks. Everything's organized in folders and labeled."

Joe noticed Colt standing in the driveway.

"Colt," she said. "This is Joe Dalton, the owner of the fencing company in town."

"Well, we started as a fencing company," Joe explained. "But we're getting into home improvement, windows, roofing and some landscaping."

"Stevie and Braden are on the same baseball team," Ellie said. "They had their first practice today."

"How'd it go?" Colt asked.

Ellie and Joe exchanged looks. Both mumbled something to the effect of: *"Good, I guess."*

"Colt's going to start as the new gym teacher at the school this fall," Ellie said to Joe.

"Are you Colt Gibson from Allentown?" Dalton asked. "The basketball player?"

"Yah, that's me, I guess." Colt looked down at his boots. "I was a better baseball player."

"Basketball?" Ellie asked, looking him up and down from head to toe and back to the top of his head.

"I reffed a lot of those games back in the day—was really into it," Joe said, "I didn't cover that one, but I was in the bleachers watching. One of the most memorable games ever."

"What game?" Ellie asked.

"Only the 4A State Championship," Joe answered like a proud dad. "They played against Norristown."

"Wow." Braden jumped into the conversation. "The State Championship?"

"I'm surprised anyone remembers." Colt downplayed the topic. "That was like ten years ago."

"Sure was," Joe beamed. "Was a big deal around here."

"Did your team win?" Braden asked.

"Did his team win?" Joe exclaimed. "Colt, here won it for them."

"Hardly," Colt deflected the attention. "I barely played. I think I had two points."

"But you won the game?" Ellie asked.

"The charge," Joe continued, his enthusiasm rising.

"The charge?" Braden asked.

"I was really more of a defensive player," Colt explained. "We had a sixteen-point lead with about ten minutes to go. Our best player was six-foot seven and a beast. More like a linebacker than a basketball player. He fouled out. He'd been battling with their best player all game. But with him out, they came back on us pretty hard. They got within one. Our guy guarding their big scorer just couldn't stop him, so they sent me in."

"This kid, Williamson," Joe continued Colt's story. "A monster. He drove the lane like a madman. He buried anyone who got in his way. That's how Harrison fouled out."

"So, they sent you in to stop him?" Ellie asked. "What're you, like six-two?"

"If I spike my hair."

"What about the charge?" Braden reminded the adults to stay on point in their story.

"Right," Joe picked up the narrative, near rabid with excitement. "So, Williamson's lighting it up. But he's got four fouls. Colt, here, goes in and pesters him. You were so quick to the ball.

He frustrated the kid. He couldn't get open. Colt did a great job denying him the ball."

"He was pretty pissed." Colt smiled, enjoying the accolade.

"The charge?" Braden asked again impatiently.

"Of course," Joe continued. "So, Williamson gets the ball off a screen with a minute left. Colt nearly got knocked to the ground. Williamson drives the lane hard, but Colt clearly gets there first and plants his feet. He covers his chest with his arms and gets blown off the court by the guy. Williamson just obliterates him. Everyone in the gym thought he was dead. He jumped so high, he nearly sunk his knee into your throat."

"I took an elbow to the eye," Colt added.

"Right." Joe laughed. "Swelled right up, all black and blue."

"So, that was the charge?" Braden asked. "The big guy from the other team got fouled out and Colt won the game?"

"They were in the double bonus," Joe replied. "Williamson was out of the game. Colt sunk the two free throws to go up by three. And that was all she wrote."

"You won the states?" Braden exclaimed.

"Sure did." Colt looked down into Braden's eyes, with a sideways glance at Ellie, who nodded her head, in acknowledgement.

"Not bad," she said, with a playful smirk.

"Hey, until school starts, what're you doing, Colt?" Joe changed the subject. "We need some help with a couple projects this summer. We could use a strong, young installer."

"I'll seriously consider that," Colt replied. "A little extra money, a chance to meet more of the people in town. I appreciate the offer. Could I get back to you by tomorrow?"

"Sure thing," Joe said, shaking hands.

Stevie, who took no interest in the conversation about basketball, said goodbye to Braden and jumped into his father's truck. Ellie went over a few additional details about the paperwork she had prepared for him, and Joe thanked her before getting into the driver's seat. As he started to pull out of the driveway, he stopped, rolled down his window and called out to Ellie and Colt.

He smiled. "How cute. You'd be co-workers."

As the car pulled away, Ellie and Colt looked at each other across the driveway and smirked at Joe's observation. The word "cute" reverberated in his mind.

"Imagine that." Ellie shrugged.

"Lehigh and Lafayette. Working together."

Ellie laughed. Her hair flung back in the breeze. Braden ran into the house thwacking the door behind him.

"Well," Colt said. "I'm off to the diner for some lunch."

"Okay." Ellie turned back toward her house, before abruptly pivoting to face him.

For a moment, she froze, like an actress on stage forgetting her lines.

"If you're hungry?" she asked after her momentary pause. "Instead of driving to the diner, I could whip you up a sandwich. I make a mean BLT."

7

THE BATTING ORDER

Colt awoke relatively early the next morning by his standards—around eight a.m. Braden hadn't even started throwing the ball against the garage wall yet. Colt flopped on his ballcap, grabbed his glove, pulled on a pair of shorts, and ventured into the bright Sunday morning sun. He stood at the top of the garage stairs stretching his arms as if taking in the fresh Pennsylvania mountain air as he eyed Ellie's back door. He placed his glove on the railing and sat at the top stair eating a stale Pop Tart from the leftover stock of his old roommate's food supply.

As if on cue, Braden bound out the door with his glove and ball, smacking it against the wall. Ellie followed behind him in grey sweatpants, a Lafayette t-shirt, and an oversized cup of coffee. Colt caught her eye as she sat in the wicker chair on her cement patio. She flashed a smile as warm as the wisps of steam that emanated from her mug.

"You're up bright and early," she called to him.

"It's a beautiful morning," Colt replied.

"That it is."

"Can you throw with me?" Braden interrupted their small talk.

"I got my glove right here," Colt replied with one last smile at Ellie.

"It's our first game today," Braden beamed. "We're playing the C-team."

"They're called the Seadogs, Honey," Ellie reminded him.

"Can you come?" Braden asked. "Mom, can Colt come to my game?"

"If he wants to." She raised her eyes to him. "You don't have to."

"Sure, I'll come," said Colt.

"Really," Ellie stammered. "If it's a bother—"

"—No. I'd love to."

Ellie smiled again and took a long sip of her coffee. Colt watched the steam float across her face and warm her cheeks a cozy pink.

"I want to go early and practice at the field," Braden said, with excitement in his voice that sounded like the hungry chirp of a bird. "Will you hit grounders to me?"

Colt noted a gleam of amusement in her eyes at Braden's infatuation with him.

"Sure will." Colt tipped Braden's ballcap forward over his eyes.

"We have about a half hour," Ellie called from the patio where she sat cross-legged with her coffee mug cupped between her hands.

For twenty minutes, they worked on his arm angle and rotating his hips on his follow-through. Colt deliberately threw the ball just out of Braden's reach, challenging him to make diving catches. Braden imitated Colt and threw the ball way off to Colt's side, forcing him to spring into the air and hurl his body across the grass to make his own diving catches. Braden laughed and cheered. After each catch by either him or Colt, he looked to his mother to make sure she saw them.

Ellie glanced at her watch and gave her son a ten-minute warning.

Braden rambled about hitting home runs, turning double plays, and stealing bases.

"We can't get there early to practice if you keep talking Colt's ear off, Honey," Ellie called to her son. "It's time. Let's go."

Braden grabbed his glove and ran across the driveway into the back seat of the car. Colt noticed Ellie watching him swat the dust from his cargo shorts out of the corner of her eye.

"You know you don't have to come with us," she said to him.

"I know," he replied, attempting to rub a stain out of the bottom of his shirt.

"You're dirty from all that diving."

"He's dirtier than I am."

"He's eight."

"It's just a little grass stain." Colt tried to fold the shirt over itself and rub away the green smudge.

"Leave it alone. You're only going to make it worse." Ellie's lips parted into a smile. "When we get back, I'll wash it for you."

Colt stopped fiddling with the shirt and instead, tucked it into his shorts to hide the mark.

"Come on," Braden called to them through the back seat window.

For a moment, Ellie ignored Braden's outburst. She stood at the top of the driveway and shifted her weight between her feet. Her smile waned as she pulled her keys from her purse.

"Quit blabbing and let's go," Braden yelled.

Ellie's face shaded red. But Colt's laugh at Braden's consternation, dispelled the flush from her cheeks.

"Seriously," she whispered to him. "Don't feel obligated."

"You kidding?" Colt replied, heading toward his truck. "I'm almost as excited as he is."

Ellie offered to drive Colt to the game. But not wanting to impose, Colt opted to take his truck and follow behind her.

They arrived before the rest of Braden's teammates. Through the woods, they could see the A-team practicing in-field drills in anticipation of their season opener against the neighboring town of Schnecksville. The Schnecksville squad had not yet arrived. But by the look of their dusty uniforms, the entire Springtown team must have been warming up all morning.

Braden ran out to the shortstop position and dug his cleats into the grass, imitating the many pros he'd seen on SportsCenter.

Ellie took the field next to him to give him pointers about getting his glove down, moving his feet and watching the ball into his glove. Colt hit light grounders to him. The lefty shortstop managed to either catch or knock down most of the balls that he faced.

"He should probably take some reps at first," Colt suggested. "The more repetition, the better he'll be there."

"But I want to play short," Braden pleaded. "That's where all the balls get hit."

"But he's a lefty." Colt looked at Ellie. "When he fields the ball, his hips are facing the wrong direction. He has to turn all the way around to step toward first."

"I think at eight, he can play wherever he wants to play," Ellie replied, her voice flat and firm.

"Most coaches are going to want him at first."

"They should want him where he can make the most plays."

"It's just not conventional, that's all."

"Well, neither is he."

"Fair enough." Colt let it drop as he hit another, harder ground ball that Braden had to run to stop.

Coach Trembley appeared next. The unathletic middle-aged man ambled across the parking lot with his nose buried in his cell phone. Ronnie, Stevie, and the twin girls followed him. Ellie lined them up in the infield. Colt conducted infield drills with Ronnie at first base, Lilly and Lainey taking turns at second, Braden at short and Stevie at third. With no coaching duties, Trembley organized the helmets in each dugout. He lined up the bats along the fence and paid the teenaged umpire who showed up to officiate the game.

By the game start time, nine players took the field for the Bees and only seven for the Seadogs, so the Bees loaned Stevie to the other dugout to even the rosters.

Colt and Ellie took seats along the fence and deferred to Coach Trembley, who led a rousing pre-game cheer and sent his players out to the same positions they had taken in the warmups. Braden gave his mom a grin and thumbs up at the opportunity to play shortstop.

A Seadogs parent, acting as the coach, lined up his players from shortest to tallest and set his batting order accordingly. Tremblay opted to line them up by the numbers on their jersey. As the shortest on the Bees, Braden would have batted first in the Seadog line-up. But, with his request for his mother's favorite number '11', he ended up last in the order for the Bees.

The first batter for the Seadogs barely looked as tall as the tee and promptly hit a ten-foot dribbler that nobody on the Bees could get to in time to make an out. The next batter, not much taller than the first, hit an equally weak grounder that barely rolled twenty feet. Braden ran all the way past the mound. By the time he reached the ball, he had no chance to throw out the runner and wisely held it in his glove. The next four batters all hit weak grounders that the Bees couldn't handle, loading the bases and ultimately squeezing in the first two runs of the season.

Then Stevie Dalton came up to bat. The heavyset eight-year-old hit a hard line-drive all the way to the fence. The left fielder for the Bees had wandered out of his half of the outfield leaving it empty. Braden chased the ball to the left field corner. By the time he picked it up and heaved it toward the catcher, Stevie cruised home with an easy grand slam.

Braden waved to the left fielder, imploring him to return to his position, and rolled his eyes at his mother. Ellie shrugged her shoulders and applauded him for his heads-up plays. At 12-0, the Seadogs had bat around their line-up more than once before the Bees could record a third out.

Like their opponent had, the Bees, hit a smattering of weak grounders, which the Seadogs couldn't handle. However, the Bees made a few mistakes, which enabled the Seadogs to record a couple outs. Willie Biegacki, forgot to run after hitting a ground ball to the Seadogs second baseman.

Lilly Yu struck out, swinging above the tee and completely missing the ball all three times.

Ronnie, who wore number ten came up to bat right before Braden with two outs. Colt watched Ellie squeeze her hands together. Braden gave her a look of dread that Ronnie would make an out and he'd miss his chance to bat.

"Come on Ronnie," he cheered for his friend. "Give it a ride."

Ronnie did just that. He socked a high, deep fly ball over second base and into the outfield. The ball sailed right at the head of the right fielder, who happened to be the tiny lead-off batter for the Seadogs. The boy stuck his glove blindly in the air and closed his eyes as the ball plopped into his web and stuck for the third out.

Braden didn't get his at bat.

Ellie lowered her face into her hands. Braden kicked the dirt with his cleat. Colt watched Braden shake his head in disappointment. He could feel the boy's despair as he and Ellie both seemed to anticipate the scene playing out.

Braden smacked his glove against his thigh and wiped a tear from his eye before trotting out of the dug out to take the field.

"Next inning, Honey," Ellie called to him. "You'll be the leadoff batter."

Before the start of the inning, Coach Trembley instructed the two left-side infielders to switch with the two outfielders. Braden begrudgingly walked to left-center field, relinquishing his spot at shortstop.

After a similar ten-run inning with the bases loaded, Stevie hit a fly ball to center field. Braden darted to his left and made a diving catch, just like the way he and Colt practiced earlier that morning. Because all the baserunners had taken off from their bases, he shouted for the infielders to cover so he could throw to them for the double play. But when they didn't heed his instructions, he simply ran from the outfield to step on second base for the double play and then tagged the runner from first base for an unassisted triple play.

Colt jumped off the bench cheering. Ellie nearly burst into tears.

"Way to go, Baby!" she yelled.

Colt found himself cheering louder than he thought he ever would at a tee-ball game.

Braden leapt off the ground, waving the ball in the air as if he had just won the World Series. The team around him barely grasped what had happened. Ronnie gave him a high five and coach Trembley awkwardly shook his hand.

As Braden took his warm-up swings in the on-deck circle, Garrett Kildeer walked onto the field and removed the tee from the plate.

"Sorry everyone. The 10-U's need the field now."

"You've got to be kidding," Ellie shouted. "We still have ten minutes."

Kildeer ignored her.

Colt pressed his lips into a straight line and made a dramatic point of looking at his watch.

"We're not done yet," Ellie repeated. "Braden hasn't been up to bat."

Kildeer unscrewed the shaft of the tee from the base without responding to Ellie.

"Coach," Colt raised his voice just enough to startle the middle-aged man into looking up at him. "She's got a point. Ten minutes, right?"

"Unfortunately, the games are only fifty minutes long," Coach Trembley answered for Coach Kildeer as he carried the bats out of the dugout. "It's ten to."

"But we didn't even finish the second inning," Ellie blurted.

"We had quite a lovely start, I'd say," Trembley continued, with his cheerful British accent lilting through the air like bad poetry.

"That's not right," Colt directed his voice toward Kildeer, who hunched over the tee with his back to the group.

"Braden didn't even get to bat," Ellie snapped.

"So sorry about that," Trembley replied, lacking empathy like Colt's father had during his own childhood. "How about if he bats first next game?"

Ellie rolled her eyes and turned her back to find Braden.

Colt walked a step behind her, unsure of what to say. As a youth, his father always batted him within the first four spots, so he'd rarely experienced the dejection he saw in Braden's face. The boy's sadness reminded him of some of the weaker players on his teams growing up who his father neglected to give meaningful playing time. He wondered if those players, he always considered 'weaker' were really as bad as they seemed, or if his father's neglect simply denied them the opportunity to develop to their full potential.

"I didn't even get to bat." Braden fought back his tears. "That wasn't fair."

"I know, Baby," Ellie said, wrapping her arms around him.

"We lost twenty-two to five." Braden's voice cracked as tears ran down his cheek. "They didn't even finish the second inning."

Colt looked at Braden's dirt-streaked face as it smudged with beads of sweat and drops of tears. It reminded him of an old picture of himself at six-years-old after losing his town t-ball championship game more than twenty years earlier.

He squatted to Braden's eye level. "You had an unassisted triple play."

Braden teetered but turned his face back into his mother's chest.

"Do you know how many times that's been done in the majors?" Colt continued.

Braden peaked out from burying his face into his mother's sweatshirt. "How many?"

"I don't actually know either," Colt answered. "I think it might have been done once in a World Series game. But I know I've never seen such an amazing play in *my* life."

Braden paused for a split second. He looked at his mom, who flashed her widest smile.

"Nobody covered the bases," Braden explained, as if snapping out of a hypnotic trance. "Did you see me make that diving catch and then tag out all the runners?"

"We sure did," Ellie said, hugging her boy. "That was the best play of the game."

Braden grabbed his baseball bag and ran over to sit next to Stevie on the playground bench. "I got an unassisted triple play against you," he called out as he bounded across the woodchips.

"Nicely done," Ellie said, peering into Colt's eyes. "You really cheered him up. Thanks."

Colt shrugged and nodded, basking in the warmth of her response. He had always wondered why his father put in so many hours coaching other peoples' kids. That one moment of gratitude from Ellie gave him a quick peek into the reward he must've felt every time a parent thanked him for his positive impact on their child.

"Hey Colt," Kildeer said as he appeared at the edge of the fence. "You want to help us out with the 10-U travel team? We could use as many assistant coaches as we can get."

"Oh, well, uh," Colt stuttered, caught off-guard by the invitation.

"If you're busy," Kildeer offered. "Got something else to get to, that's fine. I just thought with your experience..."

Colt looked at Ellie but didn't read any sign from her. He watched Braden playing on the jungle gym. He looked back at Ellie, who had turned to collect her purse and keys.

"Uh, sure," Colt replied. "What can I do?"

"We need you to warm up the Tens while the Nines finish up on Victory Field," Kildeer said. "Jog them over once you see us close out our game over there."

Ellie left abruptly, calling for Braden to come to the car. Colt tried to catch her attention, but only saw the back of her head as she walked toward the parking lot.

THE 10-U TEAM used the field for a half hour while the red and black A-team in Braden's age group finished their preceding game. Colt watched Kildeer and Smalley lecture their young crew in the dugout while the visiting team celebrated in the bleachers.

Colt finished hitting fielding practice to the 10-U's and escorted them through the woods to Victory Field. They jogged in unison over the bridge and through the woods like a military unit.

Colt glanced at the road beyond the field. He watched Ellie's little Ford Focus pull out of the diner parking lot and pass Victory Field on her way back to the house. Braden's expressionless eyes peered out the window at him as the car sped out of sight.

Kildeer neither had a child on the 9-U A-team, nor the 10-U team. But, as President, he explained that he felt compelled to make sure all the teams were coached in an effective manner. Jay Smalley assisted with both teams. In addition to his eight-year-old playing on the 9-U team that had just played, he had a nine-year-old on the 10-U team.

As the Springtown team took their at-bats at the bottom of the first inning, Kildeer asked Colt to coach first base. From his spot, adjacent to the dugout, Colt could hear Smalley question Kildeer in front of the team.

"Why him?" he snapped. "I thought I was your first base coach."

"Let's see what he can do," Kildeer replied. "We're not even an inning into this game and we're already getting smoked. Maybe a change'll do us some good."

THE 10-U TEAM HAD TALENT, but they all appeared small to Colt.

"Those guys look like football players," he said to Smalley after the other team hit their third home run over the fence in as many innings.

"What do you expect? They're eleven and we're barely nine," Smalley explained. "We play up a couple age groups. We take our lumps. But it's all about toughening them up for when they turn twelve."

After their 9-0 drubbing, Kildeer gathered the players in a circle by the dugout fence.

"We gotta clean it up," he said. "You can't make those mistakes."

"You gotta catch the ball," Coach Smalley added. "And could someone get a hit, please?"

Colt watched the grim faces of the players around the circle. He recalled the many tongue-lashings his father had laid on his college team's full-ride scholarship athletes. He'd heard the same critical feedback dating back to high school, middle school, and even elementary school.

"Good effort, though," Smalley said, looking at each player in the eye and clapping his hands to energize them. "I saw some promising plays out there too."

"Just not enough of them," Kildeer added.

Colt looked forward to returning to Ellie's house and throwing with Braden, maybe even with Ellie, he imagined. But, as the players dispersed, Joe Dalton showed up and called to him from across the parking lot.

"Any further thoughts about getting in a couple weeks of work before the school year begins?"

"Definitely," Colt replied. "I can start right away."

Dalton walked the fence at Victory Field and pointed out to Colt a number of spots where it had either curled at the bottom or tore into a gaping hole. Dalton showed him where to find wire cutters, extra lengths of fence wire, zip ties and other necessary items including work gloves and first aid supplies in the maintenance shed under the concession stand. It was about the size of Ellie's garage. Bags of infield dirt, pitching mound clay, and lime to line the field sat piled to the ceiling. Rakes, shovels, and other landscaping tools hung from the walls. He also noted the powerful ride-on lawnmower and smaller push mower as well as ten-gallon buckets of baseballs, extra catcher's equipment, and several expensive wood bats.

"Damn," he uttered under his breath.

"I know," Dalton replied. "We take good care of our ballfields here."

Colt watched Coach Kildeer shake hands with the last few parents still standing at the bottom of the bleachers.

"How come we don't fix up the other field like this?" Colt asked Dalton as Kildeer waved and walked toward them. "The grass is long. The fences are a mess. It's all weeds."

"I don't know," Dalton mused as if the thought had never occurred to him. "That's the school playground. They play soccer there."

"Plenty of room for both. You could fence along the right and left field lines at least, even if you don't install a home run fence. Or, you could put in a removeable outfield fence. I've seen these ..."

"Gibson?" Garrett Kildeer interrupted. "It just dawned on me. Are you *Colt* Gibson?"

"He sure is," Joe answered for Colt before he could even respond.

"Gibson, from Lehigh related to Butch Gibson?"

"He's my dad," Colt replied, suddenly self-conscious of the undisclosed letter of termination he received from the school.

"I thought the name sounded familiar," Kildeer said. "Good to have you on board with our organization. Thanks for helping us out. I hope you don't mind us tapping you to help with our programs as well?"

"No problem," Colt sighed, used to the common association with his father. "Glad to pitch in."

He waited to see if Kildeer would reveal further knowledge of his father or his own embarrassing dismissal from the Lehigh coaching staff. But the man's genuine cheer and authentic smile assured him that the private matter between him and the university had remained shielded from the public.

Dalton shook Colt's hand and told him to meet him at his office the next morning. Kildeer grabbed a broom from the storage room and swept sand from the area in front of the concession stand. Colt picked up his bag to leave, but Kildeer held up a finger and walked with him into the parking lot.

"Jay's pretty committed to the 9-U team, and I have to supervise him a little closer than I figure you'd need," Kildeer said to Colt. "If you want the 10-U team, you could have it."

Across the parking lot, Colt noticed Jay Smalley lurking by his car and watching the exchange.

"Oh, no," Colt replied. "I'd be happy just helping out."

"I'd love to get another college ballplayer into our ranks," Kildeer persisted.

"I'd prefer to work with that B-team you've got. You know; the Bees."

"I'll tell you what." Kildeer extended his hand to Colt. "I'll make you co-coach with Trembley. The guy's an idiot. He won't mind. In exchange, you coach this team too. They won't conflict. The 10-U's play right after the B's and C's, so it should work out great for you."

Colt agreed, shook hands with Kildeer, and hopped into his

truck. Smalley looked away as he pulled past him. He accelerated down the main road, eager to share the news with Ellie and Braden that he'd officially serve as a co-coach for the Bees.

As he pulled in, he found Braden and Ellie throwing together in the back yard. He rolled over the pebbled driveway to his spot next to the stairs. He watched Ellie glance over her shoulder and say something to her son.

He popped the parking brake, excited to tell them his good news. But, before he could retrieve his glove from the floor of the back seat, Ellie and Braden walked back toward the house. Colt exited his vehicle, with his glove tucked under his arm, ready to practice with them. But Ellie had already slammed her screen door closed, leaving him alone with the birds and crickets in the back yard.

"What was that all about?" Colt asked himself.

He stood by the edge of the backyard waiting to see if they'd return through the back door. Had he missed an oncoming rainstorm in the distance?

"I guess I'll see you guys tomorrow," he muttered to himself, as he tossed his glove back into the truck, gave one last look at the empty back yard, and withdrew up the stairs to play on his Xbox for the rest of the afternoon.

8

THE WEEKDAY GAME SCHEDULE

As with most youth baseball fields, the fencing along the base of the Victory Field backstop curled causing wild pitches to slip under the gap and into the parking lot. As a teenager in his hometown, Colt worked with his father to fix this problem at his own elementary school.

The A-team travel game had long since ended. The afternoon sun darkened the field and cast shadows from the grandstand across the backstop and batter's box.

After rummaging through Dalton's impressive shed of field repair supplies, Colt found two ten-foot-long two-by-six-inch pieces of pressure-treated wood. He grabbed a roll of stiff wire and dragged the hundred-pound lumber across the parking lot. He used one of them to push the curled section of the Victory Field fence behind home plate back into place. With the heavy-duty wire, he bound the wood plank to the bottom of the fence, creating an impenetrable wall to seal errant pitches within the confines of the playing field.

Using a pair of strong wire-cutters he found in the shed, he walked the perimeter of the field and patched holes and gaps by wrapping and twisting foot-long stretches of wire into makeshift chain links.

When he finished his work on Victory Field, he cast a weary gaze at the elementary field. The hole in the backstop was double the size of the one he had just fixed. Rather than drag the remaining two-by-six from home plate, through the woods, to the elementary school, Colt hoisted the lumber onto his back, like the crossbeam wings of a commercial airliner. He plodded from Victory Field to the adjacent run-down elementary field and dropped it behind the backstop that Braden's B-team used earlier in the day.

In the same way, Colt latched the board to the bottom of the backstop and used the wire to plug the gaping hole.

We'll call this one Winner Field.

After finishing the fence, he stood in the impression left in the grass from the home plate they had used in the game. Counting out sixty feet with twenty strides, he walked to where first base should sit. He noticed the impression from the first base used in the game was about ten feet too short. He stretched his arm outward and surveyed the precise angle and location for the placement of second base.

His concentration broke at the sight of Garrett Kildeer traipsing through the woods between the two fields.

"I saw your truck parked outside Victory," he called to Colt. "I thought you left to go home. Whatcha doing over here at the elementary?"

"Fixing the fence," Colt replied. "When I was a kid, my dad and I used to stay after each game to tend the field. We'd rake out the infield dirt, tarp the bases, and clear all the empty water bottles out of the dugout. It's amazing how many kids just leave them on the bench. Garbage can's twenty feet away."

"Can't touch this field, though," Kildeer warned. "Liability."

"I'm just wiring up the fence. No harm, no foul."

"Pretty good game earlier today." Kildeer leaned against the fence with his arms folded under his chin.

"They didn't even get through the second inning. One of the teams didn't bat all their players."

"No." Kildeer laughed. "The 10-U game."

"Oh, right." Colt nodded in agreement. "The other team seemed a lot stronger."

"This is how you build a winning program." Kildeer turned serious. "You play up. Take your knocks. They either get tougher or they quit. Either way, the program benefits."

"I felt bad for the six kids that didn't play."

"Trust me. The honor and privilege of making this team is reward enough for those kids. You think they'd make the team we just played? I don't think so."

None of them would... Colt changed the topic. "Hey, the Shaw kid, Braden; he's pretty good. You should give him a look."

"Too small." Kildeer discounted the suggestion. "What's he six? He'd never get it out of the infield."

"None of them did today. They no-hit us."

"He's a lefty, no good to me as an infielder," Garrett said. "Too small to play first base and he doesn't pitch, so, there's no place for him on an advanced team like ours."

"He could play outfield."

"Everyone who can't play infield plays outfield. I've got six kids platooning out there and they're all much bigger than the Shaw kid."

"He's a great pitcher." Colt stretched the truth.

"Is he?" Garrett asked, squinting in the sun. "I don't see it."

"You will."

"Listen." Garrett turned to watch one of his players hit a high fly ball into the outfield. "Thanks for the help. The games take place on Mondays, Wednesdays, and Fridays at six pm. The home games are all here at Victory Field. Warm-ups start at five. Good luck and thanks again for coaching them. I'll see you on Monday."

As Kildeer retreated through the woods, Colt reviewed his work on the elementary school fence. "Right," he muttered to himself. "Warm-ups at five—Monday."

As he returned to his truck, he considered hitting the diner for lunch. He noticed a text from Phil Jones.

> Phil: Beer. Pizza. Phillies-Nationals.

As he read the first text, a second appeared.

> Phil: Your new place. Game at 1. See you then.

The clock on his dashboard read nearly one-thirty as he cranked the gear shaft and spun out of the Victory Field parking lot.

Phil's yellow Jeep Wrangler sat idling in front of the wood garage. The taillights flickered red in a rhythmic pattern, as if Phil were tapping his foot to a song playing on his car radio. As Colt exited the cab of his truck, the harsh beat of rap music vibrated through the vehicle.

Though he couldn't see it, he felt Ellie's eyes roving the scene through her kitchen window. Out of his peripheral vision, he thought he caught the curtains sway.

"Dude." Phil jumped out of his vehicle wearing his brown Lehigh polo. "This is it? This is where you live? Friggin' dump."

Colt shushed him and guided him by the arm up the stairs. Phil carried a large pizza and a six-pack of beer. "You stole all my food, asswipe. I don't know why I'm the one bringing the pizza."

"The person who owns the place is really nice," Colt whispered. "Probably scared the crap out of her showing up out of the blue."

"Her?" Phil asked with a sly grin. "Is she cute?"

"No," Colt blurted before backtracking. "Well, actually, yes."

Phil raised his eyebrows.

"It's not like that. She's my landlord."

"Then maybe I'll take a shot at her."

"She's not your type."

"Think she's a gamer?"

"Dude, respect," Colt snapped. "She's a mother, and a damn good one."

"Fine, whatever. You can have her."

They entered the apartment. Colt threw his glove on the mat by the door then flicked through the channels to find the game.

"That coulda been you," Phil said as the players took the field to start the second inning.

"I wasn't good enough by a long shot."

"Coming out of high school..."

"That was a long time ago."

Phil washed down a slice of pizza with a swig of beer. He kicked his feet onto the coffee table and scratched his scruffy half-stubble beard.

"So that hot chick next door is the landlord?" he asked.

"You met her?" Colt asked, suddenly self-conscious of what his immature friend may have said to her.

"I guess so. She came right out, soon as I pulled in," Phil replied between gulps. "I didn't know who she was. I assumed she was renting the house or something. She told me to wait in the driveway. Said she thought you'da been back from some baseball game already. What're you coaching Little League or something?"

"Something like that."

EARLY MONDAY MORNING, the clouds threatened to rain out any chance of a baseball game that night. Ellie held Braden's hand as they walked from the back door to the street. The yellow school bus rumbled to a stop by the bayberry bush.

"Almost summer vacation," Braden beamed.

"Almost," Ellie said.

"Then I can play baseball with Colt in the back yard every day."

Ellie moved a strand of hair away from Braden's eyes and kissed him on the forehead. "He's a busy man. He's not going to be available to play baseball with you every day."

"But he's like me," Braden said as the bus rumbled up the street toward the driveway. "He loves to play."

"Don't get your expectations up too high, Buddy, okay."

"I won't," Braden said. "Just tell him to be ready at three o'clock when I get home."

Ellie straightened Braden's backpack and wiped some imaginary dust from his t-shirt. The boy disappeared into the bowels of the bus. A few seconds later, he reemerged in one of the windows with his little bear paw waving exuberantly at her.

Ellie stood still for a few seconds as the vehicle motored away from her driveway. Out of the corner of her eye, she caught movement in the window to Colt's apartment. She sipped her coffee and looked across her back yard at the rising sun through the trees. As she did, she stole a few quick glances toward Colt's window.

She didn't quite see him, although the curtain seemed to shift as if just having been pulled closed. She headed back up the driveway to the chores that awaited her in the house. She had to fold the laundry, make herself a lunch, and pack a snack for Braden for after school.

Her son's voice echoed in her mind.

Tell him to be ready at three o'clock when I get home.

As if sleepwalking, she found herself climbing the creaky wood steps to the upstairs apartment and knocking on the aluminum screen door.

Colt opened the door within a few seconds and flashed a cheerful smile. He wore a faded t-shirt with a picture of a baseball in the middle of it. The word CENTRAL arched above the graphic, with the word CATHOLIC in block letters below. Having showered, shaved and combed his hair, his wavy blond locks parted nicely in the middle of his forehead and dandled just below his ears. She hadn't seen him without a baseball cap covering his head and decided he looked older and more mature without it.

"I'm going to Mr. Dalton's office," Ellie said. "I thought you might like a ride?"

"I told him I'd be there by nine," Colt replied, looking at his watch. "I could go early. You could show me around the place."

"You don't have to…"

"No. It'll be fun."

"It'll take less than two minutes to show you around." She laughed. "It's a four-room office with a kitchenette and garage full of fence posts and whatever else."

"Sounds nice," Colt said, fetching a pair of work gloves from his unpacked duffel bag. "The place's a little messy, sorry."

The apartment looked much better to her than it did when Mr. Schneider lived there with his boxes of outdated paperwork from his defunct insurance agency he closed after retiring. She'd seldom visited the elderly man while he served as her tenant but recalled him drawing the shades all day and running up the heat, causing the place to seem like a dark, muggy cave.

Ellie ran her hand along the bottom of her silk floral skirt to flatten it against her legs. The ruffles extended to her ankles, obscuring her black calf-length boots. On top, she wore a thin white blouse over a thick black cotton undershirt. Despite the early summer warmth, she always felt cold sitting in Joe Dalton's dark office all day.

"So, do you want to commute together to the office?" Ellie asked him again.

Colt grabbed his wallet from the coffee table and slipped his phone into his front pocket.

"That'd be nice."

He ran his hand through his hair and slid his Lehigh baseball cap onto his head.

"Seriously." Ellie frowned in mock disgust. "You're going to wear that crap in my car?"

Colt laughed and followed her down the stairs.

"Looks like rain," he said as he slid into the passenger seat next to her.

Ellie took a moment to check the day's schedule on her phone before starting up the engine.

"Busy morning?" Colt asked.

"I've got a bunch of orders to process. Quarterly taxes are coming up. And I've got this meeting with a persistent supplier. It's gonna be a long one."

"What time's Braden get out of school?"

"Three," Ellie replied, while navigating the car out the driveway and along the main road into town. "Thank God for the Afters Program."

"Afters?"

"He plays basketball and dodgeball in the gym with other kids whose moms also work late."

"I used to love dodgeball."

"Me too," Ellie said.

"Really?"

"Sure," Ellie replied as she turned at the intersection and accelerated toward Dalton's office. "I used to have a good arm."

"Did ya?"

"Of course, I was really good at dodgeball."

"Huh," Colt said, with an under-his-breath chuckle. "That's cool."

Ellie turned into the parking lot and pulled up to the shady side of the building.

"Oh, Ellie," Colt said as she cut the engine and tossed her keys into the bottom of her purse. "Does he have his bag?"

"What bag?"

"His baseball bag. It looked to me like he only had his backpack this morning."

Had she overlooked a practice in their calendar?

Like he'd know our schedule better than me. He doesn't play on Mondays.

Then a new thought crossed her mind, tipped off by Colt's awareness of what backpack Braden had taken with him onto the bus that morning.

"Were you looking out your window at us?"

Ellie felt a jolt of nerves down her spine at the thought of him taking such interest in her. Fortunately, she'd blow dried her hair and worn her favorite cute skirt and leather boots.

"I, uh, just happened to..." Colt fumbled before changing his tone. "Seriously, where's his bag?"

"It's in the house," Ellie said, perplexed at his persistence. "Why?"

Ellie walked toward the two-story house with wraparound porch that housed Joe Dalton's office. A sign by the driveway featured the word DALTON carved and etched with sparkly gold paint against a brown stained wood background.

"He's gotta be there by five," Colt said. "Doesn't he?"

Ellie stopped walking and looked at him. She felt a wave of annoyance cloud her eyes.

"What're you talking about?" she asked, as Colt strode next to her along the brick walkway toward the front door. "Where does he have to be at five? That's when I pick him up at the Afters Program?"

"Baseball." Colt furrowed his brow in continued confusion.

"Braden doesn't have practice today."

"Practice?" Colt scoffed. "He's got a game."

Ellie looked at him. A moment of doubt crossed her mind. She dug her phone out of her purse and scrolled through her emails.

"Would it kill them to put up a website?" she muttered to herself.

Colt thrust his hands in his pockets.

"Here," Ellie said. "Here's the email from Mr. Tremblay. Practices on Saturdays. Games on Sundays."

Colt's surprised expression caught Ellie off-guard. She looked at him, not sure if he knew something she didn't or was just a bumbling, disorganized frat boy.

"What made you think..."

"Mr. Kildeer said there were games on Mondays, Wednesdays and Fridays," Colt explained. "He told me to be at the field by five."

"Not according to Tremblay's email."

They both stared at each other by the shrubbery outside Dalton's office. Ellie could nearly hear the gear wheels turning in her own head, as she tried to understand whether she or Colt were mistaken about the baseball schedule.

"I'll go home and get his bag during my lunch break," she finally said. "I'll take whatever work I don't finish with me. We can aim to get to the school by four-thirty so he can get dressed. We bought a new pair of baseball pants while you were out doing whatever you were doing yesterday. He's all excited to wear them. He said he's going to slide into first base even if he walks."

"In addition to the A-team," Colt said. "Kildeer asked me to help Tremblay coach the B-team too. I'll suggest reversing the batting order so Braden can lead off."

"That would be nice," Ellie said. "But remember, it's the Bees. And they only play on Sundays."

"Right, sorry. That's what I meant, the Bees," Colt replied with a shrug. "But, I'm still pretty sure he's got a game today."

9

THE NEW BASEBALL PANTS

Rain pattered off the sheet metal roof of Mr. Dalton's storage building. Colt sat on a wood picnic table in the break room watching puddles form in the muddy parking lot. He worked for three hours before lunchtime when the clouds darkened, and the first few raindrops dampened his cheek.

"After lunch, you can work on some pre-assemblies," Dalton told him. "Should only take an hour or two. That's all we can do unless the rain lets up. Forecast gives fifty-fifty odds of the sun coming back out this afternoon."

Colt lined up a series of posts and snapped the top caps into place. He aligned them along a wall by height and width. He caught a white flash darting across the parking lot. Ellie ran into the garage with her sweater covering her head. The bouncy, waves of her hair flattened by rainwater.

"I need a big favor." She reached into her pocket for her keys. "I'm totally confused now about his schedule. But, just in case he does have a game today and the rain lets up, can you go home and get his baseball bag? It's right by the back door."

"Sure." Colt took the keys from her hand. "You want me to drive your car?"

"I trust you. Just don't crash it, Frat Boy."

Colt laughed and shook his head at her nickname for him. "I heard there's a good chance the sun'll come out. Plus, with an all-grass infield, there's much less chance of puddles and mud."

"It'll probably get cancelled, but better to be prepared."

"We used to play on turf fields in the rain," Colt continued. "It's the dirt infield, the batter's box, and the mound that give the biggest problems. And the elementary field doesn't have any of that."

"I'm not too optimistic." Ellie shrugged.

"When we get there. Braden can get dressed in the school bathroom. I'll raid the maintenance shed and try to get the field whipped into shape."

"That's all very sweet of you," Ellie said, the playful grin from earlier giving way to a more authentic smile. "Thank you."

Colt gave her a gallant wink, nodded, and ran across the rainy parking lot to her compact car.

During the drive back to Ellie's house, the downpour intensified and flooded the pothole-laden streets. A twinge of nerves entered his system as he unlocked Ellie's house and entered through the back door. A small part of the errand felt intrusive, like he didn't belong in her home, or even in her life.

The interior exuded warmth and comfort. Colt stepped from the mud room by the back door into the quaint kitchen, which melded into an eating area and open space with a couch and television. Colt spotted a wood staircase in the center of the open floorplan leading to what he assumed were the bedrooms upstairs. He stopped at the edge of the kitchen, daring not to further invade Ellie's privacy. He wafted the faint smell of bacon and pancakes. The dirty dishes from their breakfast sat in the sink with brown bits of cured, greasy fat dripping off the plates.

The baseball bag sat exactly where Ellie said it would, tucked by the back door. As his father taught him, he checked the bag for the essentials. It contained a helmet but not a bat or glove. With a quick glimpse, he found the bat resting against the wall. But Braden's glove remained missing.

Colt scanned the inside of the cozy home. He spotted Braden's mitt on the couch in the cramped living room. After grabbing it, as he walked back to the kitchen, he glanced up the wooden staircase. At the top of the stairs, he saw a powder-blue tiled bathroom, which brightened the otherwise dark wood atmosphere of the home.

Colt could make out two upstairs bedrooms, one to the right and one to the left. But with glove in hand and on Ellie's honor system, he knew better than to explore. He returned to the back door and muttered out loud to himself as he packed the baseball bag.

"Bat, glove, helmet..."

He scanned the floor and found a pair of cleats that he added to the bag.

"Shoes," he continued his mental checklist. The image of Braden sliding into first base in his crisp new baseball pants crossed Colt's mind. "Pants."

He scoured the tiny mud room by the back door. He crossed the kitchen and searched the television room including the couch, the coffee table, behind the couch and along the stairs. Looking up at the second-floor bathroom and the two bedroom doors on either side, Colt took a breath and ascended the thirteen creaky steps.

The bright, messy room with Legos and stuffed animals all over the floor was clearly Braden's. Colt started there. He looked on the bed, the top of the bureau, the bookshelf. Nothing. He opened each drawer. But he couldn't find the pants.

Over his shoulder, Ellie's bedroom loomed like a monster with its mouth agape. Crossing the threshold seemed like an invasion of her privacy. But neglecting to bring Braden his pants seemed like the greater travesty.

He crossed the hall, past the sweet soapy scent of the bathroom and peered into Ellie's most personal space in the house. The bed, a queen, neatly made with a floral comforter, took up much of the room. Cut flowers decorated a vase on the far nightstand. A classic eighties alarm clock with big red numbers occupied the left-side end table. A picture of baby Braden resting on Ellie's chest, presumably only hours after his birth, as evidenced by Ellie's blue and pink hospital gown, protruded above the clock.

Opposite the bed, in a nook formed by the massive dormers that faced the back yard, a rocking chair, one of the plush kinds that new mothers sit in to rock their babies to sleep, held a small pile of white laundry. A blue plastic lattice-style basket contained socks, undergarments, and soft t-shirts. Colt nearly overlooked the pile, trying not to eye Ellie's delicates. But he noticed, tucked beneath the plastic basket, the tiny pair of baseball pants with the blue piping and the tag from the store still affixed to the zipper.

He gingerly slid the pants from under the pile and bolted out of the house to return to the office.

ELLIE SLAMMED THE PHONE. She took a bite of her salami sandwich and shoved it aside. As she did, the pile of orders shifted and slid off the crowded desk to the floor. Ellie scrambled across the carpet to reassemble the pile, spending several minutes matching pages to keep the orders intact. As she kneeled beside her desk to organize her paperwork, the phone rang again. She reached from her knees, grabbed the phone, and pulled it down to her spot on the carpet.

"Dalton's." She paused to listen to the customer on the other end of the line. "Yes, I know. With the rain, we've had a few calls about mudslides."

The client squawked into the phone, and she held it away from her ear.

"Listen," she said, the anger in her eyes contrasting with the syrup of her voice. "I'll get someone out there with a new stretch of fence to fix it as soon as possible."

The door swung open and magnified the rain as it pelted the awning above the front porch. A pair of light brown work boots punctuated his tight, worn jeans as Colt rounded the corner and approached her on the floor. Ellie hung up the phone and craned her neck at him, as he lowered himself to a squat. When standing upright, she thought of him as rather lean and athletic. But, hunched next to her, she noticed his broad shoulders and wide chest.

"Whatcha doing on the floor," he asked, handing her the keys. "All set on the bag."

"Oh, damn." Her mind raced down her long list of items to remember. "Was his glove…"

"Got it." Colt grinned.

"His bat? And his shoes?"

"And his pants too," Colt finished her thought.

"Oh right." A slight blush warmed her cheeks. "They were…"

"Upstairs. I thought he'd need…"

"No, right," Ellie stammered. "Of course. Nice job. I'm glad you…"

The ring of the phone interrupted her gratitude. Joe Dalton's voice sounded distressed. He was delayed at a client site and wouldn't be able to return with the truck to assist the customer whose fence had fallen over in the mud flow of the rainstorm.

"I'll take care of it," Colt said, retrieving the phone from Ellie. "Let me know what I need to do."

Ellie pulled the original paperwork from the installation. Mr. Dalton had erected the fence about six months earlier at the back of one of the properties abutting the walls of the ravine. A small tributary ran through the edge of the property, which sometimes attracted deer and coyotes. Having newly adopted a baby, the client exhibited a near-rabid need for the chain-link fence as critical protection for his budding family.

"The place is a mile away. Mr. Dalton has the truck. What're you going to do?"

Colt rubbed his chin. "We could drive back and get my pickup. Then I could throw the material in the flatbed and take care of the customer myself."

"I can't leave." Ellie frowned. "The phone's ringing off the hook and I have a meeting with a supplier in about twenty minutes."

Colt peeked out the back window into the garage. "How many feet of fencing does he need?"

"Five or six."

"And a post or two?"

"Definitely two."

"It's a mile away?"

"What are you going to do? Walk?"

"Yup." He grabbed the original paperwork and made for the back door. "That's exactly what I'm going to do."

Colt closed the door behind him and disappeared into the garage. Ellie followed him, digging into her purse for her keys.

"Colt," she called to him. "Don't be ridiculous. It's pouring. Take my car."

Colt emerged from the garage with a roll of wire fencing under his left arm. He held a toolbox in his hand. Two wood posts rested across his right shoulder with his right arm securing them against his ear. The rain spattered across his face and matted his hair causing streams to flow down his cheeks and chin.

"The wire'll cut your upholstery to shreds," Colt said with a genuine smile. "Plus, the posts would have to stick out the open window and the rain would ruin your interior. Don't worry about it. I'm good."

Ellie looked at Colt's drenched hair with a mixture of amusement and appreciation. She pictured him lugging a roll of wire fencing and two heavy posts through the mud and puddles of Springtown's back roads in his wet jeans and soggy boots.

"Don't be a hero," she said, flipping her keys to him. "Take my car back to the house. Get your truck. Come pick up the fence. Do the job. Come on back and then we can go to baseball together in the truck."

"That makes a little more sense," Colt said, smirking in embarrassment at his impractical plan.

"Don't forget to switch the…"

The bells dangling from the front door of the office jingled, breaking her train of thought. The heavy wood door bumped against the wall.

"Hello?" called out the voice of Terry Groytle, one of their main suppliers. "I know I'm early, but I have a lot to show you and new pricing to cover, so I thought we'd need a little extra time."

Ellie glanced over her shoulder at the balding fifty-something at the front door as Colt traipsed his way from the back to the front of the parking lot.

"I hope this isn't a bad time." Terry entered the building and deposited two thick binders of product catalogs. "I suppose I could've emailed the new pricing if I had to. But an in-person visit is so much more efficient."

Ellie watched Colt back her car out of its parking spot and turn onto the main road toward her house. She turned to Terry and painted a calm demeanor, offering him a seat at the conference table adjacent to her desk. As she moved to join him, the phone rang again. With a forced exhale of tense air, she raised a finger to her guest and answered what seemed like her hundredth call of the day.

10

THE BACK YARD

Terry Groytle droned about fence caps, grades of polybenzimidazole plastics and new varieties of composite faux wood end posts. Ellie took notes and asked questions, clarifying the pricing by volume and comparing the numbers to the existing cost ledgers. The constant ring of the phone interrupted their long meeting, but since the rain subsided and the sun peeked out from the clouds, the calls died down as well.

Colt blustered through the front door to the office, soaked from head to toe. His boots squished as he stepped onto the carpet. The image of him with his wet, matted hair reminded Ellie of the messy, floppy, energetic golden retriever her family owned during her childhood. The scamp drove her crazy by burying her toys in the yard, slobbering all over her shoes, shaking off the rainwater onto her newly washed clothes and chewing on the webbing of her glove. But she always knew she could count on him to greet her after school with the same heartwarming excitement no matter how bad a day she might have had.

"All set," Colt said, wiping sweat and rain from his forehead. "The Barrett's are happy and feeling safe from the wilderness for now. It's only temporary. We'll have to come back tomorrow to make it look a lot nicer."

Ellie thanked him with her eyes. Then she jolted in her seat.

"What time is it?" she asked.

"Little after four." Colt tossed his gloves on a table in the back room. "We have to go."

Ellie shrugged at Terry Groytle, who picked up on the sudden end of the meeting and quickly collected his catalogs. She thanked him and promised to review the samples in greater detail over the next few days. Terry left his business card on the desk, before existing the office and closed the door behind him.

"Anyone belong to this t-shirt?" Colt asked Ellie, holding up what looked like a rag that he found on a top shelf.

"Uh, don't think so."

Colt watched Mr. Groytle in the parking lot as he piled his catalogs in the trunk. Once the car turned down Main Street and passed out of sight, Colt peeled his soaked shirt from his body. As he lifted it past his chest, he heard Ellie clear her throat.

"Maybe I should change in the kitchen," he said.

"Yes, probably," she replied, hoping he wouldn't notice the wavering of her voice or the blush of her face.

He ducked into the kitchenette. Ellie heard his heavy, wet cotton shirt flop to the floor. She leaned over the side of her desk to peer around the corner for a split second before reminding herself to focus on her work instead of his abs.

"Let's go," he said, his new blue shirt highlighting his eyes. "Sun's out. Time to play ball."

The dashboard clock read four-forty. Colt drove through town to the elementary school, an air of familiarity settled between them in the car. Ellie adjusted the air conditioning, changed the station of the radio and triple checked the presence of Braden's bag on the back seat.

They pulled into the school parking lot with ten minutes to spare before the start of warm-ups. Braden, Stevie, Ronnie, Lilly, and Lainey fanned across the playground chasing each other in a rousing game of freeze tag. From the truck, Colt watched Braden outpace Stevie, tagging him with relative ease and then accelerating around the slide to catch Ronnie. Lilly and Lainey gave him a better run for it. By the time he and Ellie reached the playground, he had frozen all four of his playmates and stood in front of the swing set with his arms in the air like Rocky Balboa.

"Damn," Colt muttered to himself. "He's a gazelle."

Ellie held the baseball bag in the air and called to Braden. "Honey, come on, you've got to change for baseball."

He stood, frozen, as if having been tagged. Then the excitement washed over his face, and he bolted to the car.

"I have baseball tonight?" he panted, darting into the truck and grabbing his bag.

"Yes," Ellie replied, turning to Ronnie, Stevie, Lilly, and Lainey. "Where are your parents?"

Ronnie shrugged. He glanced at Stevie, who put his hands out in confusion. Braden disappeared into the school, pulling his new baseball pants from the bag and slinging them over his shoulder.

"Do you have your baseball bags?" she asked, her face darkening in a shade of hot, dawning red. "Where are your gloves?"

She eyed Colt as he rose from the driver's seat and gazed across the field at the blurs of red and black uniforms moving about on Victory Field across the woods.

"My mom said we only play on the weekends," Ronnie said as the clouds rumbled, and a light rain started to fall. "Can I borrow one of Braden's extra gloves?"

"He's lefty," Lilly giggled.

The rain intensified, enough to cause the children to scramble back into the school gym, but not enough to impact the field. Braden crossed paths with his friends, oblivious to their panicked flight from the wet conditions. Large drops of rain polka dotted his crisp new white pants.

"Where is everybody?" he asked. "Are we playing on Victory Field with the A-team?"

Wordlessly, Colt pierced Ellie's eyes. He blinked and strolled down the left field line of the elementary field toward the path through the woods. Braden called to his friends, imploring them to contact their mothers and get their gloves. He joined them under the overhang as the rain dampened the grass field.

Mr. Kildeer greeted Colt in the short stretch of woods between the fields. His red and black polo shirt splashed color through the gaps in the grey tree trunks. Colt pointed at the elementary school field. Kildeer shook his head. The rain shrouded them in a dull, misty haze.

Ellie watched from the dry confines of her car. She didn't think much of the interaction. Kildeer handed Colt one of the black and red polo shirts his coaching staff wore to the A-Team games.

With a loud sigh, she switched her attention to Braden splashing in puddles with his friends and dampening his new pants.

"Come on Braden. Let's go."

Colt approached the car. Droplets of rain soaked his long waves of hair. Ellie continued to scroll through her messages as he opened the door and slid in next to her.

"There's no game tonight is there?" she muttered.

"Apparently you were right," Colt answered. "I got the A-team schedule mixed up with the B-team."

"Let's just tell the kids it's a rainout," Ellie said, casting a scowl toward Colt. "We'll keep this little schedule misunderstanding to ourselves."

Braden ran to the truck. His cleats squished with each stride.

"Sorry, Honey," Ellie said, in a sweet voice. "You know, with the rain and all."

"We'll break in your new pants this weekend," Colt added as the boy jumped into the back.

"Looks like they're pretty broken in already," Ellie grumbled.

Colt kicked the truck into reverse and backed out of the spot.

"Wait!" Colt pumped the brake.

Startled, Ellie clutched the handle to the door. Braden jostled in the back seat.

"What?" she yelped. "Don't do that."

"We have a bunch of our players here," he said. "Braden's got his bats. Maybe we could make the best of this, uh, scheduling mishap and have a little batting practice?"

"You mean the rainout?"

"Right."

Ellie surveyed the sky. The rain had already subsided to a sprinkle. Ronnie, Lilly, Lainey, Stevie, and several others remained under the overhang by the front of the school, waiting for their parents to arrive.

"Yeah, Mom," Braden exclaimed. "Let's do it."

Ellie took a deep breath and looked at the clearing sky.

"See if your friends want to practice a little bit," she acquiesced.

"Do we have to hit off the tee?" Braden asked Colt. "Can you pitch to us?"

Colt pulled back into the parking lot and Braden pointed to his group of friends. They watched him win over the less than excited crowd and rally them to trot over to home plate where Colt had placed the tee.

"I thought you were going to pitch to us," Braden complained. "I told everyone you were the best pitcher in your college."

Colt hesitated, searching for an answer to Braden's comment. A drop of rain fell from the tip of his nose. He looked at Ellie. Her smirk revealed a mix of amusement and doubt of his ability to facilitate a rambunctious group of eight-year-olds.

"All the pros practice off of tees," he said, crouching to their eye level.

"That's lame," said Tonio Maletti.

"I went to a Phillies game," Thomas Tremblay added. "They were hitting off real pitchers. Even in warm-ups."

Colt took a deep breath. He glanced at Ellie, but her cross-armed body language emitted a potent combination of enjoyment and reluctance to help him reason with the team. He stood, looked out toward the woods beyond center field, and grabbed a ball from Braden's bag.

"I'll show you." He placed the ball on the tip of the tee and slid Braden's tiny bat from its sheath. "Step back now. Everyone against the fence."

The skinny T-ball bat looked like a little, green toothpick in his large hands.

The six of them stepped backward, intrigued by Colt as he swatted the air in a series of practice swings. He stepped up to the tee and raised it by a foot, then aligned his hands, wrists, and shoulders. With one last survey of the outfield, he drew his arms back, flexed his stomach, and whipped the bat through the air. The melodious ping of metal on leather sent the ball careening through the air in a graceful arc.

His audience gasped in unison as the little white orb sailed high against the dull, grey sky. It arched over the outfield and kept going as far as they could trace. Even Ellie caught her breath at the distance the ball traveled. It approached the woods on the fly, glanced a tall white birch and pinballed into the woods, producing a dull leafy thud somewhere beyond the tree line.

"Whoa!" Ronnie leapt. "Me next. Me next."

With a wink, he locked eyes with Ellie, who shook her head in resigned admiration. She redirected her gaze to her phone, but Colt didn't miss the smile still on her face.

Each player took turns whacking the ball into the outfield. Since Braden happened to have five balls in his bag, they played a game where the batter would take five swings with the others waiting patiently against the fence. As soon as the last ball left the tee, they all raced into the field to collect the balls. Colt awarded a point for each ball recovered and brought back to him, and the kids scrambled across the field as if racing to collect Easter eggs.

The parents dribbled into the parking lot and sat with Ellie watching the spectacle. Braden, with his speed and competitive drive, doubled the next nearest score. The kids' laughter and screams filled the air. Parents and coaches on the sidelines at Victory Field looked over to observe the fun.

Andy Tremblay, the official coach of the Bees, leaned over the fence next to Colt as he watched the players scatter into the outfield to shag balls.

"This is clearly something you're qualified to do," he said.

"Hey man," Colt replied. "You do a good job too."

"I'm more the assistant type," he replied. "It doesn't matter what the email says. This is your team."

"I don't want to step on your toes."

"I'll finally get to sleep on Friday nights." Tremblay waved his hand dismissively across the air. "The anxiety of having to pretend I knew what I was doing all weekend was killing me."

"I thought you had to go through all sorts of background checks."

"They only say that to the parents they don't like, don't want or don't trust," Tremblay said. "They love you since you played college ball."

Colt glanced at Ellie to make sure she didn't hear Tremblay's last comments.

"So, what have you, good sir?" Tremblay continued. "Will you take over for me? Maybe not officially. But what Mr. Kildeer doesn't know, can't harm him too greatly. Can it?"

Colt shook hands with Coach Tremblay as Braden ran in with three baseballs in his arms.

"That's three more points for me." He gasped for air as he dropped them in front of his feet. As he did, he stumbled over them, falling into the grass in a fit of giggles, and staining his pants from hip to ankle.

After about twenty minutes, a police car arrived on a routine patrol. Ellie greeted the officer with a hug and a beaming smile. They chatted for a few minutes. Colt watched the officer's demeanor shift from cordial to authoritative as he pointed at the field and shook his head. Ellie debated with him before hugging him a second time. The tall, athletic officer returned to his car and drove away.

"We can't stay here?" Colt asked as Ellie approached the field.

She shook her head in disappointment. Coach Tremblay called to his son to get in the car so they could return home in time for supper. Other parents beseeched their children to hurry. Colt watched them trudge along, moaning about how much fun they were having at the makeshift practice he'd conducted.

"Hey, why don't we continue at Ellie's house?" Colt suggested to the parents.

"My house?"

"Why not?" Colt flashed an exaggerated puppy dog expression as if pleading for a treat. "We've got a huge space back there."

If anything, Colt knew how to use his blue eyes when he wanted to.

"Oh, *we* do, do *we*?" Ellie projected mock indignation.

"Well, *you* do, anyway." Colt gave her a sheepish smile.

"I've got a couple dozen burgers in the freezer," Joe Dalton said. "I'll slap my grill into the back of the truck, and we can make it a team jamboree."

Braden nearly burst in excitement and hugged Stevie and Ronnie. After a brief awkward pause, he also embraced the twin girls.

"Is it alright?" Andrea asked Ellie, searching her eyes for approval. "He's not going to tap a keg or anything is he?"

Braden cupped his hands in mock prayer.

"Please, please, please?"

Colt stared at her as if daring her to say no. She returned his gaze continuing to feign disapproval of his impressive clout with the kids and parents.

"Okay." Ellie replied, raising her voice to the excitement of her son and his friends. "Let's do it."

The entire one-mile ride home, Braden jabbered about how well he hit off the tee, how much fun he had shagging balls and how dirty he already made his brand-new baseball pants. His voice raised by an octave when he marveled at how impressed he was by Colt's home run into the woods.

"Didja see it mom?" he asked her. "Didja? Didja? Didja?"

Ellie held out from giving Colt credit, until Braden's persistence forced her to call it 'very impressive'.

At the house, Colt involved all the parents to participate. While Joe Dalton set up the grill, Ellie and Andrea occupied the kitchen to pull together a large salad and organize paper plates and plastic cutlery for everyone. Andy Tremblay threw tennis balls off the barn roof with Lilly, Thomas, and Ronnie, practicing their ability to catch fly balls. The other parents shagged the baseballs hit off the tee by the remaining kids.

They played until dusk and ate burgers until the onset of night left them to the dark. As the last car kicked pebbles into the street and disappeared around the bayberry bush, Braden jumped into Colts arms and thanked him.

"That was so awesome," he shouted. "Can we do it again? Can we? Can we?"

Ellie moved her son's hair out of his eyes. She glanced at Colt as she acknowledged they would do it again the following week. Braden tossed his glove aside and returned into the house. Ellie looked back and mouthed the words "thank you," before turning and disappearing through her back door behind Braden.

Colt stood in the dark. He surveyed the back yard, lost in thought. He pictured the diamond of a baseball field, with first base adjacent to the barn, second base straight out from the back of the house. A mosquito bit him in the calf drawing him out of his early evening daydream. He noticed that Braden left his glove strewn on the ground. Conscious of the moisture in the night air, he picked it up and knocked on Ellie's back door.

"Hey." She opened the door and smiled softly with a hint of surprise.

"He left his glove out." Colt held the small leather object between them.

"Thanks," she said, taking it from him and pausing in the dim light from the mud room.

Colt lingered, hoping she'd stay and chat with him. He recalled sitting on the patio with her eating the BLT she made for him—he wanted another moment like that. A noise from behind her distracted her attention. She turned to look over her shoulder to investigate what may have fallen.

The chill of the night air cooled the back of Colt's neck. Ellie stood in the doorway with her hand on the knob. A mosquito buzzed by his head and entered her mud room behind her.

Ellie glanced over her shoulder a second time. He imagined her inviting him into her home to sit at her kitchen table and speak further about the successful baseball practice. *Think of something to say, Gibson.* Should he invite himself or suggest they hang out? Should he express a desire to keep talking about the Seabirds and the Bees?

"I'll, uh, see you... uh, later, I guess."

"Definitely," she grinned as he retreated. "It's not like you live too far away."

"I suppose not."

"Thanks again," she said.

She closed the door behind her. Her shadow passed the mud room light and then the window went dark.

"See you later?" he repeated to himself as he walked away. "I'm such a fool."

11

THE MOUND

Weeknight practices at Ellie's house grew in popularity. More players from the Bees attended. Joe continued to provide hamburgers and hot dogs, cooked on his massive Weber grill. Andrea and several other parents brought watermelon slices, coleslaw, homemade chocolate chip cookies and many other treats and refreshments. Soon, members of the Seadogs asked to join the practices and nearly a dozen parents ran stations across the yard to assist in throwing, catching, hitting, and running drills.

In the second game of the season, the Mighty Bees played stellar defense, keeping their rival Seadogs to only a few runs per inning, while racking dozens of runs on a barrage of hits. Braden missed hitting for the cycle by a home run and had the catch of the game in left field, diving into left-center to snag a fly ball out of the air.

After the game, Braden asked if he and Ellie could have lunch with Colt at the diner.

"No, Honey," Ellie replied, with a glance at Colt. "Mr. Gibson has to coach the 10-Us now."

"Actually," Colt said. "I turned them down."

Ellie looked at him, a flash of shock crossed her face, but she was quick to recover. "You took the shirt. I saw him hand it to you."

"I gave it back," he said. "I'd rather focus on the Bees."

Ellie remained quiet for a moment.

"Wow, I didn't know that." She nodded. "You're just full of surprises, Mr. Gibson. Aren't you?"

"So, we can go?" Braden reiterated his request.

"Um, yes, Honey," Ellie replied, glancing at Colt again. "As long as Mr. Gibson would like to join us."

Colt laughed. "Sorry, that's a hard pass."

A stern frown spread across Ellie's face.

"Mr. Gibson's my dad and he's not available. But Colt Gibson; he'd love to join you."

THE NEXT WEEKEND fewer Seadogs showed up for the third game, prompting the Bees to loan Stevie and the twins to maintain even rosters. Braden scored his home run, albeit on three consecutive errors that enabled him to take the extra bases on route to his first round-tripper.

The parents exhibited energetic support for the Bees as well as the Seadogs. When the parents weren't cheering for the teams, they gabbed and gossiped in the bleachers, laughing and getting to know each other. Garrett Kildeer came to watch the fourth game; a contest in which the Seadogs again struggled to field a full roster. Ronnie and Braden joined the Seadogs, to Braden's disappointment, and promptly lost by another large margin as several members of the Bees clocked long home runs to run up the score.

"Can't we play someone else?" Braden complained to his mother. "Can we play against the A's? At least they have a full roster."

Colt and Ellie approached Kildeer after the game as Braden chased Lilly and Lainey around the swing set.

"Why don't we make some calls and try to play against other towns?" Ellie asked. "There's got to be perfectly competitive teams in Revere or Coopersburg that we can play."

"Your team's not ready for that," Garrett replied.

"We're playing very well," Ellie argued. "Hitting, fielding…"

"Pitching," Garrett interrupted. "Don't forget. Other towns are playing coach pitch now and moving to kid pitch shortly."

"Then, we should play kid pitch too," Ellie said.

Colt stood by Ellie and listened to the terse discussion but resisted the urge to join the fray. It wasn't his kid. And he wasn't sure it was his place to comment. But at the mention of pitching, he couldn't help jumping into the conversation.

"Braden can pitch," he said.

"Who?"

"Braden, my son." Ellie interjected.

"The little one?"

"Trust me," Colt said, noticing Ellie's face turn red with anger. "The kid's got the potential. I've been around this sport long enough to know talent when I see it."

Garrett faced Colt. His eyes shifted between him and Ellie. He rubbed his chin for a moment.

"Can't," Garrett said, pointing to the field. "Unfortunately, there's no pitching mound."

As the weeks progressed, Ellie and Colt held practices in her expansive back yard, including members of both the Seadogs and the Bees. The weekend games devolved into scrimmages as the Seadogs fielded fewer and fewer players each week.

Colt showed up in Ellie's back yard one morning with a set of bases, which he carefully measured and installed. Ellie stood in her kitchen with a warm cup of coffee watching him through the back window of her mud room. With a shovel, he dug a shallow ditch and sunk a little metal box into the center of the hole. He inserted a casing into the hole and attached the base to the top of it.

Ellie watched him sprint gracefully with his long legs powering him up the baseline and around first base. Dust exploded from the soft bag as he pushed off and rounded second. His long strides traversed the distance between second and third in seconds. As he crossed the plate, he pumped his arms in the air in victory exactly as Braden had done in his last game.

After running the bases, he pulled the tarp from her ride-on mower and dusted off the weedwhacker. The kitchen filled with the sounds of motors and fans as he worked. The faint odor of low-grade motor oil drifted in as he lapped the property on the mower. The din of his work reached a crescendo as he trimmed the weeds along the base of the kitchen and eventually receded as he rounded to the far side of the house.

She watched him root around her oversized garage beneath his apartment. With her wheelbarrow, he trekked out to the edge of the property with a spade to siphon dirt from the glacial deposit. He spent at least an hour transporting the light brown dirt and sand before piling it between first and third base. He measured the distance from home plate and built a small pitcher's mound, complete with a long, thin rubber pitcher's plate at the top.

The weeknight practices in Ellie's back yard, with the parents all contributing to the skills-building exercises and the burgers sizzling on Joe Dalton's grill, turned out to be the highlight of the week. More players from the Seadogs showed up to join in the festivities. At the same time, attendance at the weekend games increased to the point where they could play a competitive, even-handed game and have fun in the process.

Every day after working for Dalton, Ellie drove Colt to the elementary field, where he mowed the grass, fixed holes in the fence and picked up along the bleachers. He insisted on walking back to her house at dusk, claiming he needed the exercise, but she knew he only did it to spare her the time of having to pick him up. With her busy work schedule, she appreciated the gesture. She enjoyed the rides into work with him and was surprised that they had more than enough to talk about from beginning to end of the commute. She found herself wishing he'd give in and let her pick him up at the field for that second opportunity to spend more time chatting with him in her car.

By week seven, the Bees had a 4-3 record against the Seadogs. But the Seadogs had won the most recent game by a nail-biting tally of 15-13. Braden slammed his bat to the ground after hitting a fly out to center field for the last out with the bases loaded. The Seadogs exploded in excitement. Ten minutes later, both teams engaged in a massive game of chase throughout the playground while the Red and Black 10-U team took the field for their warmups. Braden's disappointment thawed quickly, and he joined the melee.

As the sweaty, exhausted players filtered out of the playground to their parents' cars, Braden stood by the fence to watch the older team work out.

"That's my friend Mikey Wiltshire," Braden pointed out to Colt and Ellie. "How come he's playing on the older team?"

"Don't know," Colt replied. "I haven't spoken to Mr. Kildeer or Smalley. Maybe they called him up?"

"He's pitching!" Braden exclaimed, as if enamored by his favorite player on the Phillies.

"He's pretty good too," Colt echoed Braden's admiration. "He sure has a live arm."

After throwing a wild pitch past the catcher, Mikey laughed and pushed his glove in front of his face. The catcher trotted to the backstop to retrieve the ball and threw a fifty-foot relay a little high and wide of the mound. Mikey lunged. The ball tipped off his glove and careened past him to the gap between first and second base.

Braden smiled. Mikey laughed. From the opposite side of the field, Jay Smalley's annoyed voice cut the diamond.

"Catch the freakin' ball."

The caustic instruction had no effect on Mikey, who glanced over his shoulder at Braden and waved, with his toothless smile brightening his dimpled face.

"Hey," Smalley snapped. "Get your head in the game."

"Reminds me of my dad," Colt said to Braden and Ellie. "Although my dad always called it the damn ball."

Braden giggled at Colt's reference. Ellie put her arm around her boy and led him to the car. Colt followed. They could hear Smalley bark at his players as they closed the car door and exited the parking lot.

"How come Mr. Smalley said 'get your head in the game' to Mikey?" he asked Ellie and Colt from the back seat. "That was just their warm-up practice."

"Don't know, Honey," Ellie replied. "I think he was having a bad day."

Braden watched out the window as the 10-U team jogged in a line from the elementary field to Victory Field through the woods. He sat quietly for a few seconds before asking, "How come he said for Mikey to catch the ball?"

Ellie started to answer when Braden interrupted her with his follow-up question.

"It was a bad throw. He tried."

Ellie tried to offer a reply, but Braden's racing mind cut her off again.

"Did he think Mikey didn't know he was supposed to catch the ball?"

Ellie sighed. Colt grinned as Ellie struggled to explain the mindset of the overbearing coach. Their eyes met as Ellie turned to head home. His amused expression at the irony of Braden's innocent reaction prompted her to crack, and they both started to laugh. The laughter in the front seat, set a chain reaction with Braden, who burst out with a high-pitched giggle.

"What?" he asked, belly-laughing. "That's not even coaching because Mikey already knows he's supposed to try and catch the ball."

They chuckled all the way back to the bayberry bush next to the driveway. Once they were parked by the garage, Braden resumed his standard work-out, tossing his tennis ball against the side of the barn. Colt slung his bag over his shoulder as Ellie gathered Braden's bag, hat, glove, and empty water bottles.

"Thank you again for helping with the team," Ellie said, turning to go.

"Hey, Ellie," Colt stopped her. "I was putting the lawnmower away last night and I noticed you have some old plywood leaning up against the wall in the back."

"I guess." She shook the dirt from the bottom of Braden's plastic cleats.

"I also saw a pair of sawhorses."

"Ok," Ellie looked at him, unsure of his point.

"Do you have any tools?" he continued. "A bandsaw? Maybe just a regular saw?"

"There's an old saw in a bin under a tarp somewhere. Why?"

"I'm going to build a portable mound for the elementary school field," he grinned with childlike pride.

"Wow, that sounds amazing." Ellie beamed.

It had been ages since she could recall someone going so far out of their way for her, or to help her son with such unconditional care. The impulse to express her gratitude with a hug overwhelmed her. It didn't have to be a big deal. It could be a quick one. But she resisted the urge to make contact—especially in front of Braden. She wasn't sure she should even gush too much about how happy he made her by giving Braden such quality attention. She still barely knew him, and guys tended to come and go anyway—even the nice ones.

"Do what you want," she said "It belonged to my uncle. You may as well put it to good use."

Braden stopped throwing the tennis ball and raced back to the driveway. "Are you really going to build a mound for the field?"

Colt started to answer, but Braden interrupted him.

"Can I be the first starter?"

Ellie laughed and pushed her son's hair out of his eyes. "Why don't you go in and wash up? I'll be right in to fix you something to eat."

Braden started toward the screen door but stopped. He turned, ran to Colt, and hugged him around the hips, with his head pressed against Colt's belly. Colt's nervous eyes darted to Ellie. He held his hands outward to avoid enclosing his arms around the boy as Braden released him and returned to the house.

Ellie raised her eyebrow with an appreciative nod to acknowledge her approval of Braden's positive response to him. They remained in the driveway for another minute. Colt's warm smile caught the rays of the sun. His face glowed with the pale orange of the late afternoon. Ellie set aside her reluctance to express herself to him for his assistance with the baseball team.

"I really appreciate everything you've done," she said to him.

"I've got the time," Colt shrugged. "And I love the game."

"You didn't have to…"

"I start subbing for Mrs. Brewer when she goes on her maternity leave next week." He waved his hand dismissing her compliment.

"You've been here since April." Ellie laughed. "And you end up working the last week of the school year."

"I got a good seven or eight weeks in with Dalton."

"Of course," Ellie caught herself. "I just meant working at the school."

"Plus, I've worked with the baseball team for more than half a season."

"Yes, you have," she said, leaning toward him as she spoke. "That's been wonderful."

They lingered in the driveway nodding and smiling at each other. She felt off-balance, leaning forward with her weight on her toes. Braden's voice broke their moment of connection.

"Mom," he called to her through the opened kitchen window. "I spilled jelly on my pants."

They both laughed. Ellie gave Colt as sweet a smile as she could before rolling her eyes at her son's impeccable timing and turning toward her house.

"Be right there," she shouted as she walked toward her back door.

"Oh, Elles," Colt called to her as she reached the edge of the patio.

His unexpected use of a nickname for her caught her by surprise.

"How married are you to that carpet up in the apartment, the dull green one in the bedroom?" he asked.

"The carpet?"

"It's nice and plush," he continued. "It'd make a good covering for the portable mound."

Ellie shook her head playfully. Without hesitation, she raised her arm, wiggled the ring finger on her left hand, and said, "As of now, I'm definitely not married to anything."

12

THE WILD PITCH

Colt spent several hours on a Friday night after work measuring and cutting the plywood to create a flat, square top section for the portable mound. He fashioned a long, diagonal ramp leading down from the pitching platform. After ripping up a twelve-square-foot swath of carpet from his bedroom in Ellie's apartment, he cut several chunks to the exact dimensions of the portable mound, using both wood glue and carpet tacks to secure it to the board.

The contraption weighed about eighty pounds, but he dragged it out to the back yard around ten o'clock at night and left it forty-six feet from the side of the barn. He stood on the platform in the dark. The crickets cheered him on as he rose atop his creation. He pretended to take signs from an imaginary catcher, shaking off the pitch call twice before nodding in agreement.

He wound up, imitated an old-time pitcher, and raised his arms as if striking out the invisible batter.

A flash in his peripheral caught his eye. Ellie's bedroom light went out just as he finished his imaginary pitch. He stepped off the mound and trotted back to the barn. The scrape of her window sliding open cut into the crickets' cheers and her silhouette filled the window frame.

"That was a ball, Lehigh," she called to him. "High and outside."

The moonlight illuminated her pale, white robe. Her hair, up in a haphazard bun, appeared blond in the silver light. A mild breeze blew an errant strand across her shaded eyes.

"I think you need glasses, Ump," he called back to her.

"Definitely a wild pitch. Hit the showers, Gibson. Time to call it a night."

Colt chuckled as she said good night and closed her window halfway. A droplet of sweat slid down his brow above his nose—maybe he needed a shower before going to sleep after all. As he turned to head back to his apartment, out of the corner of his eye, he thought he caught a glint of her light chestnut hair and the shine of her bright, brown eyes. But when he looked back up at her bedroom window, he only saw the sway of the curtain back and forth in the breeze across the half-closed window.

Early Sunday morning, the steps to Colt's apartment creaked in rapid succession. Loud pounding on the door jolted him from his bed. He tossed on a ratty t-shirt and a pair of cotton shorts over his boxers. The relentless knocking continued as he approached the door. The shadow of Braden's small stature backlit the shade of the door.

"Just a second, Bud," Colt said, slurping a gulp of orange juice from the container in his fridge.

"Last day of the season," Braden exclaimed. "I'm pitching right? I want to practice with you again."

Colt shielded the morning sun from his eyes. "You know your mom has a pretty good glove. You could always throw to her."

"Yeah, but you're a pro," Braden beamed.

"You know I only..." he started to reply. "Right. Let's practice."

After about twenty warm-up pitches, Colt instructed Braden to jog around the field, get a good breakfast, and rest until the start of the game. Ellie emerged to watch the tail end of the bullpen session. She stood at the edge of the patio and caught Colt's attention.

"I assume you made your town's All-Star team growing up?" she shouted out to him.

"Of course."

"Do you remember how you were selected?"

"My dad was the coach," he replied. "And President of the league."

COLT HOISTED the portable mound over the liftgate to his pickup truck. Braden begged his mother to let him ride to the game with Colt and meet her there.

Both teams hovered around Colt's truck after he parked. He popped the brake and Braden jumped down and around to the back. Colt dragged the twelve-foot-long monstrosity across the grass while about a dozen eight and nine-year-olds placed their hands along the side and fooled themselves into thinking they were helping. Each player stood on the mound and took turns throwing seven pitches to Colt.

Braden and Tonio had the best arms. Cordelle Jacobs had a decent arm as well. Ronnie and Stevie, the biggest kids on the roster had power, but very little accuracy. Of the Yu girls, Lainey had power but struggled to throw strikes. Lilly hit Colt's glove accurately, but with high, slow looping throws.

Mr. Tremblay picked a starter for the Seadogs to face Braden for the Bees. Colt and Tremblay agreed to limit walks to two per inning. If the pitcher walked a second batter, they decided to temporarily take over to help speed the game along. They agreed to both stand behind the catcher and call balls and strikes by consensus.

"I'm not a great judge," Tremblay whispered to Colt after the first pitch by the Seadogs sailed through the air and fell into the dirt in front of the batter, who swung and missed. "I'll just agree with whatever you think."

The first inning took twenty minutes, but with Tremblay pitching the back half of the inning, the Seadogs managed to cobble together the three outs they needed to force their team's at bat against Braden.

Colt spotted a boy in his red and black A-team uniform standing by the fence waving to catch Braden's attention.

"Can I say hi to Mikey?" Braden asked Colt.

"Uh, you need to warm up for the inning."

"It'll just take a minute." He pleaded. "Please?"

Colt watched several Seadogs wander aimlessly from the field into their dug out. The teenaged umpire leaned against the fence texting on his phone. The next batter searched the bleachers looking for his parents to help him find his batting helmet.

"Fine," Colt, said. "But make it quick."

Braden took a detour from the mound and sprinted to the fence to smack hands with Mikey. Colt stood nearby, within earshot to gather his pitcher and shepherd him back to the mound as soon as the Seadogs appeared ready to bat. As with most innings, it looked like it could be a while as several parents invaded the dugout to provide juice boxes to their children on such a hot June morning.

"I thought you had a game on the other field?" Colt heard Braden tell Mikey.

"I do," Mikey answered. "But I heard one of the parents tell Coach Kildeer that your dad built a mound and wanted to check it out. I told him I had to go to the bathroom. I'm not up until after Damien Smalley in like six or seven batters."

Your dad? Colt pictured an older, chubbier, more wrinkled version of himself, which morphed into an image of his own father.

"He's not my dad," Braden said with a chuckle as the phrase rattled Colt's mind.

"Your uncle?" Mikey asked.

"I don't think so."

"Uncle?" Colt muttered to himself, preferring the title of 'Dad', which he found more appealing.

"Your nephew?" Mikey suggested.

"What's a nephew?"

"I don't know." Mikey shrugged.

"That's probably it then," Braden replied.

Colt shook off their conversation and corralled his player, politely telling Mikey to return to Victory Field. He directed Braden back to the mound and resumed squatting behind the plate with a catcher's mitt. He smacked the palm with his fist and called to Braden.

"Come on, Ace. Take the mound already."

As Braden threw his warm-up pitches, Colt saw Kildeer through the trees, crossing the footbridge and heading toward the elementary field.

"Batter up," he shouted.

The Seadogs' lead-off batter approached the plate, dug his cleats into the dirt, and raised his bat to his shoulder. Kildeer reached the edge of the left field fencing as Braden kicked his leg, arched his hands behind his neck, and reared back to throw the ball.

As Kildeer trotted toward third base the ball ejected from Braden's hand. The laces spun and twisted with the flick of his wrist and the friction against his three fingers. Kildeer yelled something indistinguishable that Colt chose to ignore, as the ball sailed high and inside toward the batter's face.

Colt shouted, "watch out."

The batter crumpled backwards, both swinging and simultaneously flinging his bat down the third base line.

Colt caught the ball right where the batter's head would have been had the kid not dived to the ground in fear.

"What the hell is this?" Kildeer bellowed.

"Strike one," Braden yelped from the mound. "That was a swing."

Kildeer ran along the inside of the fence toward the plate as the batter stood back up and dusted himself off.

"We're giving them a chance to try kid pitch," Colt said to a red-faced Kildeer as he stomped up to the batter's box.

"Hell no," he shouted. "Shut it down! This is a tee-ball league. Shut it down right now."

13

EGGPLANT AND OMELETS

With Braden folded into his mother's lap and bawling in the bleachers, Coach Kildeer faced a barrage of complaints. Joe, Andrea, and Laura Yu, mother of Lainey and Lilly, all barked at him from the other side of the fence. Colt and Andy Tremblay watched from behind the plate as the parents argued with the league president about his decision to ban the portable mound from the field.

Citing insurance and concerns about hurting young pitching arms, Kildeer held his ground, even raising his hand with his palm out as if to silence his critics. Sensing the need to mitigate the situation, Colt thought it best to walk Kildeer into the infield away from the fence and discuss the counterpoints to his decision. But Ellie beat him to the fray.

"I want to see the charter," she snapped at Kildeer.

"Charter?" he asked.

Andrea shouted "yah" in support of her friend.

"You're supposed to have a charter that defines the league bylaws," she continued.

"We have a..."

"And, who's on the board?" she cut him off. "The league requires a minimum of three board members."

"We have plenty of…"

"One of your board members is in a convalescent home two towns over," Ellie added.

Colt positioned himself between Kildeer and the parents. He gave Ellie a diffusive look and slung his arm around the league president, walking him toward second base. The players vacated the field and hit the playground while the parents grumbled.

"You built this?" Kildeer asked as the strode past the home-made mound.

"It's not my first time," Colt replied. "I've made them before. It's safe, sturdy; regulation. I swear."

"I can't have you going off on your own," Kildeer said. "What if the Shaw kid pegged that batter in the temple. I'd have a lawsuit on my hands. These parents are enough of a handful as it is."

"They just want the best for their kids." Colt looked back at Ellie, who had returned to the bleachers to console Braden.

The rest of the Seadogs and Bees swarmed the playground.

"You're supposed to have open board meetings," Ellie shouted across the field.

"What's with your landlord poking around asking about our board?" Kildeer asked, his tone low.

"Apparently, you're supposed to have a minimum of three board members?" Colt said. "She was telling me something about that."

"Damn it." Kildeer watched the parents' eyes follow him across the field as he and Colt ambled toward second base. "She's actually right. We've got a guy on the books, but he's not around."

Kildeer scratched his head and glanced back at the crowd of parents, complaining to each other. "I need a non-parent board member. I can't deal with them. Someone to run the B and C programs and deal with these parents for me."

It dawned on Colt what would come next. He raised an eyebrow in response.

"You in?" Kildeer grinned.

Ellie watched Colt drag the portable mound back to the patch of yellow grass in her back yard where it sat the previous night. Braden sulked in one of the chairs on the cement patio outside the back door. Ellie brought out a pastrami and cheese sandwich with baby carrots and a box of animal cookies. Colt grabbed his glove and started back toward his apartment.

"Would you like a sandwich?" she asked.

"Well, I..." Colt fumbled.

"I already made it for you, so you might as well eat it."

"Well, when you put it that way."

As Colt took a seat next to Braden, Ellie returned to the kitchen and took out a hard roll, a couple slices of cheese and deli meat, lettuce, and tomato. She noticed the half-finished package of bacon and fried it in her griddle pan.

"Just a moment," she called as she patted the greasy bacon with a paper towel.

"No problem," he answered, between speaking quietly in muted tones with Braden, who sniffled in sadness.

"Mayo?" she asked through the screen door window.

"Sure," Colt replied.

Braden didn't touch his sandwich, instead, staring blankly at the wall. Ellie slid a plate in front of Colt. He smiled at the smell of fresh grilled bacon. She brushed Braden's hair aside and tried to console him. But the despondent boy cut her off, snapping for her to leave him alone. She sat in the empty seat and gave Colt a frustrated look.

"You know..." Colt started. As he spoke, he didn't look at

Braden, instead, staring at the wall like the boy. "The batter swung at that pitch."

"I know," Braden muttered. "It was a strike."

"You didn't give up any hits," Colt added.

"So, I had a no-hitter?"

"Sure did." Colt looked Braden in the eyes. "And a zero ERA."

Appreciation and warmth heated Ellie's cheeks as Colt consoled Braden.

"I had a zero ERA and WHIP." Braden's smile penetrated his malaise. "That's Walks and Hits to Innings Pitched, Mom."

"I know what it is, Baby." Ellie's smile widened as her heart filled with an emotion somewhere between gratitude, relief, and admiration. "You pitched a perfect game."

"No, I didn't." Braden chomped on his sandwich, speaking with his mouth full. "You have to pitch nine innings for that."

"Oh," Ellie strained not to roll her eyes. "Of course."

As Braden finished his lunch, Ellie received a text from Mikey Wiltshire's mother asking if Braden could visit for a play date. At the news, he darted into the house to fetch his metal tin of baseball cards.

Colt thanked Ellie for the delicious BLT and stood to return to his apartment.

"Oh," he said to her as she cleared the plates. "Kildeer asked me to join the board."

A strange wave of either concern, confusion or anger washed over her—which emotion, she wasn't sure. She put the plates down and searched for the words.

"The board?" she asked. "You?"

Colt shifted the weight between his feet and swayed with a look of confusion in his eyes.

"I'm sorry," Ellie caught herself. "I didn't mean to sound snotty. Why you?"

"I guess he needed a non-parent?"

"He wanted someone he could control."

"Well, I wouldn't..."

"They're such bastards, those two." Ellie looked past Colt at Braden's glove sitting in the grass in the middle of the back yard. "They're just trying to get away with their own stupid agenda. I can't believe you're going to join them."

"I didn't say yes," Colt grew defensive.

"And, you didn't say no either, did you?"

"I thought this would be a good..."

"For you maybe." Ellie turned toward the house. "I have to take Braden to the Wiltshire's place."

At that, she withdrew into the back door and the screen whipped shut behind her.

As Ellie drove Braden to the other side of town, he buzzed about his no-hitter and how much he enjoyed pitching. Ellie barely heard her son's words. In her mind, she pictured Colt wearing the red and black shirt, with his arms around Jay Smalley and Garrett Kildeer, coaching the A-team to some tournament victory at Hershey Park.

Mikey Wiltshire bolted out of his house as they pulled into the driveway of his five-thousand square foot center hall Madisonian Colonial.

"Nice brush-back pitch," Mikey exclaimed. "Too bad they stopped the game."

Braden tucked his metal tin of baseball cards under his elbow, and the two boys ran into the house.

"Thank you so much for bringing him here," Mara said, her face now stern and serious. "Ever since Darius walked out, it's been so hard on him."

Ellie looked blankly at the woman with whom she had a general acquaintance, but hardly a close friendship.

"Oh, I'm sorry," she said with a blush. "I assumed you knew."

"I'm so sorry."

"I guess you'd say we're separated," Mara said, appearing to need a sounding board. "Although, he comes by quite a bit. He mows the lawn and throws with Mikey. We had dinner together as a family the other night. It's all very confusing."

Ellie withheld the commentary running through her own head.

"Ever felt like your husband is more of just a friend?" Mara continued.

Ellie fidgeted with her hair along the side of her face. Memories of caring for Braden on her own through the years flooded her mind. At least Mara had a husband that spent time with their son.

"Oh, I'm so sorry." Mara blushed again.

"It's okay."

"The baseball parents have been buzzing about us all week," Mara said, her sad eyes drooping. "They don't say anything to me directly, but I hear them whispering and looking at me with pity."

"If it helps," Ellie said. "I haven't heard a word from any of the parents."

"Maybe it's just our team. It's just so stressful. Darius almost got into a fight with one dad who planted himself next to the dugout telling Smalley what to do."

"Does Smalley listen?"

"Of course," Mara said, a tear forming in her eye. "Mikey was pitching. I think he struck out two batters. Then he hit someone on the elbow and walked the next batter. This dude started yelling loudly, 'Send him to the showers, Coach.' Mikey was so thrown off, he hit the next batter in the leg and the coach took him out of the game."

"That's terrible," Ellie clutched her hand for support.

"Darius can't make all the games with his job, but he went out of his way to see Mikey pitch," Mara continued, wiping the tear away. "He was so mad, he started swearing at this dad. Then he chewed out Coach Smalley."

"Well, of course," Ellie said, trying hard to be supportive.

"No," Mara raised her voice a notch. "We had the biggest fight about that. No matter how elitist and entitled these parents act, it's not right to stoop to their level and behave immaturely."

"Well, that's true." Ellie cringed at the thought of her badgering Garrett Kildeer about his decision not to let the Bees use the portable mound.

"We can't show any weakness to the parents and coaches on this team," Mara continued. "They'll eat you alive and blacklist your kid. We dealt with it all last year. All we ever talked about was how stupid the coaches were, how annoying the parents were, how to angle for more playing time, how to cozy up to the board members. It's like we lost our own identities and integrity, and this baseball vortex of stress and anxiety just sucked us into this pit of frustration."

The conversation with Mara swirled through Ellie's head as she stopped in town to run errands and pick up groceries for the week.

"Maybe I was too hard on him," she said to Andrea over speakerphone in the car.

"Uh, yah," Andrea answered. "He didn't ask to be on the board. They came to him."

"But why him?" Ellie pressed. "I'd love to be on the board. But they pick him, the big jock. All because I don't have a..."

"Elle, Elle," Andrea cut her off. "When are you going to attend board meetings between your three jobs and raising an eight-year-old boy."

"It's just typical, that's all," Ellie continued. "I know I don't have the time for it. But they just want to manipulate him and use him to satisfy us B and C parents while they parade their little show pony A players around the state to Hershey Park for the Baseball Bash."

"Give the guy a break and some credit," Andrea replied. "He's been amazing to our kids. They asked him to help coach that other team and he said no. He ran practices in your back yard. He built a frickin' pitching mound for you. What more do you want from him?"

"Jesus," Ellie replied. "I know you're right. He's just trying to help. And I've been such a jerk to him. Thanks, Love."

As the sun set and she returned to her driveway, Ellie's headlights spotlighted Colt hunched over the first base area in her back yard. The band of his underwear protruded from the back of his jeans as he squatted with his backside to the car. She grabbed two bags of groceries and wandered in his direction.

"Hey," Colt said, smiling softly, but restrained.

"Whatcha doing out here?"

"Measuring the basepaths. I was thinking of digging it up and installing an actual dirt infield."

"Oh," Ellie glazed over Colt's bold pronouncement. "Hey, about what I said earlier. How I acted when you told me about the board..."

"I emailed Kildeer and politely declined the board spot," Colt jumped her line of dialog.

"No," Ellie stepped forward as the last rays of the sun ducked below the horizon. "I was a jerk to give you grief about it. I think you should join the board."

"It's too late, I already sent the email."

Ellie thought for a second. The idea that Colt wanted to dig up her yard almost made it from her subconscious to her conscious mind. But her thoughts about Colt's opportunity to join the board dominated her immediate attention.

"Did he read it?"

Colt scrolled through his email app. "Uh, not yet."

"Can you recall it?"

"I think so." Colt slid his finger across the face of his phone. "It worked. Recall confirmed. You really think I should join the board?"

"I thought about it," she said as Colt took the groceries from her arms and walked them back to the house for her. "I think it would be good to have someone on the board with half a brain."

"Half, huh?" Colt nudged her.

"You did go to Lehigh, so that's probably giving you more credit than you deserve."

Colt chuckled, placed the bags of groceries on the kitchen table, and fidgeted as Ellie opened the fridge.

"Beer?" she asked, hoping the desire for him to stay wasn't obvious in her tone.

Colt helped put away the groceries into the cupboards. He held up a box of crackers and a jar of pickles, and she pointed to where she wanted him to put them. She took out two bottles of beer from her refrigerator and searched her silverware drawer for a bottle opener. As she did, Colt pulled out his keys and used the one from his key chain.

He sat at the end of the kitchen table gulping his beer. Ellie took a sip of hers and set it aside on the counter. Darkness set in outside her kitchen window. The crickets built up to their nightly crescendo. The presence of a man—one she increasingly found attractive—standing and breathing in her kitchen, set swirls of nerves afire in her stomach.

"The Wiltshire's asked if Braden could stay for dinner," she said. "They're not going to bring him back here for a couple hours, so…"

The implications of Ellie's words sunk into her brain like an explosion of tiny pin pricks. The flutter of nerves ticked her neck, and her face flushed. Colt seemed more at ease, oblivious to the overtones. He drank his beer, cool and casual, and glanced at his phone to check the time.

"I've got nowhere to go," he shrugged.

"You like eggplant?" Each word caused her throat to constrict in increments from the top of her stomach to her larynx. "I make a killer Eggplant Parm."

"As good as your BLTs?"

"Better," she replied with a twinkle in her eye. "Especially with a nice red wine."

"Sounds good. And for dessert?"

"I'll see what I can whip up." She laughed—baking wasn't her preference, but she might still have a pint of coffee ice cream in her freezer.

"Hmm, eggplant," Colt mused. "Never had it. Is it like an omelet?"

Ellie giggled, assuming he'd made a clever joke. She gave it more of a laugh than the comment deserved. But, with the boyish, confused look on his face, maybe he actually thought eggplant contained eggs as a main ingredient. At that point, she couldn't contain her laughter, which erased the butterflies in her stomach. She drank half of her beer, took out the bottle of wine, and assembled the meal while chatting with Colt about the baseball team, the other parents, and her disdain for Kildeer and Smalley.

14

UNEXPECTED MATERNITY

Colt finished his second helping of eggplant and his glass of wine. Ellie cleared the table and poured another glass. As Colt lounged in his seat, complimenting her cooking, she received a text from Braden asking if he could sleep over Mikey's house. Ellie's heart thrummed at the thought of being kid-free for the entire night, especially given the dinner and the alcohol.

"Everything alright?" Colt asked, while also scrolling through his messages.

"Sure," Ellie hesitated, pondering how to or even whether to reveal to Colt that Braden would be away for the night. She decided to hold back and see how the night progressed.

"You're great with the kids," Ellie started a line of small talk. "Are you sure you don't have a wife and family tucked away somewhere?"

Her mind screamed at her for such an awkward and intrusive comment. Colt rolled with it.

"Not that I know of." He grinned. "But I guess it's possible."

"Seriously," Ellie pulled herself together. "You've been

amazing. All the parents love you. How do you know so much about coaching?"

"My dad was a coach."

"Like father, like son?"

"Nope," Colt's face tightened. "I learned what not to do from him."

"Oh, I, uh..." Ellie didn't know what to say.

"It's alright." Colt untensed and sipped his wine. "My dad's a tool. No. He's just your classic hard-ass."

"Did you not like playing for him?"

"I never saw any other way. I played for him in Little League. Juniors. Travel. He was never the official coach. He just pulled all the strings from the bleachers. He didn't coach my high school team. But the high school coach did everything and anything my dad told him to do."

"Well, you turned out much different from that," Ellie said, the warmth of her buzz relaxing the tension in her body. She leaned her elbows on the table and peered into Colt's eyes.

"I used to dream at night about doing everything different from him," Colt continued. "You know, making it fun, low pressure, but still teaching the game."

"You have a great knack for that." Ellie dared herself to be more bold and forthcoming, but she couldn't bring herself to say the words.

By the way, Colt, Braden won't be home tonight. You know, we've got the whole house to ourselves.

The thought of such an overt admission of intention filled her head with dizziness and stirred her stomach. At the same time, the tingle of excitement ran through her neck and down her legs into her toes.

"Braden's a great kid," Colt said drawing Ellie back from her thoughts.

"He thinks you're as cool as his favorite player," she said, finishing her wine and settling into her chair.

"Who's that?"

"Some big first baseman," she replied, unable to remember the player's name, which she had only heard Braden say a thousand times. "From the Phillies a couple years ago."

"High praise," Colt beamed. "He bats left and throws right. I bat right and throw left. We're both oddballs that way."

"Funny," Ellie remarked with a soft giggle. "I throw right and bat left. I'm your complete opposite."

Colt's face brightened. His blue eyes widened. He opened his mouth as if to comment further and then stopped. A burst of blush crossed his cheeks and faded nearly as quickly as it appeared. He tipped his wine glass against hers.

"To opposites."

Ellie laughed and flipped her hair behind her shoulders. "Opposites indeed."

The phrase "opposites attract" wavered at the tip of Ellie's loose tongue. With much mental concentration, she managed to hold those words in and leave that image hovering but unsaid.

"I wondered if you played growing up," he said. "I figured you must've been pretty good with the way you can move. Did you play softball for Springtown High?"

"I played at Lafayette, Dude," she said. "You're not the only D-1 sports star in this household."

"Damn, girl," Colt leaned forward, for the first time, his blue eyes glassy with the effects of the alcohol. "What position did you play?"

"Catcher."

"No freakin' way," Colt mused. "You're too small."

"Am not."

"Way too small," he persisted with a grin. "I'd have guessed short."

"I was a perfectly good-sized catcher," Ellie insisted with more indignance than she planned.

"What are you? Five-six?" Colt asked.

"Five seven and a half in cleats," she fired back. "Five-nine with the helmet."

Colt studied her. He cocked his head sideways as if trying to visualize her in full catcher's gear. The way his eyes roamed over her sparked a tingle in her chest and sent a flush of heat over her skin.

"I don't buy it," he teased.

"Seriously, I could stop any pitch," Ellie boasted. "And a rocket arm to second. Nobody got to second on me."

"I bet. How come you don't throw with your boy more often?"

At Colt's innocent question, Ellie pulled her legs up to her chest and shuddered at the last image of her college softball career.

"I broke my arm." Her face dropped as the long-buried memory flashed across her mind. "Bad."

"Sorry." Colt's playful expression sobered.

"Two places." Ellie drew a deep breath. "The bone stuck right out. I got six pins put in, the whole works. It still hurts to throw. I tossed a couple fly balls at the first practice this spring. I thought my arm was going to fall off. I had to ice the crap out of it for three days."

"Was it a crash at the plate?" Colt surmised.

"Damn Lehigh chick." Ellie's face turned red with anger. "She was dead. I had the ball a good two seconds before she got there. She was twice my size. Freakin' plastered me. Slid right over my throwing arm. That ended my college career as a junior. Never played my senior year."

"You couldn't play first?" Colt asked. "Do they have designated hitters?"

"It doesn't matter." Ellie looked out the window, her eyes drooping with resignation. "I had Braden to take care of by then."

"Oh, right," Colt's eyes rolled upward as if calculating a math equation in his head. "I didn't think of that."

Ellie considered changing the subject. She'd enjoyed the danger of enticing Colt with her home cooking and a bottle of red wine. But discussing her painful past detracted from the excitement of their earlier banter.

"They took me to the hospital that night." Ellie considered her personal life private, but tonight she chose to reveal to Colt a glimpse into the backstory behind Braden's arrival into her life. "They asked me if I could be pregnant. I guess they always ask that. I said I didn't think so, but it was possible. Sure enough, I found out my college sports career was over and—at the time—thought my life was over too."

"Did you win?"

Colt's question snapped Ellie's reverie.

"Huh?" she asked, not having totally concentrated on his actual words.

"Did you win?" he repeated. "The game? Who won? Lafayette or Lehigh?"

As quickly as she'd tensed while sharing her story with him, Ellie felt the stiffness ease from her body with Colt's unexpected question. The frat boy jock cared more about the game than the player. Where someone else might have found his aside insensitive, she respected his competitive spirit. Not everyone got that.

"Of course, we won." She glowered at him, causing him to give her a high five across the table. "My left arm was fine. That's the glove hand that had the ball. A couple compound bone breaks wasn't enough to stop me from getting the out. That play would've tied the game. We went on to shut them down in the next and final inning for our third consecutive win over Lame-High."

Colt slid his chair closer to the table and leaned forward.

"I never lost to the Lafayette Pussycats either," Colt teased. "And I played all four years; five if you count my red shirt year."

"So, you're old," Ellie said, exaggerating the way her eyes roamed over him, head to toe. She couldn't deny she didn't mind the opportunity to take all of him in. "You probably need to lay down."

Colt chuckled before he pressed on with his teasing. "At least

I'm not brittle. We've won the Rivalry football game the last three years in a row."

"We've got an 82-73 winning record in the Rivalry games since 1884." She leaned hard on the table, wishing it would evaporate and allow her to move closer to him.

"We smoked you seventy-eight to nothing once."

"In 1917."

"Worst loss in football history."

Ellie's heart raced, sending a surge of blood to flush her skin again. Colt held her gaze. She watched his Adam's Apple bob as he swallowed, and then he stood. He ported his wine glass across the kitchen and rinsed it in the sink.

"Where do you put these?" he asked.

"You don't have to do that." Ellie also rose to her feet, wobbled slightly, and followed Colt's lead.

They stood by the dim kitchen light. The blackness of the night pressed against the kitchen window. Only a foot or two apart, they stood face-to-face. Ellie waited for a sign—a lean, his gaze to fall to her lips, the brush of his body against hers.

She hadn't had sex in months—years actually—not since Braden's dad left her. The ache to be in someone's arms traversed her body. She needed to feel desired, taken care of. And, Colt, she had no doubt, would be both happy to oblige her needs and leave not one inch of her skin untouched to make it a night to remember.

Would he lean in to her first? Would they gravitate to each other and connect like magnets? He'd only need to move toward her by an inch or two to give her the confidence she needed to throw her arms around him and pull him into her. He had to feel the same way. She ached for the moment to happen.

Instead, his phone buzzed. Sheepishly, he clutched it out of his pocket with an apologetic scrunch of his face. Ellie nodded. Her eyes said "sure" while her mind screamed "no".

"It's the Vice Principal," Colt peered at his text. "Mrs. Pemberwick went into early labor."

Braden's smiley eight-year-old face flashed across her mind, draining the nervous energy from her face.

"She's Braden's art teacher," Ellie gasped. "She not due until July. I thought you were going to sub for Mrs. Brewer's gym class next year."

"They want me to come in on Monday." Colt stared at the phone. "As an Art teacher."

"There's like a week and a half left in the school year."

Ellie stepped backward. The image of Colt in a button-down shirt and tie, standing in front of Braden and all his friends in the school's art room caused the nerves to run cold from her throat, her stomach, and her legs, down to her feet.

"You're going to be my son's teacher?" she asked.

She felt the pleasant sexual flutter wash away, draining out of her body.

"I guess so." Colt looked at her, his pained face reading first the connection that he had barely recognized in the moment, and then the lost opportunity at the news of his assignment. "I'm going to be your son's teacher."

15

MR. YANKEE DOODLE

Colt's first day of school started at nine o'clock. He aimed to be there by eight. He started his morning at six, spending an hour digging up the first base path in Ellie's back yard. He only progressed about halfway when he had to stop and shower for his workday.

He knocked lightly on Ellie's back door to offer Braden a ride to school. Ellie held the door open only a few inches. She wore a long, cotton nightgown and a sloppy ponytail.

"We're moving a little slowly this morning," she explained. "Thanks for the sweet offer, but he'll have to take the bus this morning."

By 7:58 AM, he stood in the art room surrounded by the reek of glue and paint. Childlike drawings and paintings cluttered the walls. They hung from the open space between the floor-to-ceiling shelving units packed with paintbrushes, sponges, splattered smocks, and a myriad of other supplies and instruments.

Colt stood in the middle of the room like a lost puppy. He looked at his watch. He had five fifty-minute classes on his schedule. He scanned the list and found Braden's name in his first class at nine. A barrage of game-day nerves hit him hard. He imagined himself attempting to give art instruction to a bunch of six-year-old children.

The last artwork he remembered making as a kid consisted of finger painting a picture of a baseball diamond in elementary school. His mother posted it on the side of the refrigerator, where it stayed for years. As he spun around the middle of the bright, cluttered room, Colt felt like an astronaut on a foreign planet.

What have I gotten myself into?

The door flung open and one of the librarians wheeled an old-fashioned CRT-style television monitor on a cart. It rattled and tipped as if it could fall over with a firm breeze.

"DVD player's on the shelf," the librarian said. "There's a couple dozen DVDs in the bottom drawer of the desk. Should be enough to get you through the end of the school year."

Colt thanked her and maneuvered the television into a spot that would give the students the best vantage point to view the videos. Behind him the door flung open. Braden's high-pitched excited voice bounced off the walls.

"Colt," he yelped, running through the door toward him.

"Braden, Bud."

The boy extended his arms and lunged toward him. But Colt raised a hand and made a fist in front of his body between them.

"At school, we should probably stick to a fist bump."

The class passed uneventfully. Some of the students watched the video. Others whispered to each other. One or two of them colored with crayons. Colt sat at the desk, quietly in the dark scrolling through his social media and text feeds. Since leaving the Lehigh campus, he'd received fewer and fewer invites for parties and events with his friends. His social media garnered minimal posts and mentions—he'd never been this distant with his fraternity brothers and former teammates.

A few of them announced engagements. One of his ex-girlfriends, married for just under a year, announced a pregnancy.

The day dragged. The classes ran together. He met a handful of friendly teachers, who helped him find his way through the school. Between classes, he sat with a few of them in the teacher's lounge. He listened to them discuss their curricula, new guidelines from the district and their approach to preparing their kids for next year's standardized mastery tests. He felt like he did on the first day of his freshman year at the Lehigh orientation event when he mistakenly picked up the wrong name tag and ended up at a table filled with honors students from the school of Political Science.

Throughout the day, several of the elementary students greeted Colt in the hallways, recognizing him from the Sunday baseball games. He received a few high-fives from members of the B-team that practiced with him in Ellie's back yard.

Between his fourth and fifth classes, he had an hour to kill. A ratty, old volleyball sat in the corner of the room. Judging from the dust, it had been there for a long time, certainly more than a year or two. An idea crossed his mind, and he took out a package of acrylic paints. He spent about twenty minutes creating a smiley face with a mustache and beard. He gave his cartoon face goofy, crossed eyes and wild, blue mangy hair. He set it on a back shelf to dry until the end of the school day as his next group of students filtered into his classroom.

By 2:30, as Colt made his way toward the parking lot, a tall, athletic boy approached him in the back hallway. He had a Phillies backpack slung over his shoulder and a black and red Springtown A's ballcap.

"Mr. Gibson," he said in a soft, respectful voice. "I'm Braden's friend Mikey."

"Right, sure. Mikey Wiltshire, right?" he asked, recalling Braden's admiration of the kid and his prowess on the field from watching the A-team play.

"That's right." Mikey said. "Um. I know the practices you run in Braden's back yard are just for the B-team and the C-team. But I was wondering if I could practice too?"

"Sure, Mikey," Colt replied. "Anyone's welcome to join us. Come by today."

Since Colt's last class finished an hour before the school bell rang to end the day, he was able to leave the building and finish digging out the basepath to first base. Ellie wandered out to the field and peered over his shoulder.

"Jesus," she exclaimed. "You're digging up the whole lawn."

"What did you think I was going to do?"

"I don't know." Ellie scrunched her face. "Honestly, I wasn't totally listening to you when you told me about this. I'm not sure I would have agreed to it."

Colt cocked his head, unsure of where she was going with this.

"I was a little distracted," Ellie murmured.

"Oh. The wine?" Colt laughed.

Ellie lowered her eyes and hid a shy smile which he found adorable. "How was school?" she asked. "I can't imagine you in a beret and paint-splattered smock."

"I showed videos all day."

"Seriously, though." Ellie nodded to Colt's landscaping project. "You're going to dig up my whole back yard like this?"

"Just the infield. You've got a hundred yards to the woods. I'm only digging out like seventy square feet."

"Seventy?" Ellie's eyes widened. She surveyed the property trying to imagine Colt's handiwork spread across a much larger area.

"I'm going to dig out an extra wide infield so it can be used for both sixty-forty and fifty-seventy. That way, no matter which age, the basepaths will be the right dimensions."

"Where are you going to get the dirt?"

"The big hill behind those trees at the end of the property." Colt pointed.

"Is it safe?" She raised her hand to her forehead to peer through the woods. "At first, we were just inviting people over to play. I don't want any liability."

"It's a huge glacier deposit." Colt squinted in the sun. "Beautiful, soft, fine sand. It'll be perfect. And nice and safe."

Mara Wiltshire pulled up in her black Mercedes. Mikey spilled out as Braden's bus arrived to drop him off across the street. The two boys hugged. Mikey grabbed his baseball bag and waved to his mother. Ellie walked over to her and beckoned Colt for an introduction.

"My husband played a little high school ball," Mara said. "He was really good. He works most evenings, so it's hard for him to help out."

"He can come by any weekend," Colt said. "We usually practice here after the games on Sundays."

"If he can. He works a lot of weekends too," Mara said with a quick, glance and a head shake at Ellie.

"He's the Sheriff for the county," Ellie explained. "I'm sure he's busy."

"I can't speak for his time commitments. He's, uh, not always around."

Colt noticed the two women flash knowing looks at each other as they communicated some wordless message that only a pair of mothers might understand.

"Still the same," Mara murmured to Ellie, before brightening her eyes and smiling at Colt. "I know Mikey's excited to be here."

Mara pulled out of the driveway and other cars took her place. In addition to Mikey and Braden, Ronnie, Stevie, Lilly, and Lainey all showed up to practice.

As the players congregated in the driveway, Colt lugged the tee to the far end of the yard near the woods. They followed him like a herd of deer. He grabbed a bucket of old, worn practice balls and angled the tee toward the trees.

"Reverse Home Run Derby," he announced.

"What's Reverse Home Run Derby?" Cordelle Jacobs asked.

"We start really close," Colt replied. "Everyone hits ten balls.

Every time you hit a home run into the woods, you get a point. Hit a tree, you get an extra point."

"How is it reverse?" Ronnie asked.

"After each round we move back farther from the woods," Colt replied. "So, it gets harder."

The kids all cheered.

"You all have very nice swings," Colt said. "But it's time to learn how to get the ball out of the infield. You don't have to hit it into the woods on the fly. Line drives and hard grounders travel farther than lazy flies. So, keep a level swing and follow-through for power."

As each player took their turn, the rest of the players stood in front of the woods to retrieve as many of the balls as they could find. As expected, they lost a lot of balls to the "Woods Monster", as Colt called it.

Mikey won the derby, followed by Ronnie, Stevie, and Lainey. Next, Colt brought the players and the tee back to the side of the barn. They stood along the portable mound facing the broad side of the wooden structure that Braden typically used as a back stop.

"This game is called... Perfect Pitch," Colt announced, pulling the painted volleyball out of his bag.

When Braden noticed the goofy face, he laughed, which created a chain reaction of giggles throughout the group. Colt placed the volleyball, face outward on top of the tee.

"This is Mr. Yankee Doodle," he said.

"Yankee Doodle?" Mikey repeated.

"You guys like the Yankees?" Colt asked.

The kids responded in a chorus of jeers and boos.

"Well, the point of the game is to pitch from that mound and knock Mr. Yankee Doodle off the tee. Five throws each."

The purpose of the contest elicited another bout of giggles and cheers.

"How many points is this one?" Braden asked.

"Hmm... Let's say a hundred."

Mara's black Mercedes appeared in the driveway soon after Braden and Mikey tied at 300 points for toppling Mr. Yankee Doodle to the ground three times each. With her arrival, Mikey hunched his shoulders and frowned. As he gathered his bat and glove, Ellie stood by Mara's window to chat with her while Colt walked with an arm around Mikey's shoulder to the car.

"Is Braden's team going to this tournament at Hershey Park this weekend?" Mara asked. Ellie shook her head from side to side.

"Tournament?" Colt mouthed to Ellie in confusion. *What had he missed?*

"I guess a couple of the players can't make it," Mara continued. "I thought they were going to contact other players."

"Uh, tournament?" Colt repeated louder.

"No one's contacted us." Confusion wrinkled Ellie's brow.

"Hopefully they'll give you a call," Mara said, getting out of her car to place Mikey's baseball bag in the trunk. "I'll send an email to our coaches and suggest they ask Braden. Mikey would love that."

"Is there a tournament somewhere?" Colt asked again.

"I'll explain later," Ellie said with a pat on his arm as if an old wife silencing her husband.

Ellie thanked Mara and gave her a warm hug.

"What about the summer and fall travel teams they're putting together?" Mara flopped into the driver's seat of her car. "Has anyone from the league contacted you about those programs?"

"He should definitely play summer and fall ball," Colt said.

Ellie nodded as Mara waved goodbye.

"Maybe." She mustered a faint smile.

16

THE BOARD

Ellie left countless messages for both coaches Kildeer and Smalley to find out about the tournament. They didn't respond to her until the Friday before Memorial Day. The hasty, bordering on terse, voicemail indicated that they had enough players and didn't need additional subs.

The weekend passed uneventfully. With Mikey away, Braden went fishing with Stevie and his father, Joe. Colt mentioned something about a party with his roommate Phil. His truck disappeared from Ellie's driveway for the entire weekend. As she sipped her coffee on Sunday morning, she pictured them passed out on the floor of some sorority house. Ellie shook her head as she watched him return, looking haggard and worn in the same Phillies t-shirt he wore when he left her place forty-eight hours earlier.

All day on Monday, she watched him dig up the new infield. He made his way around first and over to the second base area. Ellie sat in her house, planning her reply email to the coaches. She wrote numerous drafts, set them aside, and revisited them throughout the brutally hot holiday.

Ellie decided to copy the President of the GPYBA in her

message to Garrett Kildeer and Jay Smalley. Noting that she hoped to attend and vote for the new board member they proposed, she asked for the date of the next board meeting. She knew Kildeer hadn't convened a meeting in several years, at least the last two since Braden joined the league. Her short, three-sentence memo conveyed a positive, cheerful voice, indicating that she hadn't seen the notice of the latest monthly board meeting and must have just missed it in her inbox.

Kildeer's equally short reply appeared later in the same day that there would be a board meeting in the school cafeteria the following week. Ellie laughed—he'd obviously concocted his last-minute response to pacify her. She glanced out the window at the sweaty frat boy working in her back yard. Maybe she should show him the printed email and gloat about her ability to force Kildeer's hand. But she opted not to interrupt him and kept her thoughts to herself.

In a separate voicemail, Jay Smalley told her the summer program was an offshoot of the Springtown Youth Baseball Program for select All-Stars only, and that they didn't have room on the roster for Braden. Ellie spent most of the day and worked into the evening researching the GPYBA bylaws to arm herself with as much knowledge as possible in advance of the upcoming meeting. As she did, she stewed all week without sharing her angst with Colt. In fact, she barely spoke to him, as he finished digging out the infield and lugged wheelbarrows of sand from the hill in the woods to the yard.

ELLIE AND COLT drove to the board meeting together in Ellie's car. They hadn't spent more than a few minutes together since their eggplant dinner two weeks earlier. A weird reluctance settled over Ellie to pursue a relationship with her child's teacher. And yet, a flutter of excitement ran through her as she sat in the car only a few inches apart from him. Colt appeared tired and preoccupied with school, building the backyard diamond, and conducting the practices.

"So, school," Ellie said as they drove through town.

"Yup," Colt answered. "School."

"It's good?"

"Sure, you know, can't complain. Work?"

"Good."

Ellie scoured her mind for something less superficial to discuss. She recalled a funny interaction she had with a client earlier in the day.

"I had a customer call complaining that someone was peeping at them through their fence."

"They called you?"

"I know," Ellie said with a laugh. "I told them to call the police. She said she already did but wanted me to send a crew to fix the hole in the wood."

"Well, that makes sense."

"Turns out." Ellie giggled. "There was no hole. It was a knot in the wood." They shared a laugh, which loosened the awkwardness and eased the flow of conversation. "You like teaching art?"

"It's okay, I guess," Colt answered with a shrug.

"What do you know about art?"

"About as much as I do about eggplant," Colt joked as he shifted in his seat to face her. "Actually, I'm starting to figure out how to teach it. Today, I started out by asking them to draw their favorite cartoon character. First, we used crayons, but then we switched to colored pencils, and then chalk."

"Braden showed me a picture of the Philly Fan mascot that he drew." Ellie's nerves eased as the conversation flowed.

"I'm realizing that teaching is just like coaching."

"Well, they're both pretty much the same, right? Isn't the objective for the kids to learn and grow?"

"I guess so," Colt mused as they pulled into the parking lot. "I told them I'd pose, and they had to draw me, but they had to make me look either funny, goofy, mad, mean or sad."

"I'm sure they all picked goofy," Ellie teased. "A pretty easy assignment."

"Oh, so I'm goofy now?" Colt retorted, while feigning offense.

"Totally." She pivoted in her driver's seat to face him as he had. "But, in a good way."

Ellie softened her smile and raised her eyes to meet his. Colt's brow flinched. She couldn't read his expression.

What had he thought of her flirtation? Had she come on too strongly?

"Well, they loved the assignment." Colt smiled, unaffected, as he clutched the door handle to exit the vehicle.

Nope. Clueless.

"They were laughing, looking at each other's work, giving suggestions." Colt continued to describe the reactions of his students to his fun assignment. "It was really rewarding to see them respond that way."

Colt moved toward the door handle, but Ellie remained in the passenger seat. She made no attempt to exit. Instead, she held him in place with her eyes. Frozen in the front seat of her compact car, they resembled a pair of high school kids at a drive-in or the back of a mall parking lot.

"Who would have pegged the frat boy jock as an art teacher?" Ellie continued to tease him. "If only the sorority sisters could see you now."

"I know," Colt agreed. "It's like I'm almost a fully-functioning adult."

"Almost," Ellie giggled. "Fully-functioning, maybe, but adult, I think that's a stretch."

"Ouch." Colt pretended to stab himself in the heart again, feigning offense. "You're harsh tonight."

"Oh, you haven't even seen my harsh side yet. You'll know it when you see it."

"I bet I will." Colt laughed. "I'm starting to see a couple different sides of you."

"Oh?" she asked, turning from right to left. "Which side do you like best?"

"Both." Colt gave her a grin before finally pulling the handle and exiting the car.

THE SPARSELY ATTENDED meeting took place in the school cafeteria. Kildeer and Smalley sat at a table by the entrance to the kitchen. Colt, Ellie, Laura Yu, and Joe Dalton sat around a table ten feet away. A few other parents congregated at another table. Ellie smiled at Mara Wiltshire sitting with the parents from the red and black team and gave her a subtle wave. Each parent wore either a black and red t-shirt, golf shirt, or windbreaker.

"First order of business," Kildeer opened the meeting. "Starting next meeting, we'll be adding another member to our board in order to comply with our league charter."

Ellie flashed hopeful eyes at Joe Dalton.

"At least we'll get someone with half a brain on the board," she whispered to him.

The parents at the other table didn't appear to listen. Some scrolled through their phones. Others whispered and chuckled softly.

"I've asked Colt Gibson, who's been helping us with the developmental program," Kildeer continued. "He played D-1 ball at Lehigh and will give us an advantage over other town programs. We need a motion and a second."

Smalley said "motion," and Kildeer said "second."

That's when Ellie spoke up.

"Excuse me," she said, standing from her undersized elementary school cafeteria bench. "You don't have a quorum."

"Come again?" Kildeer asked.

"You need a minimum of three people for a quorum."

"Then how do we vote in our new member?" Smalley asked.

"According to your GPYBA charter, for lack of a quorum at the annual meeting, you can pass motions based on the general consensus of the membership in attendance."

"Where'd you get a copy of our charter?" Kildeer asked, staring at Ellie, while Smalley rolled his eyes.

"I got it from Frank Fioretti," Ellie replied. "He's the commissioner of the GPYBA."

"I know who he is," Kildeer snapped.

"Jesus," Smalley muttered, under his breath, unconcerned that the first few rows could hear his outburst. "I don't even have a copy of the charter."

Ellie raised an eyebrow at Colt. Kildeer subtly shushed his fellow board member.

"It's not like we even go by it," Smalley added.

"It's in the charter you signed and renewed every year, including the start of this year." Ellie motioned to a stack of papers on the table in front of her. "It governs how you have to act as an affiliate chapter of the GPYBA, not to mention as a 501(c3) charitable organization."

"That's just a guideline," Smalley started to say.

"As a 501(c3)," Ellie continued. "And the fact that you take tax-free donations from the public, there are very strict laws..."

"Fine," Kildeer cut her off. "Does anybody oppose the appointment of Colt Gibson to our board?"

The room remained silent. The A-team parents looked blankly at each other. Nobody opposed and Garrett said "approved," to make it official.

"Is that your harsh side?" Colt whispered to Ellie.

"Not even close," she replied.

Kildeer shuffled a pile of papers at the front table. He slid a packet in front of Smalley and spoke to him while pointing at the next agenda item.

"Ok, up next," Smalley announced. "We thought we'd run down the results of the season. We had the Seadogs in second place with a record of 3-7. The Bees came in first place at 7-3. Congratulations to both teams. Our A-team competed last weekend in a very competitive tournament at Hershey Park against some of the best ten-year-old teams in the state. We played well, especially in the double consolation game where we lost a close one by only a few runs."

Ellie raised her hand. Kildeer tried to ignore her, but she also stood and cleared her throat demonstratively.

"Yes, Ms. Shaw?"

"Can you explain to us the evaluation criteria used to select the team that attended the tournament?"

"That's our own private process," Kildeer replied. "As, I'm sure you know from reading the bylaws, we're required to have an analytical process, which we do. We're not, however, required to share that formula with the parents."

"That's ridiculous," Ellie retorted. "Why wouldn't you be honest and open about it?"

"We've done this for a long time, ma'am," Kildeer replied. "Frankly, I'm offended at the suggestion that we're somehow dishonest."

"If parents understood our process for scoring the kids, they'd coach them to the numbers rather than teach them the game," Smalley added. "It might make the parents feel good for their kid to be selected to a better team—"

"But it's not in the kids' best interests to know that we rate them and rank them like cattle at the county fair," Kildeer concluded Smalley's thought. "And then dissect and debate them by probing their flaws and inabilities. At some point, Ms. Shaw, you have to trust the process."

"Can you share with us the end results of this *evaluation*?" Ellie stressed the word *evaluation*, in what could be construed as just less than a mocking voice. What she really wanted to call it was a farce.

"Of course not," Smalley spoke up. "If those scores got out, they'd devastate the kids. I know you think you're trying to help here, but we know what we're doing. We've been doing this for a long time. We're all about nothing but the kids. And you parents may not always understand or like what we're doing. But we have a plan, and we know how to give the kids the best possible experiences while helping them all develop in their own way and reach their goals and objectives."

Ellie looked around at the parents at her table and the one adjacent to her. The A-team parents seemed disinterested. Colt looked at her with helpless sympathy. A tall A-team parent nodded approvingly. Joe Dalton crossed his arms, staring at Smalley with a stern expression. But only Ellie spoke.

"Fine." She changed her tactic—if this was how they wanted to play it—she could play hardball too. "I'd like to raise a motion, please?"

"A motion?" Smalley scoffed.

"Yes, a motion." Colt stood next to Ellie with a mocking smile—innocent yet earnest—as only he could pull off. "It's when you..."

"I know what a motion is," Smalley snapped. "I literally just made one. It's just that, um, Ms. Shaw, you can't just..."

"Yes, I can," she said, picking up her printed pages. "At the annual meeting, non-board members may petition motions for consideration by the board."

"What's your motion?" Kildeer asked.

"I propose that any player in town interested in playing on the summer or fall travel team should be granted a spot on the roster and allowed to play."

"Jesus," Smalley slumped in his chair. "We already set the rosters."

"Do I have a second?" Ellie turned to the audience.

"Let me share our philosophy with you." Kildeer stood and

stepped toward the crowd of parents. "We work tirelessly to give every player the experience they deserve."

Ellie snorted, but Kildeer ignored her.

"Second," Joe called out.

"Hear me out first," Kildeer continued. "We have the unenviable responsibility of recognizing the players with the potential to grow and succeed at the highest level of competition and giving them the guidance and support to reach their potential."

"You have a motion and a second," Ellie interrupted him. "Now you vote."

Behind her, the B-team parents grumbled. She heard Joe Dalton and Laura Yu repeat the word "vote."

"Now wait, just a moment," Kildeer continued, looking to the A-team parents on the other side of the room for support, "We can't just... We can't include... Not every player is cut out for year-round baseball. It's not... They're not... In the interest of safety and fairness to the kids who might want to focus on other activities, we have to be selective. That's why it's called a selection process."

"How's it a selection process if you always select the same kids year in and year out?" Ellie asked, as the grousing of the parents behind her continued to escalate.

"Listen, we give the weaker players the opportunity to compete in a safe, controlled setting," he said, with another glance at the A-team parents, some of whom looked up from their phones to observe the tense exchange. "We keep the environment fun and low pressure. We identify the players who will most likely stay with it, usually the bigger, more athletic boys in town and give them the opportunity they need to grow. It's so important not to hold back the better players. We have a responsibility to the town, to the high school team, to the sport itself, to produce the best possible product we can."

"It's time to call the vote," Ellie announced.

"Not all the parents understand how much we agonize over

these decisions," Kildeer spouted, walking closer to the A-team table. "I know most of you get it."

A few A-team parents nodded in agreement. The noise level in the room rose. Voices echoed off the drab cement walls of the cafeteria. Both tables conducted their own side conversations about the fairness of the selection process at issue.

"Come on, vote," shouted Joe Dalton.

"Fine," Smalley said. "I vote no."

"It's not fair to our A-team parents and players," Kildeer continued to direct his commentary to the parents in the red and black swag. "We need to foster a growth environment where the better players can experience the challenging competition they're ready to handle. Not all players in town are equipped for the intensity and demands of travel ball. We play 10-U teams that could have eleven-year-olds on their rosters throwing gas depending on their birthdates. You know how much bigger an eleven-year-old's going to be than your son."

"It's not about my son," Ellie snapped. "It's about what's right and fair."

"Be that as it may," Kildeer replied. "I vote Nay as well."

Ellie stared at the two league administrators for a second. She picked up her paper and read a different passage.

"In a non-quorum scenario in which fewer than three board members are in attendance at the annual meeting and in which more than six attendees are present, the board must recognize the majority vote of both the board members in attendance and the attending non-board members."

Kildeer and Smalley looked at her incredulously.

"Harsh," Colt whispered into Ellie's ear, eliciting a mischievous smirk from her.

"We do have a quorum," Kildeer said. "We have Colt, who we just voted onto the board."

"I haven't accepted the position yet," Colt spoke up. "I'd like to think about it for the next twenty minutes or so. I'm just here as a concerned non-board citizen tonight."

"We all get to vote." A hint of triumph glazed Ellie's words. She had him.

"Fine," Kildeer said. "We have two board members voting 'no' and four other A-team parents. That makes six. You've only got four parents at your table."

Ellie glanced sideways at the A-team parents. Two of them were on their phones not paying attention.

Mara Wiltshire stood, raised her hand, and said, "Yes." Her voice echoed off the glass behind the board's table. "I vote yes. We should let others play if they want to."

"Two votes on the board and three out of four from the A-team table," Smalley said. "With only four parents at the B-team table, that's still not enough to pass."

Colt looked from side-to-side and raised his hand.

"Just because I'm not a parent, doesn't mean I'm not voting."

Ellie beamed at his support as he spoke his vote.

"I don't have a dog in this fight," he said, flashing that innocent sheepish smile again. "But I say yes. Let 'em play."

Kildeer and Smalley glared at Colt as he lowered his hand and crossed his arms. A few of the B-team parents repeated Colt's pronouncement to "Let 'em play." Kildeer looked at the A-team parents and then over his shoulder at Smalley, who leaned back in his seat, nearly toppling.

"That still makes it five to five. Still not enough to pass a motion," he said with a smug sneer. "I'm sorry Ms. Shaw, but…"

Mara patted the arm of the parent from the A-team table sitting close to her. She gave him a nod and a directive flash of her dark brown eyes. The tall man, dressed from head-to-toe in a Lehigh Valley Sheriff's uniform loomed high above the other parents in their red and black garb.

"You didn't count my vote," he said with a quick glance at Mara. "Like my wife, I say let the kids play."

In the parking lot after the meeting, Ellie gave a modest hoot as the parents filed out of the school. She waited until the A-team parents she didn't know reached their cars. Mara Wiltshire approached them and gave Ellie a hug. She introduced the tall, athletic man that voted in favor of Ellie's motion as Darius Wiltshire, Mikey's father. As Ellie thanked Darius for his support, a grim-faced Kildeer and Smalley called to Colt for a word.

Ellie stood with her back to them but strained to listen to their conversation. They were visible from the reflection in the eight-foot plate glass window to the school foyer.

"What was that stunt you pulled tonight?" Smalley poked a finger in the air as if wishing to jab it into Colt's chest.

"We brought you onto the board for your baseball background, the good credibility you can give us, and the fact that you're not a parent," Kildeer spoke in a sharp whisper. "We expected your loyal support. We're going to need you to help us keep your big-mouthed landlord in check."

"She just wants the best for her kid," Colt said. "That's all any of them want."

Colt's support of her efforts as a parent chilled her spine.

"We run the league the way it's always been managed," Smalley snapped. "Not everybody gets to be an All-Star. It's about giving these kids confidence and a sense of pride. Otherwise, there's nothing special about it."

"All I'm saying is that you should give the other kids a look," Colt said. "Some of them are pretty good. Braden's got a good arm and a great head for the game."

Ellie's throat constricted and a tear formed in her eye at Colt's gallant defense of her child.

"He's four feet tall and barely fifty pounds," Smalley scoffed. "He hasn't seen pitching like this. He's not ready."

"I disagree," Colt said. "And I'm glad you'll get the chance to see him play. I think he'll surprise you."

Ellie closed her eyes. She felt the flutter in her stomach return stronger than she'd felt it earlier in the car before the meeting.

"He's not going to play," Smalley sneered. "They voted to put him on the roster. He'll dress, warm up and keep the scorebook for us. He won't see the field unless you count carrying the team bag around."

Colt stared at Smalley. Ellie's positive vibe disappeared. Her face flushed in anger. She wanted to scream at the two imbecilic coaches. But her instincts told her to trust Colt. So, she bit her tongue, stood by the side of her car, and continued to eavesdrop.

"At this level, we have to put our best nine on the field." Kildeer interjected, his voice soft, almost snake-like. You played your whole life. You've seen benchwarmers. It's part of the deal with travel baseball. It's a privilege to even be on the roster."

"You should check him out before you pass judgement," Colt said. "He'll surprise you. The kid's going to be an ace."

"If you're going to join us..." Kildeer caught Ellie watching them in the reflection. "We need you to be one of us."

Ellie wandered toward the back of her car and pretended to appear unaware of the ongoing debate.

"Let's just run a good program." Colt paused and made eye contact with Smalley and Kildeer before adding, "Together."

Ellie waved goodbye to the Wiltshire's and ambled toward Colt. As she approached, all three stepped apart. She leaned close to Colt and resisted the impulse to place her hand on him.

"Welcome to the board." Smalley spat the words as he and Kildeer walked away toward their cars.

17

ELLIE'S PIE

Braden sat the bench for the entire first game of the summer season.

He'd worn his red and black jersey to bed the night before. Ellie had to soak it with dish detergent and dry it with her blow-dryer after he spilled maple syrup on it during breakfast. He and Colt played catch in the yard before the game. Only minutes after Ellie managed to stamp out the amber stain, Braden scuffed it again on a diving snatch in the new dirt-covered infield that Colt installed.

Before leaving for the game, Ellie took pictures of her boy standing in the driveway with a large azalea bush by the side of the barn in the background. Colt snapped a few pictures of the mother and son duo. And then Ellie urged Colt to pose with Braden.

Colt reluctantly stood next to the boy with his arms awkwardly dangling at his side. After a few snaps, he suggested they get in the car to avoid being late.

Braden chattered the entire ride to the field in Stockertown. He waved to his mother as they lined the field and called out each player by name. The euphoria of making the A-team and warming up with the alleged best players in town kept the smile on Braden's face throughout four of the first six innings. By the fifth, he cast a look of concern at his mother. That cherubic gaze morphed to sheer disappointment by the end of the game. Three other players sat on the bench with Braden the entire contest, which seemed to comfort him a little bit.

"It probably means I'll play the whole game next weekend," he said to Ellie as she and Colt tossed his gear into the trunk.

"Don't get your hopes up, Honey," Ellie's voice cracked as her stomach churned.

"Let's get pancakes at the diner," Colt changed the subject, catching a faint glimmer of an appreciative smirk from Ellie in the driver's seat.

Ellie's heart broke every time Braden beamed about playing a whole game—or as he put it- "at least most of the game." The coming weekend featured a home game. He asked Ellie if she thought Lainey and Lilly would come to watch him play. Ellie's mind raced as she saw the weather report. She hated to think this way, but she secretly hoped for a rainout. And, when she awoke on Saturday morning to the sound of driving rain against her thin roof, she couldn't help feeling relieved—even elated.

"You gotta get him into a game—even just an inning," Ellie said to Colt outside her car as Braden waited for them in the back seat. "Maybe at the next board meeting you could talk to them?"

"If we ever have a next board meeting." Colt's shoulders slumped in defeat.

Two more weekends went by with Braden riding the bench for every inning.

"Three games," he whined to his mother during the hour and a half drive from Ephrata. "That's eighteen innings in a row. When am I gonna get to play?"

The rhythmic hum of the engine and the pale light of the setting sun dimmed his sad demeanor as his breathing lengthened and his little eyes drooped to sleep.

"Can you talk some sense into these guys?" Ellie asked Colt as

Braden slept draped across the back seat of her car in his uniform. "You're on the board. How can they look these kids in the eyes after making them drive two hours to east nowhere?"

"West," Colt corrected her. "Ephrata's west of..."

"Whatever," she continued. "How can they look themselves in the mirror knowing they made a kid waste five hours of a beautiful fall weekend in a cement dugout, watching other kids get to play and have fun."

"You think those kids had fun?"

"What was Smalley saying about a refrigerator?" Ellie pulled memories of details from the game.

"That big ten-year-old kid..." Colt paused as if trying to recall his name. "Grounded out. Ran the best he could."

"That's right. He told him to take the refrigerator off his back."

"The 'Goddam' refrigerator," Colt added with his fingers making air quotes.

As he spoke with Ellie, he scrolled to a message on his phone. While stopped at a red light, Ellie caught a glimpse of the invite but pretended not to read it over his shoulder.

She could only make out "Party at the apartment," and "Lehigh PT staff."

Ellie pictured Colt with mussed hair and a misbuttoned shirt like he'd appeared in her driveway after his last campus party. She cast the image aside and finished her train of thought.

"They shouldn't be allowed to speak like that," Ellie continued her affront on the A-team coaches. "Who was that big kid anyway? Was he the one who hit the ball off the fence for that double?"

"That's the kid," Colt said. "I assumed you knew him."

"I've never seen him before." Ellie pulled into the driveway. "Weird."

The rumbling of the car caused Braden to stir and then slump his face back into the side of his glove against the upholstered back seat bench. Ellie grabbed the baseball bag. Colt lifted Braden from the back seat, carrying him across the patio to the patio door and into the house.

As Colt creaked each step of the exposed wood staircase, Braden's face buried deep into his chest, with his limp arms draped over his shoulders. From the bottom of the stairs, she watched him carry the boy into his room. The floorboards shuddered and the bedsprings squeaked. She heard two hushed voices, one high pitched and sleepy, the other deep. Colt reappeared outside Braden's door a few minutes later.

"Did he wake up?" Ellie whispered.

"Just for a moment," Colt replied, padding quietly across the upstairs hallway.

"What'd he say?"

"He thanked me for being his coach. I told him it was my pleasure."

Ellie's heart skipped a beat at the thought of Braden, with his puppy-dog eyes, expressing such gratitude to the gentle father-figure that spent so much of his time working with him.

The varnished pine creaked under Colt's weight as he descended the stairs toward her. She stood in his path at the bottom, clutching the knob on the banister like the swinging door to a gate. Their eyes met for a brief moment. He slid his palm along the handrail and moved slowly enough to minimize the echo of the distressed wood against the upstairs walls. As he reached the second to last step, his gaze caught a dish on the counter. He nearly walked through her extended arm, which she dropped to her side just in time to let him pass.

"Is that cherry pie?" he asked, eyeing the golden crown of crust on the counter. He moved past her to take a closer look at the dessert she'd baked earlier in the day.

"Uh, sure," she muttered with a sigh. "Want some?"

Colt took a seat. She cut him a large slice and served herself a smaller sliver.

They sat across from each other at the table eating their pie.

"Delicious," Colt said, his smile as wide and genuine as ever.

Ellie watched him down the dessert in seconds. "Another?"

Colt glanced at the pie on the counter, appearing to consider it for a moment before nodding and rubbing his stomach.

"It's delicious," he said. "I could probably eat it all. But you should save the rest for your boy."

Ellie cleared the plates and stood by the sink, buying time as she rinsed them under the faucet. With her back to her guest, she exhaled and closed her eyes. She turned to see him reclined in her kitchen chair with his arms behind his head.

"Uh," Ellie's voice cracked as she lowered her voice. "Thirsty? Something to drink?"

Colt shrugged. An awkward silence lingered between them. His phone buzzed in his pocket for the third time in as many minutes.

Colt fidgeted with his phone. Ellie's brow crinkled in doubt. To her delight, Colt slipped his phone back into his pocket and nodded.

"Sure," he said with a warm smile.

As she turned to search the fridge, she spied him type a quick message to his former roommate. *Maybe later.*

Ellie offered him a beer, but he asked for milk instead. With a shrug and a movement of his eyes across the counter, Ellie thought she noticed a blush in his cheeks.

"I suppose if I had just one more little sliver of pie, there'd still be plenty left for Braden tomorrow."

Her face brightened as she poured two glasses of whole milk she'd picked up from the local farmers' market and cut him his second slice of pie.

"No frat party tonight?" she teased him, as she slid a fresh new dessert plate and milk glass across the table in front of him.

"No, there is."

"You chose milk and cherry pie over booze, and Lord knows what else?"

"It's good pie," Colt replied, before downing another chunk of crust, covered in bright red filling.

"I'm keeping you from the fun?"

"You should come with me some night."

Ellie withheld her smirk as her mind cycled through all the hoops she'd have to jump through to free herself for an evening at a party. She hadn't visited a sorority or frat house in years.

"You could get someone to watch Braden," Colt continued. "When's the last time you cut loose?"

Ellie resisted the impulse to laugh out loud at the idea that she would have the time or energy to cut loose, as Colt suggested. She recalled herself drinking all night and dancing on top of the bar at the local night club in college.

"I'm well past that part of my life," she said. "When you have three jobs and a nine-year-old to manage, it's just 'no' in my single mom's handbook."

"Isn't he eight?"

"Whatever," Ellie laughed. "Next month."

"I think it'd be fun to go out to a party together. After seeing Harsh Ellie, it makes me wonder what Party Ellie might be like."

"Party Ellie hasn't gone out in a while." Despite her rejection of the idea, she still pictured what she might wear to such an event. "I'm pretty much a sweatpants on the couch type of girl at this point."

"I bet Party Ellie has great outfits up there, just waiting to be taken out."

"I'm a mom now," she scoffed. "That's hardly the life I live anymore."

Colt sized her up, maybe imagining her as a college student. Ellie couldn't tell if his scrutiny made her self-conscious or his attentiveness gave her confidence.

After she made a mental map of her closet and possible outfits, she replied, "It's been a while since I threw on my leather mini skirt."

Did her legs still look as athletic as they did when she played softball?

"There you go," Colt egged her on. "I bet you clean up pretty good."

"Or my little black cocktail dress," she continued, "as long as it still fits."

"I'm sure it does."

"It's been a while since I broke out my heels. With three inches added to my height, I actually look like a catcher."

"I don't know about that, Lafayette," Colt replied. "You still look like a shortstop to me. Thin, wiry, and quick."

Ellie blushed at his compliment. Colt slid his empty plate aside and glanced at a photo on the refrigerator of Ellie and Braden standing by the barn.

"Where's his dad?" he asked.

The image of her son's smug, self-centered father wiped away any thoughts of her wild days in college.

"Gone," she replied, as she cleared his second plate and ran the water with her back to him.

"Not involved?"

"At first." Ellie returned to the table and peered into Colt's eyes, challenging him to probe deeper.

"What happened?" he asked.

"We gave it a go. He lived here for a while with me and my aunt before she died."

"Sorry."

Ellie nodded in acknowledgement of Colt's condolence. "He worked a couple hours away, at Penn State as an adjunct philosophy professor; stayed there during the week and visited on the weekends."

"Long distance. That's tough," Colt said.

"I left Braden with my aunt and went up to visit him when I could." Ellie gazed past Colt and recalled her first year as a mother, including the late Friday night drives through nowhere

Pennsylvania to visit him in his studio apartment, followed by the long, lonely early morning returns to Springtown.

She snapped out of her glazed expression and fixed her eyes back on Colt. "He was cheating."

"Damn. That sucks."

"It's not like she was there," Ellie continued. "But I knew. The place was too clean and organized."

"That doesn't mean—"

"He was a slob with me," Ellie interrupted him. "I had to keep his head glued on for him."

"Was that it?"

"He had two sets of keys," she continued. "And only one car."

"You mean like a spare?"

"I mean like a Honda and a Subaru."

"Oh, man," Colt replied. "Busted."

Ellie dropped her eyes as a wave of sadness washed over her. "I eventually had to explain to Braden that his dad's job was just too far away, and he couldn't visit as often as he used to."

"How'd he take it?"

"He didn't understand at first. He was just a toddler. As he got older, he wanted to move to where Jeffrey worked. Or he wanted him to quit and move back here. Eventually, he just accepted life without a dad. But it's affected his confidence and his ability to make friends."

"How so?"

"It doesn't help that he's small," Ellie replied. "Or, that he's so nice and innocent. Other boys tease him, or just don't include him. It's not a big problem, but sometimes I wonder if having two parents—you know, a dad, who better understands how boys tick—would give him different tools to use in social situations; different ways to establish himself other than just the way I try to guide him."

"So, like, if his dad were around," Colt reassembled Ellie's thought process. "He could teach him to be more of a guy's guy?"

"I don't know?" Ellie wavered. "It sounds stupid. The world's full of amazing single mothers who raise strong, confident boys."

Ellie once served as the center of the softball team, ordering the infielders around, directing the outfielders to shift for each batter, and calling the pitches. Now, she'd faded from such an authoritative, decisive leader to this worried, exasperated, downtrodden single parent, who struggled daily to live up to the life her son deserved.

"You're one of those amazing single mothers." Colt cocked his head to the side as if surprised that she would doubt herself. "And you've got a wonderful, happy, confident little boy up there."

Ellie raised her eyes to meet his, appreciative of his compliment.

Colt's phone buzzed again in his pocket. Ellie heard it, but ignored it, lost in the confluence of her painful recollection of the departure of Braden's father from her life, and the glow of Colt's effusive support.

"I'm just frustrated with how Jeffrey conducted himself." The admission darkened her mood, and she lowered her tone. "And I hate cheaters."

18

THE NEXT SEASON'S ROSTERS

The fall baseball season flew by. Braden played right field for an inning or two in the last blow-out game. At the plate, he struck out in his only at bat, fouling several pitches before buckling at a called strike curveball.

The next board meeting for the league took place in December, two months after the last game of the fall season. Jay Smalley proposed a new position called Evaluations Officer and nominated himself. Garrett Kildeer seconded his motion and the measure passed with their majority vote. With three board members present, Kildeer and Smally had an easier time passing new measures, simply by outvoting Colt two-to-one. In his new position, Smalley gave himself sole control over the analytical ranking methods used to justify their All-Star selections.

Next, Smalley presented the rosters for the next year's teams, which were identical to the ones from the previous year, with all the same players picked for the "A's", "Bees" and "Seadogs". The rosters appeared on a single piece of paper with names hand-written and initials next to each name to indicate their positions.

Kildeer made a motion to end the meeting and Smalley seconded it, but Colt raised his hand.

"Wait," he said. "There are no ratings assigned to these players."

"They're just not listed," Smalley replied.

"Was there even a tryout?" Colt asked.

"We evaluated the players during the season," Smalley said. "We know every player in town inside and out."

"You need to hold a tryout," Colt scoffed. "You can't just decide at seven or eight who makes the best team and stick with that for the next ten years."

Smalley and Kildeer glanced sideways at each other. Smalley pulled out another photocopied, handwritten page and slid it across the table. Colt scanned it. Each name had a number from one to five for hitting, fielding, and pitching with a total score ranging from three to fifteen. He found Braden about halfway up the page with a total score of nine.

"How'd you come up with these?" Colt asked.

"We have a process," Smalley sneered.

Colt paused to change his approach. "I'd like to make a motion. We should have a well-defined and documented set of evaluation criteria, and an actual tryout event at the beginning of the season. Team selection should be done by consensus of the board."

"We're not doing that." Smalley crossed his arms in front of his chest.

"Why not?" Colt asked.

"We have it covered," Smalley replied. "Don't worry about it."

"I made a motion." Colt looked to Kildeer.

"He made a motion," Kildeer repeated and turned to Smalley. "Do we have a second?"

Smalley smirked at Colt.

"I'll second my own motion," Colt snapped.

"Can't," Smalley said with a sly, smug grin.

"Why the hell not?"

"Charter says you can't second your own motion." He laughed. "Maybe your girlfriend should read it to you."

Colt's nerves frayed. He clenched his fists and grit his teeth. He shifted his appeal to Kildeer, who looked away from his stare.

"I will second Garrett's motion to close the meeting though." Smalley chuckled at Colt's powerlessness.

Kildeer, looking more sympathetic, but still avoiding eye contact with Colt, announced the end of the meeting. He took the evaluation page back from Colt and wrapped his scarf across his neck before donning his coat and leaving the room with Smalley tagging closely behind.

"That's it?" Colt called to them as they wordlessly exited the empty cafeteria and closed the heavy doors behind them.

Colt stewed as he drove through town to Ellie's house. As he pulled into the driveway, his headlights illuminated her athletic silhouette. She pulled her winter coat across her mouth to shield the winter wind.

"How'd it go?" she asked him as he emerged from the cab.

"Fine." He grabbed a duffel bag and slung it over his shoulder.

"What'd they talk about?"

"They made the teams for next year," Colt replied, turning toward his apartment.

"And?" Ellie asked, apprehension in her tone.

"He's on the Bee's again."

"How'd they..."

"I don't know." Colt turned to face Ellie. "They just did."

"But you were there? You're on the board."

Frustrated and tired from the hectic school day, Colt felt like a witness under a cross-examination. The lasting image of Smalley's curled lips and beady eyes flashed across his mind.

"Up against those two, my presence on the board may not do us a damn bit of good."

Ellie shuddered in the cold. With her black, leather-gloved

hand, she adjusted her fur-lined hood in the dark of the December evening.

"I made meatloaf," her voice softened. "My mother's recipe. Braden hates it, so I have plenty extra if you'd like some."

Colt saw Braden's head bop across the kitchen window. The brisk winter air caused a shiver to race down his spine. He found himself wanting to return to his apartment, take a hot shower, catch a basketball game on television and go to sleep.

"School's off next week." He shrugged. The wind blew Ellie's hood, obscuring her face. He was thankful he wouldn't see her expression when he relayed his plans. "I was going to spend some time up in Bethlehem with my old teammates."

"Ah, right." Ellie shifted weight from one foot to the next, keeping her head down. "Well, have fun then."

"You wanna—" He stopped when he saw Braden's shadow in the window again. "Maybe tomorrow, or…"

"No," Ellie retreated. "Go have your fun. I'll see you whenever you get back."

19

JUICEBALL

At the turn of the year, Colt found out that Mrs. Pemberwick decided not to return to her job as the Springtown Elementary School art teacher. Soon after, he received an offer to teach the subject on a full-time basis for the remainder of the year. He spent his evenings reading about art history and concepts. He even took up painting, albeit badly, where he sat at the top of the steps to his apartment and muddled through an impressionist representation of Ellie's house.

He had little artistic talent but learned quite a bit about teaching it to others. As a sports coach, he had never believed that adage that you didn't have to be a great player to be a great coach. But his experience as an art teacher caused him to reevaluate the phrase and give it greater credibility.

For the first game of the new 10-U season, ten out of thirteen players showed up. Only six members of the Seadogs made it. As they had the previous year's opening day, they combined teams, split into even groups, and played eight against eight. The merged team arrangement proved a permanent change as the Seadogs folded except for one or two players.

Ellie took the field and helped coach. She directed baserunners and guided players where to throw the ball in each play. Colt brought his homemade pitching mound and gave several players, including Braden, the opportunity to hurl from the hill. The advent of kid-pitching produced more walks than hits. Braden's first pitch sailed high and inside and pegged Stevie Dalton on the side of the helmet.

Despite the erratic pitching and the handful of beanballs, nobody cried for long, and everyone enjoyed the game in the warm, breezy April weather. After the first game, the players ran around the playground in a rousing game of tag while the parents thanked Colt and Ellie for their energy and dedication to their kids.

Several parents joined them for pancakes and milkshakes at the diner. The kids giggled, squirmed, and spilled food all over their booths. The parents congregated at one table, deep in conversation as Andrea served the big group and raked in the sympathetic tip.

"Maybe this year, we can play for the championship and get our pictures on the wall," Braden pointed at the frames that covered three walls of the diner. "We'll be famous."

As Colt pulled his car to the far edge of the driveway, facing Shaw Field as the Bees had come to call it, he saw Braden with a bucket of baseballs and a tee, standing at home plate. He placed a ball on the tee and whacked it into the outfield. Several dozen balls scattered about center and right field.

"Looking good," he said, as he slung his duffel bag over his shoulder, feeling the excess oranges, apples and pears from the day's lesson plan roll around and batter his neck and back.

"I'm good in the field," Braden said before teeing the ball, lining it up, and smashing it over second base. "But I have to hit better."

"If you level your swing, you'll hit line drives and they'll go farther." Colt approached him. "Tee another one for me."

Braden dropped his bat and held his arms outward. "That was the last one."

Colt reached into his bag for a baseball but grabbed an orange instead. Braden giggled. Colt snickered as well and placed the orange sphere onto the tee.

"Can I smash it?" Braden asked.

"Only if you have a nice level swing," Colt replied. "Keep your head down, use your hips and swing all the way through the ball."

"You mean the orange," Braden corrected Colt as he narrowed his gaze to the top of the tee.

"Head down," Colt instructed him. "Smash it into orange juice. You'll want to watch it explode and you can't do that looking up and out into the middle of nowhere."

"Explode?"

"Of course. Like a big orange firework."

Braden grinned as he aligned the bat with the side of the orange and set his feet in the dirt.

"Plus," Colt continued. "I've got more oranges and a couple apples in my bag."

"Can I smash them too?"

"Only if I like your swing," Colt said. "Level. Turn your hips. Head down on the ball. And follow through. Then we'll make more orange juice."

"And apple juice?" Braden giggled.

"And apple juice."

The kitchen door clapped against the distressed wood frame behind Colt. Ellie's footsteps ambled across the porch as Braden splattered orange pulp across the batter's box and toward the mound.

"What are you guys doing?" she asked.

"Making orange juice." Braden belly-laughed with Colt.

"We've got the team coming over soon." She shook her head at what resembled a small child and an overgrown one laying on their backs laughing. "I know you got home late. Are you all set for practice?"

"Actually," Colt dusted his shorts and stood. "Could you run out to the store? I'll text you a list."

Ellie disappeared for about a half-hour fulfilling Colt's strange list of requests. While she shopped, Colt, towered over a dozen nine and ten-year-olds deep in center field. They made a semi-circle around him and erupted in wild cheers.

Colt watched Ellie's tiny car pull into the driveway and stop at the edge of the grass. She lugged the bags of groceries into the kitchen while Colt managed the practice. He caught her looking out the back window.

"Why hit way out in center field?" she asked Colt as she wandered across the patio toward the groomed infield dirt. "Won't you lose the balls in the woods?"

Colt held his hand up to his ear in the universal sign that he couldn't hear her. The cheering grew louder and more frequent. He observed her standing at the end of the field watching the practice play out. Eventually she moved to the middle of the diamond.

"What are you guys doing?" she asked, standing atop the Pitcher's Mound.

"Home Run Derby," said Ronnie.

"No," Braden corrected him. "Reverse Home Run Derby, like before."

Ellie looked at Colt in amusement at the enthusiasm of the players on his team.

"Ronnie and Tonio are winning." Braden said. "Then Lainey. I'm in fourth place."

He listed each player's score before asking his mother if she "got the food from the store."

"I did," Ellie replied. "I'll bring it out after you finish your hitting practice."

"No," Braden pleaded. "We want to play juiceball now."

"Juiceball?" she asked.

"You got the two dozen apples and oranges?" Colt asked her.

"Yes."

"And the twelve watermelons?"

"Twelve watermelons?" she asked. "I got enough watermelon for twelve kids."

"You didn't get twelve?" Braden asked.

"I just got one big one."

"Aw, mom," Braden whined.

"I was going to bring out a big bowl of fruit cocktail during your water break." Ellie raised an eyebrow at Colt.

"You don't get it, Mom." Braden said, with slumped shoulders. "We're each supposed to get our own watermelon."

"That's too much, honey," she said, looking confused and annoyed. "I'll just slice it up into chunks and everyone will get plenty to eat."

"It's not for eating," Braden groused. "We wanted to smash them up into chunks ourselves."

Ellie looked to Colt for help. He shrugged his shoulders and laughed.

20

THE SPECIAL RINGTONE

With the merger of the Bees and the Seadogs, Kildeer agreed to schedule exhibition games for the consolidated squad to square off against the weakest spring-league A-teams in the travel program. The arrangement gave the Bees an opponent each week and a higher level of competition to face. In exchange, the A-teams with losing records across the league licked their chops for the chance to gain confidence and a winning experience by thrashing the Bees.

Braden stewed after each defeat. His teammates also groused afterward but moved on from the hard feelings of losing more quickly than he did. Many of the parents, as relaxed as they had been over the past season and a half, grumbled about the inequity between the teams in town, venting their frustration about having the weakest roster in the league.

Between the games, as April flipped to May, Juiceball became a big hit at the Shaw Field practices. Reverse Home Run Derby and Juicepitch, which, like Juiceball, challenged the pitchers to knock apples and oranges off the tee by hurling a baseball at them from the mound, also generated significant excitement among the players.

Colt placed funny objects on top of the tee including a beachball, a volleyball, a watermelon, apples, oranges and even a large strawberry. The smaller the object, the more difficult the challenge for the pitchers. While Ronnie, Stevie, and Lainey tended to win the hitting competitions. Braden, by far, excelled as a pitcher.

Braden even invented a variation of Juicepitch. He called it Juicebomb, where instead of throwing a baseball at an orange and trying to explode it off the tee, the pitchers threw oranges against the shed and tried to create the best orange explosions.

Juicebomb only lasted a week until Ellie calmly but firmly suggested the players who made the biggest messes would also be the ones to clean the side of the barn. Between the larger practices, Colt worked one-on-one with Braden, training him to throw with precision and mix his pitches across different locations over the plate. He suspended a watermelon from the rafters of the barn to create a fun new target. Braden practiced nearly every day trying to obliterate the watermelons, until Colt forced him to rest once or twice per week to avoid injury. To circumvent Ellie's scorn, Colt made sure to scrub away all traces of the watermelon before she returned from work each day.

The team workouts continued in full momentum, paying dividends in a variety of ways. The players blew off their frustrations and lost track of the beatings they took during their Sunday contests. And the parents appreciated the excitement their kids exuded about the creative workouts at Shaw Field.

The Bees started hitting the ball in their games more consistently. Ellie snickered from the patio one morning when Colt threw practice pitches, and Stevie plunked him in the shoulder with a line drive. After that he started using his L-screen for protection from the batted balls that now sailed closer past his ear when he threw to the stronger batters.

At the same time, scores of the Bees' losses grew closer each week. They went from a 21-0 drubbing in their first game to a 10-1 loss in their second and an 8-2 deficit in their third. As they warmed up for their fourth game of the spring season, Colt received a last-minute call from the opposing coach cancelling the game. Word about the all-grass infield, with its excessive weeds, uneven divots, and dangerous patches of hard clay, caused several local coaches to trade emails cautioning each other to avoid the Springtown Bees.

Ellie and Colt frantically reworked their schedule, seeking teams willing to play at their field. They sent an email to all coaches in the league and offered to travel to away games rather than serving as hosts. They also contacted Smalley to inquire if they could play on Victory Field.

He replied by email several days later:

That's the A-team field. It's tightly scheduled and needs downtime between games and practices for grooming, watering, and settling.

Ellie didn't respond to Smalley's ridiculous message about the field, but his follow-up email caught her by surprise.

He wrote: *You could play against us at Victory if you like.*

Ellie stared at the words on the screen. The blinking cursor taunted her. She forwarded it to Colt, prefaced by a single word; "*Thoughts?*" She next considered how to concoct a way to float the idea by Braden.

"How's the A-team doing?" she asked over dessert before bedtime.

"I think they might have won one," he answered, with a blob of ice cream spilling out of his mouth.

"It would be fun to play on Victory Field."

"That would be awesome," he agreed.

"How do you think you'd do against them?"

"Against who?" Braden asked.

"The other team," Ellie replied, "You know, the A-team."

Every time she said A-team, a pit formed in her stomach as if referring to them as *"the team that doesn't lose all the time like your B-team."* But then, she registered Braden's response that Kildeer and Smalley's squad had only won a single game and felt less jealous of them. *A-team, my ass.*

"They'd kill us," Braden answered. "They have Mikey Wiltshire and Damien Smalley as their pitchers. And they have that big kid from Ferndale, who hits home runs."

As Ellie cleared the plates, her phone beeped in her purse.

"That's Colt," he said, leaping off his chair and retreating to the television room.

"How did you know that?" she asked, with a nervous chuckle.

"You programmed a special ring tone for him," he replied.

Her playful laugh morphed to embarrassment as she answered the incoming call.

"Got your email," Colt shouted, over the sound of pounding music.

"Where are you?" she asked.

"Uh, nowhere. Just this club."

"I see. We can talk another time."

"About playing Smalley's team," Colt continued. "I'm not sure we're ready for that. It might be tough on them in school."

"What do you mean?"

"You know," he replied. "The teasing and taunting. There's enough of that already."

"Do they tease our team?" Ellie asked.

"Hey, listen," Colt cut her off. "It is pretty loud here. Let's talk after the weekend."

"Sure." Ellie shook her head and tossed her phone into her purse before joining Braden on the couch to watch his show with him. As the hypnotic blue glow from Braden's cartoon strobed through the house, Ellie pictured Colt in a similarly lit room, but more spacious and crowded with people. She pictured a throng of young women in their early twenties, dancing to loud, pulsating music, smiling, laughing, and drinking. She imagined them scantily clad, curvy, and easy.

"It's loud here," she sneered, imitating Colt's impish voice. "I've got shots to drink and twenty-year-olds to hit on. Blah, blah, blah."

The thought transported her to her junior year of college; back when she was young, smiley and curvy, before childbirth, motherhood, homeownership and career. She recalled meeting Jeffrey in a Data and Analytics class during her junior year and joining him in the library to study for the final.

He wore dark clothes, black skinny jeans and a white t-shirt. His hair, thick and artistic, jetted from his head in different directions. He seemed distant, like he had bigger plans for himself and always wanted to be somewhere other than his current situation.

With Jeffrey and his ambition, she imagined a future. She pictured him working as a college professor and her as a high school softball coach. He appeared much more serious and responsible than her old high school boyfriends.

But it was all a load of crap. He only cared about himself. By the time she figured it out, she already had his baby growing in her womb.

I should have read him better. They're all the same.

Ellie sighed in reflection of her past mistakes. Braden lay slumped sideways with his head against a throw pillow, his eyes drooping. The scratchy hum of crickets surrounded the house from the outside. The moonlight competed with the glow of the television. She tapped him on the shoulder, nudged him to consciousness, and guided him up the stairs to brush his teeth and snuggle into bed.

After kissing him and turning out his light, she stood in his door and watched his eyes close for the night. The moonlight illuminated the curve of his cheek and nose. Thoughts of her ex dissolved from her mind as the flutter in her stomach filled her with love and pride in the wonderful young boy that comprised her two-person family. She couldn't tear herself away, longing to hold him, lay with him and ensure his utmost happiness in life.

And yet... She watched her boy's chest rise and fall with the soft breath of slumber. *I wouldn't change a single detail about how it all happened.*

Her mindset shifted from her own past to her son's present. She ran through her mental checklist. Should the Bees take on the A-team? That dilemma popped up in her mind for the third time that day. She ignored the debate and focused on her tasks for the next day. She had to confirm who would attend practice after school. She had a long list of fruits and vegetables to buy at the market so they could bat them all around her yard. Concerns of liability crossed her mind. With so many kids practicing as a team on her property. What exposure could she face if someone sustained a serious injury?

Unable to resist returning to Braden's side, she kissed his cheek again and brushed his hair away from his eyes.

Damned baseball coaches. How can they not see how amazing he is?

Her phone chirped from the kitchen table downstairs. The noise startled her as if breaking a trance or shaking her from a dream. She recognized the special ringtone as Braden described it. She closed the door and padded down the stairs to catch it just in time.

"Hey there," Colt said, his voice much clearer, with the pounding dance music replaced by the hum of his truck engine. "I know you wanted to speak with me about the team. I left the club and I'm on my way home now. Hopefully you can hear me better."

21

THE HOME TEAM

Ellie couldn't figure out how the switch took place. She hadn't committed to playing against the A-team. And yet, somehow, she received an email from the GPYBA league administrator that due to a last-minute schedule change, the Springtown A-team would play the Springtown Bees instead of the first-place Allentown A's as Coach Smalley's original schedule indicated.

She looked up the standings and figured out that the Allentown A's posted an undefeated record, beating most teams by double digits. The Springtown A's had a 2-4 record, beating two of the lower-ranked teams by a run or two each. Her mind swirled in conspiracy theory. Had Smalley orchestrated the switch to avoid playing the superior Allentown team, using the GPYBA executive to force her into submission?

She emailed the league administrator and asked if she could play a different opponent, but only received a terse response.

"It's a scheduling nightmare to keep making changes," he wrote. "Get your act together over there in Springtown."

The next day at practice, Ellie and Colt broke the news to the

Bees that they would play the A-team later that weekend. The team cheered in excitement at the prospect of playing at the "stadium."

"We're gonna get whooped," Ronnie said after the cheering subsided. "But at least we get to play on a field with a home run fence."

Colt aligned his infield and hit groundballs to them, working on their fielding technique and their throws to first base. Ellie took the outfielders into deep right and worked on hitting off a tee into the woods.

Ellie had her back to the infield but sensed the yelp even before she heard it. She swung around just in time to see Ronnie Pawlecki go down. He writhed on the ground like a firecracker, whining, moaning, and holding his mouth. Even from two hundred feet out, Ellie saw the brightness of Ronnie's fresh red blood against his white t-shirt.

"What happened?" she screeched as she sprinted across the grass.

"Took a wicked hop off a divot," Colt said, as he whipped off his t-shirt and pressed it against Ronnie's gushing lip.

Caught off guard, Ellie stared at Colt's curved chest muscles and rippled stomach, before her mommy instincts wretched her back to the situation at hand.

"Are his teeth ok?" she asked, as Ronnie cried uncontrollably.

"He got his body in front of it just like he's supposed to," said Lainey, seated at her shortstop position.

"Braden," Ellie snapped. "Get the bag of frozen peas out of the freezer, wrap it in a dish cloth, and bring it out here."

Braden trotted in from the outfield. Lilly offered to help. She jogged with him to the back door and into the kitchen to abide by Ellie's instructions.

"I think practice is over for tonight," Ellie announced to the team as she and Colt helped Ronnie to a chair on the patio. "Call your parents and let them know we're ending early."

ELLIE SAT on her couch late that night with her laptop resting on top of a blanket draped over her thighs. Hours after Andrea picked up Ronnie with his purple swollen lip and package of frozen peas held against the side of his face, her heart still raced. Even with Andrea's reassuring text that Ronnie's teeth were unharmed, and he just had a fat lip, she continued to tremble as she typed 'personal liability' and 'injury lawsuits' into her browser's search engine.

She found an article about a Connecticut homeowner who successfully petitioned the town to sanction a four-acre backyard playing field as a designated recreation site covered by the town's liability insurance. She also stumbled onto the site for the Greater Philadelphia Elite Baseball League, also known as the GPEBL, which listed both public and private fields on their page of sanctioned venues covered by the league's insurance waiver.

As much as she scoured the GPYBA website, she couldn't find evidence of any private fields covered by the league's insurance. Returning to the GPEBL site, she discovered a form for new entries to join the league. Team Administrators could log their zip code or range of zip codes and apply for a charter to enter a team into the upcoming season.

The rules specified that the town could not already be affiliated with another league. Teams accepted for the upcoming season of the GPEBL would be entitled to insurance covering both away and home games as well as practices occurring at both public and approved private fields.

Ellie's heart soared. She typed a text to Colt but stopped when she noticed the qualifiers regarding acceptance of private fields including the length of the basepaths, the dimensions of the infield, and the distance between the natural mound and the plate. The rule specifically banned portable mounds from use on sanctioned fields.

Additional rules read: *Must be completely fenced with a*

backstop no less than twenty feet high with designated dugouts and bullpen areas also fenced from the playing area. Must allow for ample parking to accommodate at least as many vehicles as players attending each event.

She looked through the kitchen, out the back window. Darkness shrouded the field. The moon lit a path from Colt's makeshift homemade mound to the plate, which reflected the silver glow.

Ellie erased her text to Colt and clutched the top of her laptop screen to close it for the evening. An email caught her attention, followed by another that appeared after the first.

Frank Fioretti, the head of the GPYBA, copied both her and Jay Smalley and wrote: *Who should I list as the home team this weekend.*

Smalley replied in about a heartbeat: *It's our field. We're the home team.*

Braden's warm-up ritual started at six o'clock, sharp.

Thwack. Thwack. Thwack.

The pounding against the façade of the garage snapped Colt out of a deep sleep.

Thwack. Thwack. Thwack.

After a few moments of burying his head under his pillow, Colt sat upright and eyed the clock.

Thwack. Thwack. Thwack.

The sound of the tennis ball against the faded wood of the garage called to him. He descended the stairs and rounded the corner to the yard where he spied Braden in his baseball pants and bright blue jersey.

"All warmed up?" he asked the boy.

"Almost."

"Not until you knock the ball off the tee."

Colt positioned Mr. Yankee Doodle and handed Braden a fresh baseball from the bucket by the side of the barn. Braden cast aside his tennis ball and eyed the volleyball. Colt chuckled at the boy's resolve. Braden wound up, cocked his arm, torqued his hips, and hurled a strike right over the tee, knocking the volleyball to the ground on his first try.

"Wow," Braden beamed. "First pitch."

"Jeez," Colt muttered.

"I guess I'm ready to strike everyone out today."

"I guess so," Colt replied, scratching the back of his neck in shock.

Ellie, Colt, and Braden arrived at Victory Stadium first of the Bees. The A-team already occupied the field, running sprints across the outfield in unison. Their black and red uniforms contrasted with the green grass and the beige infield dirt.

Kildeer ran a tight and efficient infield practice while Smalley used a pitching machine angled into the sky to project fly balls to his outfielders. Three pitchers warmed up, throwing to three back-up catchers in the bullpen adjacent to the dugout.

A row of A-team parents hung over the left field fence where they scrutinized every throw and catch. They gave about as much coaching feedback as the actual coaches and in the same negative phrasing.

"Catch the damn ball."

"What kind of throw was that?"

"Get your ass down on those grounders."

The remaining Bees rolled in about twenty minutes before game time. Colt asked Tonio Maletti to warm up as the starting pitcher. He put Braden at first base, Lilly Yu at second, her sister Lainey at short, and Ronnie at third.

"How come I'm not the starting pitcher?" Braden asked Colt in a hushed voice, with a side glance to his mother, standing next to the dugout fence. "I thought I was going to strike everyone out today."

"I need you at first to get us some outs," Colt replied.

He knew Braden would want to pitch. But he couldn't bear to feed the exuberant young boy to the wolves of the A-team that might rock him, discourage him and then tease him at school.

"Plus, if we're winning... I mean *when* we're winning in the last inning, you can be the closer and strike out whoever you face."

"Got it," Braden said, with a smile and a wink before trotting back to his spot in the infield.

As Colt watched Braden run to his position, an impulse to show confidence in him by letting him start the game on the mound conflicted with his decision to protect him from the scorn and abuse of his classmates. He noticed Ellie leaning against the fence shouting encouragement to her son and his teammates. He watched Tonio finish his warm-up pitches in the bull pen, looking strong and fairly accurate.

"Hey Braden," he called from the dugout. "The first baseman is the leader out there. Take charge."

Braden gave a thumbs up as he warmed up his infielders.

After five minutes of infield practice, Jay Smalley asked Colt to move his players off the field so he could hose the dirt to minimize the dust. They played the Star-Spangled Banner with each starting line-up standing along the basepaths. The players held their caps over their hearts. And then the umpire shouted, "play ball."

From the start of the game, Ellie, Colt, and all the parents of the Bees felt the other team's momentum build from the first few batters. Leading off in the first inning at the plate, the Bees went down on three straight strikeouts as Mikey Wiltshire blew his fastball past Lilly, Braden, and Ronnie. He ended the inning on ten pitches.

Tonio took a couple batters to settle in. He hit the first batter, walked the second and gave up a single to the third. With the bases loaded, the big kid that Braden referred to as 'the dude from Ferndale' stepped up to the plate.

On Tonio's first pitch, the boy smacked the ball into the leaves beyond the fence. Colt watched helplessly as four runs crossed the plate and the stadium erupted in raucous cheers for the other team.

"That's what I'm talking about," yelled one parent.

"Keep 'em coming boys," yelled another.

Braden's shoulders slumped. Tonio hung his head. Ellie and Colt exchanged wary glances. The A-team made a ring around home plate and mobbed their clean-up hitter as he crossed the plate.

Colt visited the mound and brought the whole team together. "Don't worry about the score. Focus on getting one out. Who's going to catch the next ball?"

Lainey and Lilly raised their hands first. Then Braden and Stevie and the rest of the outfielders followed.

"Ok, good," Colt said. "One point for each person who makes a play in the field. I'll keep track on my clipboard and post it in the dugout. Now, go make an out."

After running to a full count, Tonio threw a strike down the middle of the plate to Damien Smalley, who chopped a hard groundball into the hole between third and short. Ronnie couldn't reach it. But, ranging behind Ronnie, Lainey Yu backhanded the ball and made the throw to Braden, who stretched to make the catch in time.

As the umpire shouted "out," Lainey held up a finger into the air to let Colt know she wanted her point.

"Me too," Braden yelled to the dugout. "I made the play too."

By contrast, Smalley shouted something at his kid about how his grandmother could run faster than him.

"And she's dead!" he added.

The Bees escaped the first inning down only 6-0. But the next three batters for the Bees all struck out in much the same manner as the first three.

Tonio fared a little better in the second inning, only giving up three runs. But rather than fret about the score, the Bees focused on making defensive plays so they could earn their points.

"You know we've got the ten and two rule in effect," Coach Smalley shouted to Colt between the innings.

"I know," Colt replied. "If we're losing by ten after four innings or two hours goes by, the game's over."

"We'll try to stretch it to the full two hours," Smalley winked.

"Just swing away," Colt replied. "We'll get the outs."

The Bees had completed three innings at bat without registering a hit. The top of the order came up to bat in the fourth inning down 9-0. Smalley replaced Mikey Wiltshire on the mound with his son Damien, who threw even harder than Mikey.

"Watch out for his curveball," Braden announced to the team as Damien warmed up.

"Don't think of them as curveballs," Colt told them. "Think of them as juiceballs."

Lilly and Lainey giggled at the suggested image of hitting apples and oranges out of the air.

"Hey," Colt said, pulling a twelve-pack of eight-ounce plastic apple juice bottles from his cooler bag. "Free juice for anyone who makes apple juice out of Damien's pitching."

Damien whizzed a fastball by Lilly's nose, which scared her into jumping out of the batter's box and falling to her back in the dirt. The Bees shouted encouragement to her from their dugout. So rattled by the first pitch, the next one scared her out of the box again, even before it left Damien's hand.

Colt called time out and greeted her next to the plate.

"You can do it, Lilly," Laura called to her daughter.

"Picture the ball as an apple," Colt told her. "Remember how much fun it was to smash the apples in practice?"

Lilly nodded.

"Just go smash that apple," Colt completed his pep talk.

Damien's next pitch came in a little slower. Lilly torqued her hips and caught the ball on the end of the bat. It bounced and rolled thirty feet down the third base line as she propelled her wispy frame toward first base. After sprinting to field the ball, Damien's throw smacked the first baseman's glove late. The umpire shouted "safe."

As the Bee's erupted in cheers, Smalley's voice bellowed across the field.

"Jesus, Damien," he shouted. "Seriously? You knock her on her ass with your fastball, and then think you're going to trick her with a slower pitch? You know she can't catch up to the heat. What the hell's the matter with you?"

Kicking the dirt, Damien smacked the ball into his glove and gave Braden a wicked stare as he stepped into the box. Colt called time and walked out to give Braden some instruction.

"Are you afraid of this kid's fastball?" he asked.

"No," Braden replied.

"Good, cause it's coming right down the middle on the first pitch," Colt continued. "It'll be your best chance to hit him. He gets that first fastball by you, then you're stuck guessing on the next one. You understand what I'm saying?"

"So, swing at the first pitch?" Braden asked.

"That's right," Colt answered. "Swing early and hard."

As the fastball left Damien's hand, Braden started his swing immediately and hit the ball square in the meat of his bat.

Smalley yelled for his third baseman to make the double play. But Braden's one hop line drive was not an easy play for either the third baseman or the shortstop. Instead of fielding the ball cleanly, it careened off the third baseman's shin and kicked into the outfield past the shortstop.

Smalley slammed his clipboard onto the dugout cement as Lilly advanced to second base and Braden safely reached first.

"That's a hit," he called to Colt. "That's not an error. That's a hit. I'm batting five hundred today."

Emboldened, Ronnie hit a deep fly ball to right field, but the outfielder made a running catch. Tonio and the next batter each struck out and the Bees failed to score. Despite the nine-run deficit, the team and parents all cheered as if they had taken the lead.

"That's an hour forty-five," Kildeer called across the diamond to Colt. "Bottom of the fourth will probably be the end of the game."

"This game does not end by the two-hour rule," Smalley announced to his own team, but loud enough for all to hear. "We walk off with a ten-run mercy score. You hear me. This game ends on a walk-off."

As Tonio grabbed his glove to return to the mound, Colt stepped in front of him.

"I think that's enough pitches for one day," he said.

Colt noticed Ellie in the bleachers beyond the fence. She strained to peer into the dugout with a stern, worried expression.

"Braden, warm up to pitch the last inning," Colt continued.

Colt glanced Ellie's way, as if feeling the weight of her stare. As furtively as he caught her eye, he looked away. He cast two hands atop Braden's shoulders at the steps of the dugout.

"You've got the last inning, like I promised," he said.

"Maybe if I had started…"

"None of that matters," Colt interrupted him. "In sports, and in life, what happened before means nothing compared to what's about to happen."

Braden nodded in understanding.

"We can't win," Colt continued. "At the end of this inning, the time will be up."

"So, what's the point of…"

"The point is that you don't have to feel any pressure other than throwing strikes."

"I'm not going to let them get to ten," Braden said.

"I like the attitude," Colt said with a pat on his back. "Just remember throwing the ball at Mr. Yankee Doodle."

Braden smiled and trotted to the mound to take his warm-up pitches. As he did, Ellie stared at him, her tense expression reflecting the nerves that ran through Colt's spine.

"Come on, Kid," Colt muttered to himself. "Do what I know you can do."

22

THE CONFERENCE

In the wake of the showdown between the A-team and the Bees, Colt kept an eye out for teasing and taunting in the hallways of the school.

Damien Smalley bragged in the lunchroom about his team's 9-0 domination. He wasn't verbally offensive enough to garner disciplinary action. But the young lout was annoying enough to be hurtful to any Bees within earshot of his obnoxious, boisterous voice. From what Colt could tell, the boasting didn't bother Braden as much as he expected, despite the constant barrage of A-team players reiterating stories of their victory to anyone who would listen. At one point, he had to send one of the A-team players to the principal's office for dumping Lainey's books out of her hands and calling her an 'Error Machine'. He also reprimanded another A-team player for calling Stevie an "Automatic Strikeout."

He recalled Braden taking the mound in that last inning against the top of the A-team's line-up. He pictured Braden digging his cleats into the dirt and facing Mikey Wiltshire with the bold confidence of a bullfighter.

His first pitch, a decent inside fastball, sailed a bit too much past the edge of the plate and clipped Mikey in the elbow. Mikey laughed it off and gave Braden an encouraging thumbs up as he trotted to first base.

Braden regrouped and managed to pitch Damien Smalley to a full count. With a sideways glance at Mikey on first, he gripped the ball, wound up and fired it right by Damien on the low, outside corner. Damien argued the umpire's call. Coach Smalley screamed from the dugout. But the umpire stood his ground and awarded the out to the Bees.

The next batter, the big home run hitter from Ferndale that nobody seemed to know, stepped to the plate. He whacked a hard line-drive up the middle. But Lainey lunged to snare the ball on a short hop and flipped it to her sister at second base for the second out. Lilly swiveled her hips like a gazelle and whipped it to first base for a double play to end the inning.

"Ten points," Colt shouted as he and the rest of the team sprinted across the field. It looked as if the Bees had won the World Series the way they hugged each other and threw their gloves and hats in the air. The B-team parents cheered as the A-team hung their heads and walked back to their dugout with their disappointing 9-0 win.

At the lunch period, Colt flipped the lights to his classroom and pulled his door closed from the hallway. The birdlike voices of Braden and Mikey chirped around the corner at the water fountain as they discussed the game. He stood by his door, pretending to scroll through e-mails on his phone as he eavesdropped.

"Just ignore stupid Damien Smalley," Mikey said. "You guys played a great game last weekend."

"Thanks," Braden replied. "How come your team had to run so many sprints after the game?"

"Two sprints for every error, three for each time anyone struck out and four just because Damien threw a changeup instead of a fastball."

"We went to the diner for pancakes after the game," Braden said. "You should've come."

Colt leaned closer to the corner of the lockers to differentiate Mikey and Braden from the sound of other students emerging from their rooms.

"I wish I could have come with you guys," Mikey said. "I'd rather just play on your team instead."

Mikey's words, *"I'd rather just play on your team instead,"* repeated in Colt's mind throughout his lunch break. For the rest of the day, he wondered how he could help make Mikey's desire come true. Not only would he love to have the talented pitcher on the roster, he was a nice kid that Braden adored.

"Win-win," he told himself.

After the bell rang to end the day and his students bolted out of his class, he sat at his desk, in a smock splattered with rainbow-colored bits of paint, picturing Mikey Wiltshire on the mound in a blue Bees uniform. Streaks of pink and green acrylic paint decorated his nose and cheek as he tried to rub speckles of gold and silver glitter out of the palm of his hand.

"Hello," said Andrea Pawlecki as she knocked on the door. "Sorry to bother you."

"Come on in," Colt replied with a smile. He discarded his smock and wiped his face to remove the paint stains. "What can I do for you?"

Andrea, looking less carefree than usual, sat in one of the undersized chairs at a desk across from Colt.

"It's about Ronnie," she started. "Have you noticed any behavior problems in your class?"

"No," Colt replied. "He's a joy. Not the best painter in the world, uh... well, uh ... I mean, he's a great kid. Why?"

"I just had a conference with his teacher. She says he's acting out." She looked down in embarrassment. "You haven't seen that in your class?"

"No, nothing." Colt softened his voice out of respect for her unusual vulnerability. "He's a sweet kid. Gets along with everyone. I'm surprised to hear it."

"He's in class with Damien Smalley and a couple kids from that other baseball team. And they keep telling him they're this semi-professional A-team because they're the best and the B-team sucks. They're losers. Stuff like that. It really bothers him."

Colt took in the feedback and nodded his head in thought.

"I tried to explain it to the teacher," Andrea continued. "But she said she hadn't observed any offensive behavior between the kids. Have you seen any bullying around the hallways? Or am I just crazy?"

"They're eight years old," Colt replied.

"Most of them are ten now," Andrea corrected him.

"It happens. You can't stop it."

"It sucks," Andrea snapped. "He has enough trouble with his schoolwork. He's pretty down on himself about it. Then they tease him and laugh when he gets answers wrong. One asset he always had going for him was that he was big and strong. But now, when they make fun of his baseball playing, it takes away that confidence too."

"I'm sure it's just typical eight-year-old behavior," Colt tried to comfort her. "I'll keep an eye out for it and put a stop to it if I see it."

"Damien accused him of cheating off him on a test. He's not a cheater. He struggles with math. But it's not because he's not bright."

"Sharp as a tack," Colt agreed.

"He just doesn't like math. He doesn't see why it's even important in life. But he didn't cheat. I know that little punk is lying."

"What did the teacher say?"

"She believes me," Andrea replied, a tear forming in one of her eyes. "This time."

"The answer's not to stop them from saying what they're going to say—"

"It would be nice to beat them on the baseball field and shut them up," Andrea interjected with a subtle wipe of her eye.

"You can't count on that," Colt replied. "And it never solves the problem. A bully finds their cause no matter what."

"So, what do we do?"

"There's no easy answer." Colt's nerves encroached on his stomach as he realized he had no idea what to say next. "I'll think about how to help him with his schoolwork. The more he focuses on what he's happy about, the more he won't care about what he's not happy about. Maybe that'll help restore his confidence."

"Well, he loves playing on the Bees and practicing at Shaw Field."

"That's a start," Colt said.

"And Juiceball?" Andrea continued, her familiar smile returning to her face. "You have them hit apples and oranges instead of baseballs?"

"Well, it's just something fun that I made up." Colt blushed.

"He loves it," Andrea said, before shifting the glint in her eyes and changing the topic. "What do you think of Ellie?"

Colt felt a whoosh of mental whiplash at her new, unexpected line of discussion.

"Ellie?" he asked as if hearing the name for the first time. "I, uh, we get along really well. She's a great landlord."

"That all she is?"

"Yes, of course," Colt stammered. "Why, what did she say?"

"You know, she has a history with immature guys." Andrea's smile faded. "She's got a kid to take care of and it's a serious responsibility."

"Of course," Colt replied, crinkling his nose at the implied inference from Andrea's line of dialog. "Ellie's a great mom."

"Just don't be a frat boy with her," Andrea outright lectured him. "Braden adores you."

"I've been nothing but respectful."

"Keep it that way," Andrea snapped before softening her smile. "It's my job to protect her from getting hurt."

Colt nodded like a child taking direction from a parent. How had the dynamic of authority shifted so quickly from him guiding her to her giving him direction?

"It's fine if you want to go for it. I don't know how she feels."

"Go for it?" Colt muttered, his face shading red. What did Andrea's idea of 'going for it' even mean? *Go for what?* It's not like he hadn't thought about Ellie as more than a landlord or a parent of one of his players. But he also hadn't thought out loud about any feelings he might have harbored for her and definitely preferred to keep them to himself.

"Well, how about that," Andrea said with a knowing smile, not unlike the one in the diner when she read his mind and predicted his dinner order. "I've never seen you so tongue-tied before."

"I'm, uh fine," Colt stammered. "She's... uh... We're... uh. I don't know. Maybe?"

"That's all fine and good, but, if anything does happen, you better treat her right." Andrea stood to bring the conversation to an end. "She's had some real losers in her life. If you get with her and then turn out to be just another cheater, you won't only be letting her down, you'll be hurting her kid even worse."

Andrea's face hardened. The shadows from the overhead fluorescent lights shaded her eyes under her thick blond hair. "Plus, you'll have me to answer to. And all these other kids that look up to you too."

Colt sat, rattled at his desk. He tried to speak. Andrea's posture relaxed as she patted him on the shoulder and turned to leave the room.

"And. If you wouldn't mind watching out for Ronnie?" Andrea added, over her shoulder as she walked toward the door. "I'm always reminding him how important it is to behave with other people's best interests at heart. I know he didn't do what Damien accused him of, but I still reminded him that nobody likes a cheater."

23

THE EXHIBITION TEAM

For the games following the loss to the Springtown A's, the Bees gelled and played stellar ball. They lost to Elizabethtown by one run. They took a tie into the last inning against a solid team from Milford before dropping a heartbreaking walk-off loss.

Braden emerged as the team's ace pitcher with Tonio and Lilly both pitching well in relief. With three games left in the season, the Bee's faced two teams at the bottom of the rankings and beat them both. The streak included a tight 3-2 win over Frenchtown, in which Braden had to pitch out of a bases loaded jam in the second to last inning. They followed the thrilling victory over the Frenchtown Terriers with a 4-1 win over New Hope, in which Ronnie broke a fifth inning tie with a double off the wall to score Lainey and Lilly. Against Doylestown, a team with a 5-3 record, Braden pitched a complete game one-hit shutout to notch the 1-0 win against the fifth-place team in the league.

Colt didn't tell Braden that the Doylestown Marauders had beaten the Springtown A's until after the game concluded.

"We're on a win streak going into the playoffs," Braden

beamed. "Mikey Wiltshire told me if you win the regional championship, you get to play at the states under the lights at Hershey Park. How cool would that be?"

The parents threw an ice cream party to celebrate the end of the regular season. They brought tubs of vanilla, chocolate, and strawberry ice cream from the Springman Dairy Farm and set up a table with bowls, spoons, chocolate sauce, whipped cream and sprinkles.

Each kid piled their bowl much higher than their stomachs could handle. The trash can soon filled with gooey bowls of half-eaten ice cream mud, which overflowed and attracted a swarm of flies and bees.

Colt watched Andrea maneuver Ronnie behind the bleachers to wipe the chocolate sauce off his face. Giving them privacy, he stood nearby and pretended to run into them by accident as they rounded the corner.

"Great game, Ronnie," Colt complimented him with a sly glance at Andrea. "You got two hits today, right?"

"Yup," he answered. "A single and a double."

"So, you had a three hundred batting average today?"

"Uh, Coach," he said, "That's five hundred."

"Oh, right," Colt said. "Four divided by two. If they didn't throw you out in your last at bat, you would have batted six hundred."

"No, Coach," Ronnie replied. "Three for four is a .750 batting average."

Colt glanced across the parking lot as if letting Ronnie in on a secret.

"I'm also trying to figure out Braden's ERA," he whispered, dramatically. "You know what that is?"

"Earned Run Average," Ronnie replied. "It's the number of runs a pitcher gives up in a game."

"Do you know how to figure it out?"

Ronnie looked at his mother as if she would give him the

answer and then back to Colt.

"I think you add up all the runs in the game and that's how you do it?"

Andrea smiled at Colt and shook her head as if to tell him his transparent ruse wouldn't work. But he stuck to it.

"If a pitcher pitches a full game, then, that's right," Colt explained. "But, if the pitcher only pitches a half of a game, then you have to use division to figure out their average runs for a single inning and then you use multiplication to figure out how many runs they would have given up if they pitched the whole game."

Ronnie stood, temporarily fixed. He looked at his mother again, but this time, not in seek of the answer, but rather to give his eyes a focal point in the air as his mind calculated.

"So, against Frenchtown," Ronnie said. "Braden gave up two runs in four innings. That's like one run in two innings. So, his ERA is a half?"

Colt didn't respond.

"Oh, then I have to multiply it times nine to get his ERA for the full game."

Colt nodded with enthusiasm and encouragement.

"What's nine times a half?" Ronnie asked. "Oh, half of nine is like four point five. So, he had a four-point-five ERA?"

"Yes, although, they call that four-fifty."

Andrea looked like she was waiting for Ronnie to grow bored of the conversation. But Colt changed his tactic just in time.

"I didn't know you could figure all that out on your own. I have a big important job..." Colt stopped and looked away as if he'd changed his mind. "I bet you're too busy."

"I'm not too busy," Ronnie blurted, his eyes widening at the prospect to take on a special function.

Andrea's expression changed from dubious to impressed.

"You see," Colt said. "I'm an Art teacher, so I'm not so good with numbers."

"Me neither," Ronnie agreed. "Math's my worst subject."

"But you're clearly a lot smarter than I am when it comes to figuring out batting averages."

"Yup," Ronnie agreed, causing Andrea to stifle a chuckle.

"Any chance I could give you and Braden all the stats for the season written down on a big piece of paper and have you add them up, figure out each players' batting average, and write down the ERAs for all the pitchers?"

Ronnie looked up at his focal point as his inner computer churned through the ramifications of the request. Andrea arched her eyebrows at Colt as Ronnie nodded his head in acceptance of his task. He turned to his mother and asked her a question that she didn't expect.

"Can I have a playdate with Braden today," he asked. "We gotta get started figuring out all the stats."

Andrea locked eyes with Colt.

"Of course, Honey," she said to her son.

"Cool," said Ronnie with an excited pump of his fist. "I gotta go tell Braden."

As the boy ran off, Andrea gave Colt a pat on the back of the shoulder. "Nice job, Coach," she said with a beaming smile. "I'm impressed."

Following the last game of the season, Colt attended the coaches meeting to determine the playoff format and seedings. Braden visited the Wiltshire's for the evening so Ellie could accompany him. With their 3-7 record, Colt didn't expect a high seed.

"I just hope they don't have to play the Springtown A's, again," Ellie said what weighed heavy on Colt's thoughts.

After sharing a small pepperoni pizza in the quaint center of town, Colt pulled into the parking spot at the Levittown Community Center. Ellie hopped from the passenger side of his truck with her notepad tucked under her arm. They saw Garrett Kildeer across the way and waved to him. He approached them with a quizzical look on his face.

"What are you guys doing here?" he asked.

"It's the coaches meeting tonight," Colt replied.

"I know, but it's only for playoff teams."

"Everyone makes the playoffs," Ellie said with the annoyed edge to her voice that she usually reserved for Smalley.

"I know, but you're not eligible," Kildeer retorted

"Why not?" Ellie asked. "We beat Doylestown. We have a chance to actually win a game or two."

"It's not that," Kildeer replied. "You're a second team; a B-team. We petitioned the league to get you the games you played."

"That shouldn't matter," Colt replied. "Doylestown beat you guys and we beat them. I think we're as much an A-team as you or any other team."

"You don't understand," Kildeer continued. "Each town is only allowed to have one team in the playoffs. You're officially listed as an exhibition team. None of your games counted. And you're not eligible for the playoffs."

THEY RODE in silence from Levittown to Springtown. Ellie piloted the car with her head fixed forward and her foot pushing the gas to speed the car down the windy, rural streets. At one point, as the car screeched around a sharp bend, Colt had to clutch the handle on the door to steady himself. For much of the ride, the soaring hum of the engine presented the only sound that reverberated through the cabin of the compact car. The sharp voice from Colt's phone barked directions as they approached each turn and cut the thick air between them.

"Sucks about the playoffs, huh?" Colt tried to engage her, receiving only a "yup" in response.

"They never said anything about us being an exhibition team," he continued.

"Nope." Ellie turned up the radio and shook her head in agreement.

Colt tried again to spark the conversation and crack past Ellie's hard exterior. "I had no clue about this, but there's nothing we can do about it now."

"Right," Ellie uttered.

"You believe me?" Colt elevated his tone, frustrated at the monosyllabic interaction. "Right?"

"Sure." She slowed the car to rumble over the train tracks by the diner.

Colt placed his hands on the dashboard to stop from lurching forward. "I'm just as pissed about it as you are."

Ellie didn't respond. She passed the yellow blinking light onto Main Street and accelerated toward her farmhouse.

"Elles," he said, calling her by the nickname that Andrea, her childhood best friend used.

Colt paused for a split-second, surprised at the ease the pet name rolled off his tongue.

"I'm just as pissed as you are," he continued.

Ellie remained tight-lipped. The shadows from the spotlights filled in the reservoirs of her tightened cheeks. As she pulled into the gravel driveway, those shadows dissipated when she opened her mouth to speak.

"Whatever," she said as she squeaked the breaks to a stop.

Ellie exited the car in a rush and slammed the door behind her. Colt scrambled to get out of the tiny vehicle, first forgetting to unlatch his seatbelt and then having to unfold his legs out of the well beneath the glove compartment.

Ellie stalked off to her patio back door.

"You're mad at me?" Colt asked as she set foot on the cement.

"No, just the situation." The orange light above her patio softened her face with a warm glow, like the morning sunlight. "It's not your fault."

Colt stood in the dark next to the car. The crickets roared in the trees and bushes around them. Overhead, the stars coated the sky like a splatter of white paint on a black canvass.

"There was nothing I could do," Colt said.

Ellie closed her eyes and nodded her head. "I know." Her voice lost its edge. "You've been great."

Colt exhaled.

"But what's the point of you being on the board if you don't know what's going on and you can't help fight back against these jerk coaches who run everything and make all the decisions about who gets to play and who doesn't."

"I... I..." Colt struggled to formulate a response.

"Thanks for everything you did with the team," Ellie cut short the small talk. "It was a nice season and I appreciate it."

Colt nodded and stepped toward the front of the car.

Ellie stepped back toward her house.

"I have to go figure out how to break this to Braden," Ellie said as she skulked back through her screen door and spoke over her shoulder. "Good night, Colt."

The screen door slammed, leaving Colt alone in the driveway. Even the crickets silenced their constant scratching. The stars glowed bright white as Colt stared across Shaw Field. He scoured his mind for a solution to how he could fix the situation embroiling Ellie, Braden, and their plucky B-team. He resolved to research summer tournaments so he could enter the team into one of the regional showcase events that attracted All-Star programs from all over the state.

He recalled, from playing in many showcase tournaments as a youth, that most teams came with a roster made up of the best players from four and five towns. Some represented city areas where more than a hundred players would try out.

He read about a tournament at Clarion University that hosted teams from as far away as California, where the winning team from Pomona flew in a starting pitcher specifically to win the championship game.

Colt climbed the stairs to his apartment. At the top, he glanced at Ellie's kitchen window in time to watch it snuff out, like a candle losing its flame in the wind.

He sat on his couch and flipped his laptop onto his thighs. He browsed the internet and reviewed regional baseball tournaments throughout Pennsylvania, New Jersey, and New York. They appeared too advanced for the novice Springtown Bees.

He closed the browser window and tossed a rubber ball against the bathroom door in his apartment. The memory of his days as a ten-year-old and the many travel teams he played on during his youth spurred the Greater Philadelphia Elite Baseball League to cross his mind. He entered the URL for the league and reviewed their home page. He read up on the teams that made up the standings and reviewed the guidelines for entering a new team. One page provided guidelines for a private field to be sanctioned and covered through the league's insurance. He paused, reading and rereading the page to understand the criteria.

His phone buzzed. Phil's face appeared on his screen. He bookmarked the page and closed the laptop screen. Phil's text message invited him to an outdoor bonfire and keg party with a group of clients from his physical therapy practice. Colt turned the phone upside down on his coffee table and tossed his rubber ball against the refrigerator, lost in thought.

ELLIE HAD the weekend trip circled on her calendar. She'd told Braden about it on the patio a few mornings after the devastating coaches meeting where they learned they wouldn't be able to play in the spring league playoffs. She and Andrea had planned the long weekend around the baseball schedule. They decided to take their kids to an indoor water park with an attached hotel. Colt looked it up on his laptop. The facility looked like a wilderness lodge with a log cabin exterior, dark wooden interior, and large fireplaces in the giant lobby. The kid in him wished he could go too.

If only they had a place like this fifteen or twenty years ago.

He watched them pack the car and disappear around the bayberry bush.

As Colt had planned, Joe Dalton and his crew arrived less than an hour after Ellie backed out of her driveway and sped off for the three-day weekend. Three trucks crowded into the driveway. Five installers emerged from the vehicles and unloaded shiny silver poles and large rolls of fencing just behind home plate of Shaw Field.

"You ready to work?" Joe asked Colt as he descended the stairs in work boots and gloves.

"Sure am," he replied. "Positive we can get this done in three days?"

"You'll be giving Stevie private hitting lessons for the next year," Joe chuckled with his arm around Colt. "You better be right that she won't mind."

"She's going to love it," he answered.

Even as he projected his usual confident swagger, his mind wavered.

I hope.

The construction team spent most of Saturday measuring and planning. They dug the holes for the infield fence and poured cement to secure the tall backstop poles into place. On Sunday, one crew erected the backstop fencing and infield support poles while a second crew measured and dug the holes for the outfield fence. Colt watched as Joe's expert installers dug up Ellie's property and poured concrete into the holes they formed in her yard.

His stomach sunk at the realization that she might freak out at his overstep.

Who am I to decide what to do with her back yard?

A pit grew in his stomach.

What the hell am I doing?

Despite his misgivings, he pushed forward and directed Joe's crew as to how he wanted them to configure the fencing.

By the time, they hoisted the twenty-foot-tall backstop and wired the fencing to it, he panicked at what he thought was a rash and stupid idea. But, by then, it was too late to turn back. Joe had invested the time, donated the materials, and completed most of the work over the course of the long weekend.

As the sun faded below the tree line, an eerie reddish-purple hue illuminated the yard and refracted off the shiny poles that dominated Shaw Field. Joe's crew cleaned up the work area and pulled out of the driveway about an hour before Ellie's Ford rounded the bayberry bush and kicked up a cloud of dust to signal her arrival.

Colt sat at the top step to his apartment out of sight. Heavy clouds had moved across the sky and shielded the moon from alighting the back yard.

Braden rubbed his eyes as he lumbered from the back seat of the car to the back door of the house. Ellie helped him along.

"I'll tuck you into bed and then empty the car after you fall asleep," Ellie said, her soft words drifting up the apartment stairs.

Colt's nerves swirled. The cloud cover that obscured the moonlight set him at ease.

Maybe she won't notice until tomorrow. His nerves continued to flutter. *What was I thinking?*

He sat atop his staircase for twenty more minutes and waited for Ellie's reaction when she returned to the car. He looked out at Shaw Field, realizing he could barely make out the aluminum poles and fencing that covered most of her property.

The back door slammed. Ellie ambled to the car. She opened the trunk and pulled out two suitcases.

Colt broke out in a sweat as the clouds moved away from the moon and the pale glow glinted off the twenty-foot-tall silver backstop.

Colt watched Ellie stop and notice. She stood in silence for a long pause before walking toward the backstop. She ran her hand along the pole and walked the first base line to the visitor dugout and bullpen area. She had her back to him; her chestnut hair and athletic shoulders rotated. Like an owl, she trained her gaze toward his second story apartment and stomped toward him.

Colt scrambled to his feet and hopped two stairs at a time to meet her by the base of the garage door. She quickened her pace and stared right through his eyes.

"Listen, I'm, uh, I can explain," he stammered. "There's this league..."

"I know," she said, not slowing her pace toward him. "The GPEBL, the one in Philly."

"You just..." Colt continued to babble as she approached. "They have this requirement."

"And, so you decided to fence the entire field?"

"The outfield fence is removable," he stammered.

"I see." Ellie invaded his personal space, her forehead nearly contacting his nose.

"I'm so sorry." Colt said, facing her for a moment, before stepping back and continuing to try and explain himself. "I never should have... I'm really... You're not gonna hit me, are you?"

Ellie giggled and surprised him by hugging him. Her lean arms wrapped around the small of his back and her chest smooshed in a perfect fit against his.

"It's amazing." She pulled back and looked into his eyes. "You did all that for Braden?"

"Well, yeah." Colt's nerves subsided with Ellie's hug. "And for you."

24

THE JOB OFFER

Colt sat on his couch. He could still feel the brush of Ellie's hair against the side of his cheek, and the blaze of her eyes peering into his. The hug lasted a second longer than short, and yet a few seconds shorter than long. Though he'd silently watched her return to her house, he wanted to invite her up to his apartment to continue their conversation.

It was just a hug, Dude. Can't get involved with her. It's too complicated—she's in a vulnerable spot. And I'm too much of a bonehead for her. Plus, I'm her kid's teacher and coach. And I love that kid too much to ruin what we've already got. God knows, I'd screw it up. There's a million reasons to avoid it."

He tossed his t-shirt into a pile and brushed his teeth.

The floors creaked and the windows whistled from a strong wind. The noises of his apartment overshadowed the sound of cars passing by Main Street. He tossed his shorts aside and flopped on the couch in his boxers. He grabbed his Xbox controller to play a game but cast it aside and decided to read up on the teams in the GPEBL instead.

Like the faint smacking of Braden's tennis ball against the side of the garage, a similar light knocking caught Colt's attention. He glanced through his shaded front door window and saw a silhouette. His stomach lurched at the thought of Ellie sneaking out of her house to visit him.

Maybe I didn't read too much into that hug. I knew I should have kissed her.

Colt scrambled to find a clean shirt. As he made his way to the door, he realized he was only wearing underwear and scanned the floor for his shorts, which had clung to the back of the couch.

The knocking continued, a little louder. He darted into his bedroom and grabbed a pair of sweatpants from a shelf. After yanking them up to his waist, he pawed at the waistband for the drawstring only to realize they were on backwards.

The figure in the door loomed in the moonlight. Looking more closely, he made out a pair of broad shoulders and a larger-than-life-sized head. His guest shifted from one foot to the other, creaking the wood platform.

After righting his pants, Colt flung open the door. His smile drooped at the sight of the stern-faced visitor that blocked the moon with his square jaw and full beard.

"Dad?"

Butch Gibson stood at six-foot-three, two inches taller than his youngest son and a good fifty pounds heavier. He looked more like a linebacker than a baseball coach. He wore his Lehigh windbreaker over a brown and gold shirt with the words "Coach Gibson" embroidered over the chest.

The man didn't smile or embrace his son. Colt considered slamming the door in his face. With a nod and a curious scan of his apartment, Butch edged forward. Colt stood still for a moment, sizing up his father, blocking him from entry with an edge of defiance.

He can speak first.

"Well, can I come in?" Butch finally asked.

"What do you want, Pop?"

"I want to come in," he replied. "I have something to tell you."

"How'd you even find this place?"

"I work at the school, remember?"

"Fine." Colt conceded and flicked on the light to his apartment. "Come in. Say what you need to say."

Butch entered the room then took off his windbreaker and hung it on a hook next to the door. He glanced from the open kitchen to the office space to the couch facing the large television and Xbox console. "Not bad. Kinda rustic. Very PA."

"What do you want?" Colt asked, moving toward his kitchen. "Need a beer or anything?"

"I didn't come for a long visit. I just came to tell you I got you a job."

Colt took a beer out of the refrigerator and popped the cap for himself. "I already have a job," he said between swigs from his glass bottle.

"As a gym teacher?" Butch sneered. "Playing kickball with a bunch of six and seven-year-olds?"

"They're eight," Colt fired back.

Butch's beard twitched for a millisecond like a facial tick at his amusement in Colt's curt response. He took a seat on the couch. Colt straddled his coffee table and placed his beer on the floor by his foot.

"This is what you want to do?" Butch asked.

"For now."

Butch paused and regarded his son with that far-off look he'd often give him on the playing field after a bad loss or a game where he made too many mistakes. His shoulders slumped, and he exhaled perceptibly.

"Look, I hate the way it went down..." he said, his voice softening in contrast to his hard, weathered exterior.

"You survived just fine." Colt looked away to shield his angry eyes.

"I want to help you out of your jam."

"I'm not in a jam," Colt shot back, his face expressionless. "Don't go worrying about me now. It's too late for that."

Butch frowned and leaned forward. "You're a ballplayer. And a damn fine coach. You should be on the field with another team."

"It's over Pop."

"I hope not."

"You know what I mean." Colt peered through his father. "It's behind us now."

"Is it really?"

"What do you want me to say? I'm here and you're there. You're still the great Coach Butch Gibson. I don't want a pity job you set up for me to make up for what happened."

Butch didn't respond. Silence filled the apartment as father and son stared at each other.

"Really, Pop." Colt mustered a smile. "I've moved on. It's alright. You can too."

Butch looked up with sad eyes. For the first time in a long time, Colt felt strong in the man's presence.

"Your mother misses you," Butch said.

"Are you back in the house with her?" Colt asked.

"Nah, I'm still in the apartment. We're trying to work it out."

Colt finished his beer and walked to the kitchen to throw it in the recycling bin. Butch stood, shifting his balance between his feet. He appeared less stable than twenty years earlier when he coached his Little League teams with the ferocity of a lion.

Colt stared out the kitchen window into the blackness of the night. He exhaled as much of the tension from his shoulders as he could and turned to face his father. "I like what I'm doing now. But what's this job you have for me?"

"It wouldn't impact your teaching gig," Butch said. "It's a summer assignment in Altoona, working at a camp. They need another hitting coach. It'd be a good way to showcase yourself, maybe hook in with a DIII school or an independent league club as a coach. I'll pull strings."

Colt gauged his father. Two decades of throwing with him, hitting his pitches, running sprints after each game, and hustling to impress Coach Butch flooded his mind. He recalled long conversations about how they'd work together at Lehigh for years until his retirement—so much for that. Butch grabbed his jacket from the hook. "You want the job or not?"

Colt recalled standing in his cap and gown after his Lehigh graduation ceremony with his father, a few years younger, a few pounds lighter, and fewer grey hairs, asking him the same question. *"You want the job or not?"*

"I gotta think about it," Colt muttered.

"They need an answer in a couple weeks."

"I'll get back to you."

Butch dropped his eyes. He slipped each arm back into his jacket and nodded goodbye.

"And don't forget," he said as he exited the apartment and creaked back down the stairs. "Call your mother."

25

THE DOMINO EFFECT

With the spring season concluded and school set to finish in a few weeks, Ellie conducted her research and officially applied to register the Springtown Valley zip code with the GPEBL. She kept Colt informed of the status of her actions to place the team in a league that would enable the Bees to play as a full-fledged team.

Tommy Porchetti, the head of the Philadelphia league, indicated Springtown was already registered with the GPYBL. After informing him that Springtown Valley had a different zip code than Springtown Hills, even though they shared a common town government and school district, he asked her to seek written approval from Garrett Kildeer to leave the existing program and join his league.

Tommy also asked for pictures of the private home field they'd be using and a tentative roster of players. She and Colt assembled their team for a special practice at Shaw Field and shared their plan discreetly with the parents. It was too late to enter the summer league, but starting in the fall, they'd play 11-U ball in the GPEBL.

News of their plans set off a barrage of reactions across the schoolyard and the network of parents. The first domino fell when Mara Wiltshire told Ellie that she and her husband decided they'd prefer the opportunity to join the Bees if they had a spot on the roster.

Braden's cheer boomed from across the driveway into Colt's apartment as Ellie informed him that his friend had switched teams.

Soon after, the retribution from Kildeer and Smalley happened fast. They scheduled an emergency board meeting and invited every parent from both teams. Right after calling the meeting to order, they made a dramatic point that they had achieved a three-member quorum.

"The bottom line is that the GPEBL is an inferior league and not in the best interest of our Springtown boys," Kildeer announced to the crowd. "The games are much farther away. You could find yourself driving three hours to play a four-inning blowout or get rained out once you get there."

He went on to call the GPEBL disorganized, dishonest, and corrupt in the way they favored teams from the immediate area around Philadelphia.

"Their pet Philly teams get the more convenient time slots, the nicer fields and the better umpires," he continued. "Their schedules match them against weaker teams, so they have better records and higher seeds going into the playoffs. I'm not even sure all their players are the right ages."

He raised additional concerns about hidden fees, travel costs, dangerous turf fields and an unrelated point about property taxes that nobody quite understood.

"The B-team is not ready for this level of competition," Smalley added. "You'll get your asses kicked every game. Every coach will exploit you to pad their records and run up their kids' stats. Nobody wants that. We're only looking out for your own good."

At that, Mara Wiltshire raised her hand. Smalley acted as if he didn't see it, but her husband stood. His imposing physique,

Sherriff's uniform, and wide-brimmed hat created an unmistakable marker for his wife's question.

"Thank you," she said to her husband with a pat on his forearm. "Uh, Mr. Kildeer and Mr. Smalley, you said this Philadelphia league is inferior, but then you seemed to imply that the Bees would not be able to compete."

"Yes, that's right," Smalley answered her.

"But why would we be able to compete any worse in a league that's inferior, according to you, than in the existing league."

"Look, Mrs. Wiltshire," Kildeer answered for his partner. "We got the B-team into the GPYBA as a favor from the league President. He didn't have to set up those exhibition games. We were all perfectly content having them play house league games and intra-squad scrimmages here in town. But they wanted to travel and give their boys some better competition. So, we hand-picked the opponents to make sure you didn't get beat too badly. The EBL won't do that. You'll be cut loose and totally on your own."

"We beat a team that beat you guys," Joe Dalton called out. "We're a lot better than you think."

"And it's not just boys," Laura Yu added.

"I hate to tell you," Smalley snarled. "We had an off game against Doylestown. We were missing a couple players, and they used their best pitcher. The weather didn't help either. The mound was a little soggy, which was a disadvantage for Damien with his long stride and high leg kick. Under better conditions, we'd have crushed them. I'm sure they were missing their best players against you guys. Good for you, you played the game of your lives and had a freak win. It happens. Even a blind squirrel finds a nut from time to time. It doesn't change the fact that you're the B-team in town and don't belong in an elite program like the GPEBL."

"I'll make it simple for you," Kildeer added. "You want your kid to make the Springtown High School team? You have to play for us. Bennie scouts our games. He drafts his freshman team from our roster. If you leave our organization, I can't be responsible for your kid getting cut on day one of the high school tryouts. Just think about that."

"We're going to increase the size of our roster to account for anyone who wants to stay with us," Smalley continued.

"Is everyone going to play?" Ellie asked.

"Everyone gets playing time on our squad," Smalley snapped back. "Commensurate to contribution and talent, of course, but we are, by far, the fairest team in the league. You think those regional All-Star elite showcase teams in the Philly league let their benchwarmers even sniff the field. We're the best program in the state and you're crazy to look at other options."

Then they voted 2-1 not to endorse the plan to register the Springtown Valley zip code with the new league.

ALONG THE RIDE to Andrea's house to pick up Braden, Ellie fumed at the deceptive fear-mongering and contradictory statements that Kildeer and Smalley made at the meeting.

"Oh, the Philly league sucks," she mimicked Kildeer. "They cheat. They kill people. They're murderers and thieves."

"He sure laid it on thick," Colt agreed.

"They're inferior, but you'll have a better chance to win in our league," Ellie continued to bluster, mocking Smalley's deep, scratchy voice. "Nobody gets off the bench on our team, but we're going to make our roster bigger, and everyone will magically get to play all of a sudden. They're so full of crap."

"I talked to my father," Colt interjected. "The Philly league is a bit of a mess. The great teams are like world-class superstar programs that draw from hundreds of kids trying out. Some of them have pro scouts watching them. They don't schedule the games for the coaches. It would be up to us to arrange our own games. And they charge three times what the existing league costs."

"So, we just stay the way we are?" Ellie snapped at Colt. "The second-class citizens of Springtown baseball?"

"I think we have to find a situation that works best for our kids."

"News flash." Ellie's frustration boiled over. "None of them are your kids."

Both she and Colt remained quiet for several minutes as they rounded the corner to Andrea's cul de sac. Ellie watched Colt's jaw clench as he stared at the road. Her comment cut too deeply into a man who'd dedicated so much of his time to helping her kid—and her.

"I'm sorry," Ellie said as they approached Andrea's ranch-style home at the end of the circle.

"It's alright. These guys piss me off too."

"I'm glad to have you as an ally. I couldn't get through all this without you."

With a brief squeeze of his hand, Ellie turned on the radio and flipped to the sports channel to listen to the Phillies game.

"I met your father in the driveway," she said.

"Did you?"

"Nice guy."

"Sure you weren't talking to the side of the barn, maybe that big azalea bush?"

"I gave him my business card. He might email me about hiring Joe's crew to fix the fence at his practice field."

"Great, I can work for my dad again." Colt sighed. "Doesn't matter because he won't email you."

"Well, you never know. Maybe he will." Ellie shrugged. "It'd be good business for Mr. Dalton."

"He doesn't even call me."

Ellie pulled into the driveway. Andrea waved from the door as Braden darted out. His backpack wiggled on his back as his glove nearly fell out the unzipped top.

"What did Kildeer mean when he said you had to play in his program if you want to make the high school team?" Colt asked. "I didn't understand that point."

"Bennie Richards, the coach at SHS," she replied, as Braden reached the car and tugged at the door handle. "It's his brother-in-law."

AFTER THE BOARD MEETING, the dominoes toppled. First, Robert Biegacki sent Ellie an email to inform her that his son Willie preferred to play on the A-team. Two outfielders also informed her of their intention to join Smalley's squad. With the loss of the three players, plus the addition of Mikey Wiltshire, their roster dropped from twelve players to ten; still enough to field a nine-player starting line-up, but with little wiggle room to account for injuries or missing players.

Colt remained upbeat and positive as Ellie received calls from various nervous parents seeking her advice on what to do. He assured her it would all work out in their favor, and they'd figure out how to field a full team. But in his mind, he felt like the co-captain of a sinking ship. His heart dropped when she received a call one morning from Dina Maletti, while they ate breakfast together on her patio.

"I'm so sorry," Dina said. "Tonio loves playing on the Bees. And he's heartbroken to have to switch teams."

"Then why switch?" Ellie asked.

"It's just that he has his heart set on playing for the high school team," Dina replied. "My husband, Danny, and his brothers all played on that team back in the day. Tonio's brother is a senior captain and his other brother is on the freshman team."

"This is what Tonio wants?"

"Well, uh, yah," Dina hesitated in giving her answer before replying with more confidence. "It's the only way to get what we want in terms of playing in high school. I'm so sorry. Good luck with the Bees next season."

26

THE ILLUMINATION

Ellie tossed her phone onto the kitchen table and yanked the refrigerator door open. In all the chaos around Braden's baseball league, she neglected to stock the groceries. They had nothing available for dinner. She took out a package of English muffins and toasted a few in the toaster oven.

The hum of the lawnmower filtered into the house as Colt mowed the field. When he finished, she watched him take off his shirt and pour a bottle of water over his head to cool off in the sun. Little rivers ran down his muscled pecs like baby waterfalls. She imagined his skin like one of those old-fashioned glass bottles of Coca-Cola, ice cold with droplets of condensation glistening in the sun. She paused to soak in the sight before shaking her head to cast away the image and focus on her task at hand.

After searching for a bag of shredded mozzarella cheese, she watched him rake the infield. The dust flew around him, shrouding him in a cloud of grey and gold mist. It stuck to his sweat like the golden rub on a prime cut of steak.

It occurred to her that either Colt had a great body, or she was really hungry for dinner.

Braden emerged from the garage holding a smaller rake and joined him in primping the field. She laughed as Braden also removed his shirt and poured water over his own head just like his coach had.

Colt dragged his L-screen in front of the mound and pitched a round of batting practice to Braden. Ellie watched her son launch Colt's left-handed pitching from behind the cutout in the screen past his head into center field.

She reached into her tiny pantry closet wedged under her wooden staircase and found a jar of tomato sauce. She selected oregano and basil from her spice rack. On the top shelf of the pantry, she found a red and white checkered tablecloth and set the table on the patio for three. She poured herself a glass of red wine and added a beer for Colt and a plastic cup of skim milk for Braden.

"Dinner time boys," she called to them.

Braden ran to her, boasting about how he and Colt made the field look as beautiful as a professional stadium. He added that they had a surprise for her. Colt sauntered toward the patio with his shirt tossed over his shoulder. The dust clung to the sweat on his chest, neck, and face.

"Looks like you're expecting company," he said, pointing at the beer.

"I am," she answered.

"Anyone special," Colt asked.

"Maybe," she replied.

"You know I'm not one to turn down a beer," he smiled. "Can I shower first?"

"Please do," she teased him.

"What's on the menu?"

"English muffin pizzas." She blushed at how lame the makeshift dinner sounded.

"Classy." Colt winked. "Give me five minutes to cleanup. We have a surprise for you."

HEADING FOR HOME

THE SUN DROPPED below the tree line. The orange glow of the evening sky faded to red, then purple. Colt descended the stairs with his hair wet and slicked. He wore fitted jeans and a yellow and black, plaid short-sleeved button-down shirt, untucked. Braden served him three pizzas from the main platter. He took three for himself and placed two on his mother's plate.

"She doesn't eat as much as us guys," Braden said as Ellie brought out a small salad. "She's watching her figure."

"Am not." She glared at him. "I never had to worry about that."

"Well, you, look damn—" Colt cleared his throat. "Uh, I mean darn good to me. Or rather that you look like you're still in playing shape."

Braden giggled at Colt's off-color word.

"What's this surprise you have for me?" Ellie asked as she picked through her salad.

Colt and Braden shot sideways glances at each other as they held back their giggling like school children.

"It's too early to show you," Braden replied. "Maybe after dessert."

"Dessert?" she asked. "You think there's dessert tonight?"

"There's always dessert at our house," Braden answered.

After his sixth English muffin pizza, Colt thanked Ellie for the tasty meal. She gazed at the baseball diamond with its trim grass, shiny new fence, crisp, dark clay, and sand basepaths.

"Braden, you've heard about how we're thinking of joining the Philadelphia Elite League?"

"Yup," he replied.

"Is that what you want?"

"Uh, I dunno," he said with a mouthful of pizza. "I guess so."

"You want to play travel baseball and make it to the playoffs, maybe play a game under the lights?"

"Sure," he answered. "I just wanna play. I'm happy I get to be on the same team as Mikey Wiltshire."

"Does it matter to you what league you play in?" Colt asked, gathering Ellie's swirling thought process.

"I don't know," Braden replied. "Not really. I like the league we're in because the games are close by, and we have a good chance of beating all the teams. With Mikey on our team, we're going to be so much better. We might even win if they let us in the playoffs. When Ronnie and I figure out the stats, ERA will be so easy 'cause it'll be zero."

Ellie cleared the plates and brought out a small peach cobbler she made with the last of the peaches. She served a blob of peachy goop topped with brown sugar, oat crumble, and a scoop of locally churned vanilla ice cream.

Both Braden and Colt scarfed their desserts in minutes, scraping the plate for every last morsel of sweet, peachy sugar.

"My God." Colt tapped his stomach while lounging in his chair. "I'm not teasing you this time. This cobbler rocks."

The moon cast its silver light on the patio. The stars above the roof of the house pricked through the sky. The crickets roared. Bats hovered and flittered overhead. Ellie asked Braden to bus the dessert plates and dress in his pajamas for bed.

"You think it's the wrong move?" Ellie asked Colt while Braden scurried up the stairs to his bedroom.

"It's a tough league," Colt leveled with her. "The more I learn about it, the more I think our mighty Bees are fine where they are."

"I was so caught up in fighting for what I thought he wanted, I never bothered to ask him."

"He says he just wants to play." Colt glanced at the kitchen door. "But what he really wants is the *opportunity* to play."

"What's the difference?" Ellie asked.

"Anyone can *play*," Colt said. "Get a ball and a dozen kids—you've got a game. He's special. He's got ability, heart, and desire. He wants the *opportunity* to play in a structured format against challenging competition with something at stake."

"He wants what the A-team has."

"But without the negative coaching style."

"What do we do?" Ellie asked as her son reappeared through the screen door.

"About what?" Braden asked, his baseball pajamas reflecting the white light of the moon.

"About this surprise you have for me," Ellie said, poking her son in the stomach and chest. "That's what."

Colt asked Ellie to stand. He placed his large, callused hands over her eyes. The warmth from his chest pressed against her back. His breath rustled a few errant strands of her hair next to her ear.

Braden counted back from ten. Ellie's hair twisted in the breeze and brushed against Colt's forearms. Her eyelids beneath his fingers fluttered against the skin of his palms.

At 'zero', Colt let his hands slip from Ellie's face. Braden plugged an extension cord into the outlet next to the screen door, and a barrage of yellow light brightened the baseball field.

"It's just for decoration," Colt said as Ellie focused on the long string of Christmas lights that edged the outline of the backstop and ran all along the infield fence and around the arc of the outfield.

The green grass danced in the confluence of light and shadow. The back of the house reflected the dim illumination. Each bulb twinkled in Ellie's dark, brown eyes. She stood speechless as Braden ran to home plate and proceeded to trot around the bases as if he had just hit a home run during a night game.

"You did all this?" she asked Colt.

"Well, me and Braden."

She watched her boy cross the plate with his arms extended into the night air and basking in a bath of golden lights around the batter's box. Her eyes turned from her boy on the field to Colt at the edge of the patio. Her smile brightened her face like the twinkle of Christmas lights around her.

"I love it."

27

THE REVELATION

The moon rose in the sky. The illuminated baseball diamond behind Ellie's house burned against the silhouette of the woods.

"Stay here," Ellie said to Colt before leading Braden into the house with a handful of dirty dishes. "I'll be right back."

Colt sat on the patio drinking his second beer. The clank of plates in the sink and muffled talking in the kitchen drifted through the screen door.

"Do I have to?" Braden whined.

"Yes," Ellie replied. "It's late and past your bedtime."

Through the screen door, he could see them cross Ellie's bright kitchen and climb the creaky wooden stairs together. While Ellie managed Braden's bedtime routine, Colt leaned back in his seat and downed a deep gulp of his beer. The alcohol relaxed his nerves, which raced at the thought of Ellie's imminent return to sit with him on the patio under the moonlight.

We're just hanging out. Two adults shooting the breeze. That's all.

After a few minutes, Ellie emerged from the house. She'd

changed from her skirt and flowered blouse into a thick, grey hooded sweatshirt over a tight, black pair of yoga pants, that hugged her curves. The cool evening breeze blew the screen door closed behind her. Colt pointed at the word 'LAFAYETTE' in bold maroon letters across her chest. She glared back at him in defiance as if to say, *"Take it or leave it, Dude."* The lights from the field brightened her hair and softened her eyes from dark mocha to warm hot chocolate.

They didn't speak at first, instead staring at each other while Ellie tugged at the bottom of her sweatshirt. Colt took the last sip of his beer and sat upright in his chair, biding time to think of a natural opening line that wouldn't sound like idle small talk.

As he pondered where to start the conversation, Ellie took a step into the darkness of the shadows. For a moment, he lost track of her eyes. As she approached the empty chair next to Colt, she brushed past it and made her way to the field.

Colt watched her walk beyond the edge of the patio toward the lighted fence.

"It took us all day." He stood from his seat and followed her into the yard. "We did it while you were working on your computer."

"I was finishing up processing Dalton's invoices. I saw the work order for the install."

"He said he wouldn't charge."

"He didn't," she replied as she ran her hand along the fence by the first base line. "He coded it as a training expense for his crew."

"It was three day's work for five guys," she continued. "That's more than a hundred bucks an hour. It had to set him back a couple thousand. How'd you get him to do it?"

"He wanted to," Colt replied, then gave her a sheepish grin. "Plus, I promised to give his kid private lessons from now until he gets to high school."

Ellie walked farther into right field. "I guess that's what

everyone's worried about now that they're almost ten and playing 11-U. In only a couple years they'll be in high school."

"There's nothing like playing for your high school team—" Colt's phone buzzed in his pocket; a text from Phil Jones about some party he assumed. Ellie heard it as well and looked away.

"I know," Ellie said, stooping to pick up a ball that Braden left in the grass. "I played for SHS, God, like fifteen years ago. Seems like yesterday."

Colt took out his phone and made a dramatic gesture to turn it off before shoving it back into his pocket. He stood shoulder to shoulder with Ellie, facing the field. "I miss playing in high school. Maybe even more than college."

"Not me."

"At least in high school, everyone came to the games and cheered for us," Colt finished his thought.

"Not us," Ellie said. "Nobody came to see us play in high school, even though we were division champs all four years. But, in college, everyone came to our softball games. The bleachers were packed."

"Nobody came to see us at Lehigh." Colt laughed. "We kinda sucked my senior year."

Ellie let out a sigh. Her shoulder brushed against his. She continued walking across the field and rotated to take in the full effect of the lights.

"You rarely throw with Braden," Colt changed the subject.

"I told you. It hurts my arm."

"You should get it looked at," he said, walking to catch up to her. "You need a trainer that can design a program for you. My dad has access to some of the best specialists in the country."

Ellie wandered across the infield, past the mound and stopped at home plate. Colt stood on the mound as if he'd pitch to her in the darkness. He imagined her in her Lafayette softball uniform with a ponytail pulled through the back of her cap.

"My arm's just too messed up," she said. "I don't think I'll ever throw like I used to."

Colt approached her and reached for her shoulder. "Where does it hurt?" He rolled up her sleeve and lightly pressed different spots on her elbow.

"I don't know," Ellie answered, her voice reduced to a whisper. "I don't think it matters."

Colt ran his hand under her sleeve and up her bicep. He massaged her triceps like the physical trainers used to do for him after long, hot double-headers. The warmth of her skin, under her thick sweatshirt radiated in his hand. A tingle in his neck ran down his back. He raised his eyes to meet hers. The hundreds of golden lights around them gave her face a magical glow. Her eyes twinkled like the stars in the distance above them. A jolt of nervous adrenaline washed over him. Did she feel the same electricity that he did?

Ellie's lips twitched, and she moved an errant strand of hair from the side of her nose. She swiveled her shoulders and tipped her head to one side. Her eyes locked with his. The nerves along his spine dissipated as instinct took over. He slowed the rhythm of his touch along her arm, shifting from a strong massage to a light caress.

As he did, Ellie leaned toward him. He slid his hand from her upper arm, along her forearm to her soft, warm hand. As if in slow motion, their fingers interlocked. He heard a light thud of Ellie dropping the baseball from her other hand.

She reached for his cheek, her soft touch lighting his face on fire. Colt wrapped his arm around the small of her back and moved in to kiss her. Soft and short, their lips meshed. Their fingers untangled. Colt wrapped both arms around her waist as she cupped his face in her hands. They moved in unison—natural, familiar—as if they'd been together for years. Their kiss moved from sweet to frantic. He pulled her tighter into his body. She slung her arms around his neck and squeezed.

They stood over home plate, melting into each other. The

gravity of the moment left him feeling both weightless and heavy at the same time. In that moment, she ceased to be a busy single mother with real-life problems and important responsibilities to him, but instead, a woman unlike any of the girls he'd experienced in college.

This is real.

After a minute she pushed away from him, breathless. Her eyes roved the back of her house and landed on the dark bedroom window above the television room.

A new emotion crept into his mind: fear. Had he pushed her too far? Was he mature enough for a woman with so much at stake? Had he ruined the one opportunity he might have with someone as amazing as her?

"I'm sorry." Colt pulled back. "I shouldn't have."

"No," Ellie replied.

"Right," Colt acknowledged. "I get it. No is no."

"No," Ellie repeated. "That's not what I..."

"I didn't mean to do something you didn't want to do," Colt continued, glancing with her towards Braden's bedroom window. "I get it. It's probably not... You probably don't want to..."

"No, it's totally fine." Heat flared in Ellie's eyes. "And I totally do want to."

"But, you can't?" Colt expected her to play the card of the single mom not able to get involved.

"No. I can."

"Oh?" Colt's mind spun, unable to read Ellie's intentions.

She stood in front of him. The amber glow of the twinkling lights gave her an angelic aura. His lips craved to reconnect with the soft warmth of hers. His muscles desired the feel of her lithe but firm body against his.

"So, it's okay?" he asked.

"Yes, it's more than okay."

Colt smiled and leaned back toward her. But she put up a

hand, again enforcing the distance between them. His eyes flinched in confusion.

"Where do you..." Ellie whispered, her words deliberate, albeit tentative. "Uh... where can we... uh, you know, other than here?"

Nerves jolted Colt from his knees through his stomach and up his spine. He scanned the back of Ellie's house before gesturing his head toward the stairway to his apartment.

Ellie nodded in enthusiastic agreement. He clasped her hand, and they hurried up the stairs to the door. Colt opened it and held it for her as she passed under his arm into his cozy apartment. He closed the door and pressed her against the shaded window. Again, her hands found his neck, drawing his lips to hers, in fervent passionate kisses. The taste of her, the crush of her soft curves against his hips, every bit of him wanted to feel every inch of her. He tugged at her sweatshirt. She obliged by raising her arms and letting him pull it over her head, revealing a soft, pink cotton t-shirt with the word "LOVE" printed across her chest.

As he dropped her sweatshirt to the ground and moved in to kiss her neck, her cell phone flipped out of her pocket to the floor. It clattered across the knotted clapboard and started ringing. The shrill tone scared the nerves back down his spine in retreat. She recoiled at the sound and jerked away from Colt's embrace.

"Jesus, what am I doing?" she yelped. "Oh my God. Is it Braden calling?"

"It's ok," Colt said and handed her the phone.

She looked at the screen. Her expression twisted in confusion.

"Hello," she said, flustered. She gazed past Colt to the back of the apartment, a worried look on her face.

Neither Colt, nor Ellie expected the next words that escaped her mouth. "Mr. Kildeer?"

They exchanged perplexed glances.

"Uh, well, it's a little late, but it's fine," she said before pausing to listen. "Another emergency board meeting? We just had one last week."

Ellie placed her hand over the phone and opened the apartment door.

"No," she said with a furtive glance at Colt and a finger across her mouth, calling for him to remain silent while she took the inopportune call. "He's not. I don't... uh... I haven't seen him."

Ellie walked down the staircase with her sweatshirt under her arm. "And what did you find out?" She took a seat at the patio table.

Colt followed behind her, trying to catch her attention with his eyes.

"I see." She looked intently off into the woods. "Are you positive?"

Colt sat across the table from her. The blood that had coursed through his face settled back into the rest of his body. The subtle fruity flavor of her lip gloss and the taste of minty toothpaste on her tongue lingered on his lips.

Ellie turned away from Colt, her back to the lighted field. A shadow crossed her cheeks and hid her expression. "Ok. Thanks for the heads up. I appreciate you letting me know."

Colt leaned back in his chair with his arms behind his neck. "What did the weasel want this time?"

Ellie didn't answer, her features still hidden and her gaze in the distance. As she turned to face him, the light from the field brightened her cheek as if by firelight. Her cool brown eyes darkened, likening to black coffee.

"Did you get fired from your coaching job at Lehigh?" she asked him. "For cheating?"

28

THE TWIN BED

The school year ended the day after Ellie chewed Colt out for lying to her, Braden, and all the players and parents of their baseball team. Colt opted to pay Ellie the rent even though he hadn't inhabited the apartment in two weeks. Ellie had no idea if or when he'd return and he gave her no indication. A big part of her didn't care. By the morning, he'd left his electronics behind, packed a duffel bag of clothes, and cleared out early the next morning.

Ellie watched his truck kick up the dirt and pebbles of her driveway. He accelerated past the bayberry bush onto the main road. He revved the engine and disappeared into the distance.

Later that night, at the emergency meeting, Ellie informed the board that Colt had left and that the Bees no longer sought to cede from the GPYBL. Kildeer and Smalley agreed to reassemble the two teams and proceed with the next season in the same format as the last with the A-team representing both sections of town and the Bees registered as an exhibition team.

Neither Kildeer, nor Smalley revealed to any of the parents the reason behind Colt's departure, saying only that he received an opportunity to coach professionally at a showcase summer camp and they weren't sure if he'd be coming back. They also informed the parents that Tommy Tremblay had decided not to continue playing baseball and that coach Andy Tremblay would not be back the next season either.

When nobody offered to step in and coach the Bees, Ellie raised her hand and agreed to fill the role. Andrea laughed out loud at her. Ellie's shoulder ached thinking about running a practice, and her head spun at the prospect of taking on a fourth "job". But her inner mom justified her overextension as part of the burden of a single parent doing whatever she had to in order to support the love of her life. Every time she worried about her damaged throwing arm, Braden's smiling face kept her grounded and motivated.

Soon after the board meeting, Ellie invited all the parents to her house for a team meeting to discuss how they would proceed. Andrea brought a tray of cookies and offered to help with any of the administrative tasks. She also agreed to supply the fruit so that the tradition of juiceball could continue. Other parents agreed to serve as base coaches and fill-ins when Ellie's work demands precluded her from attending a weekend game.

A sleek black Mercedes pulled into her driveway and parked next to the bayberry bush. To her surprise, Darius and Mara Wiltshire emerged together.

"I thought you guys were separated." Ellie nudged Mara after Darius walked out to the field to check out the fencing.

"It was so stressful on us to be associated with that A-team and those coaches." Mara shook her head in disgust. "Those other parents are animals, telling the coaches they shouldn't let Mikey pitch, sniping about who should play which positions, what the batting order should be. The whole experience took its toll on us."

"You're back together?"

"Darius was so convinced that Mikey had to be the star of the A-team," Mara continued. "I vehemently disagreed. He wasn't there on the sidelines, listening to those parents grumbling and complaining about everyone else's kids. They're ten-years-old. They make mistakes."

"So, what changed?"

"Darius works evenings, weekends and holidays, right when all the games take place," Mara said. "I finally convinced him to just call in sick and come to see for himself."

"I didn't realize it was that bad." Ellie squeezed her friend's shoulder in support.

"Mikey kept saying for weeks that he wanted to play on your team—the Bees," Mara said, checking to make sure her husband remained out of earshot. "He wouldn't say it to Darius, because he was always on A-teams and All-Star programs as a kid. He thought I was overdramatic.

"Then there was an accident in the parking lot at our game against New Hope. Darius responded to the call. After he finished, he was able to watch a little bit of the game. I think we lost that one and the coaches were really on the kids; yelling, swearing. He got so pissed off at the attitudes of the parents and especially at Jay Smalley, he wanted to punch him in the mouth."

"Glad he didn't," Ellie said. "It's youth baseball. There should never be a reason to throw a punch."

"You're so right," Mara replied. "And Darius knew that. He'd never actually do that. He'd lose his job."

"We're just happy to have you with us." Ellie gave her a warm smile. "I promise you…"

"Thank you." Mara returned the smile. "Ever since we decided to switch teams, Mikey's been so happy, D and I are back on the same page, and he's been staying over on the weekends to see how we fit back together."

"How's that going?"

"Oh, I'd say pretty, uh…" A blush brightened Mara's cheeks. "Hot and heavy."

The memory of making out with Colt jammed against the back of the apartment door flashed through Ellie's thoughts. She could feel his lips pressed against hers and the sensation of her sweatshirt sliding up her arms and over her head.

She reached into her pocket and fingered the envelope that had arrived in the mail earlier that day; a letter from Colt, apologizing for the way she found out about his cheating scandal. Beyond his words of contrition, he stapled a one-page worksheet instructing her how to properly stretch and warm-up her arm and a business card for a physical trainer.

"He owes me and my dad," he wrote. *"You should call him."*

Mara leaned in and whispered to Ellie, "Were you and Colt? I mean, you seemed really close and so cute. Honestly, you'd make a great couple. Did you guys ever?"

"No," she answered flatly. "He's not my type."

COLT AWOKE to the sound of the nearby highway as the morning commute escalated and the buzz of trucks filled his open window. He rose from his twin bed and dressed in a pair of gym shorts and plain white t-shirt. The sun streamed into his window, reflecting off a shelf of trophies.

The smell of bacon wafted under the door to his wood-paneled bedroom, and he trod along the shag-carpeted hallway to the kitchen. He sat on a stool at the breakfast nook and watched a cardinal fly across the above ground pool in the back yard. The crimson bird perched atop the feeder outside the sliding glass doors and looked right into the house at him.

"How'd you sleep?" his mother, Doina, asked him.

"Fine. Two weeks and I'm finally getting used to the twin bed again."

"How was your trip to Altoona?" she asked.

"Dad's still pretty pissed I didn't take the job out there."

Colt's phone buzzed. He took a quick glance at it; an email had come from Garrett Kildeer.

"How does he look?"

"Huh?" he asked, distracted by his phone.

"Your father?" Doina raised her voice. "Is he eating right? Is he getting puffy again?"

"I don't know, Ma?" Colt replied while crunching on a mouthful of bacon. "He's fine. You know how he is. He's Butch."

Doina scoffed as she poured herself a cup of coffee.

"He's too proud for his own good," Colt added. "I know he should come to you, but you could drive out to Altoona and go see him for yourself."

"Maybe I will." She huffed, then mumbled, "Someone's cranky this morning."

Colt took a second glance at Kildeer's email. Given lower than expected registrations for the upcoming baseball season, Kildeer called another emergency board meeting only two weeks after the previous one to discuss plans for the next year.

"He never eats well when he stays at these camps," Doina continued as she scrubbed the grease from the frying pan into an empty tin coffee container. "Six, eight weeks, all he eats is cereal for breakfast, lunch, and dinner."

"He looks fine, Ma," Colt said, without looking up from his phone. "He misses you."

"Right."

"He does, Ma." Colt drank a gulp of orange juice. "He just wants to know what it's going to take to get past this."

"He said that?"

"Yes, he said that. And he said he'd do anything. He just doesn't know what you want."

Colt read the email further, noting the date and time of the upcoming meeting which was set for the next day. He scanned the agenda for the meeting. There was an item about voting on the constitution of the board. Then a second item that referred to disbanding the B-team program, consolidating the travel-quality players into the A-team, and setting up the remaining players as reserve "Practice-Only" participants.

"Mom, listen to me," Colt continued. "You and Dad were the best parents a guy could have. I know he was a hard ass and didn't always pay enough attention to you, especially during the season."

"And recruiting seasons and summer camps," Doina added as she wiped her hands on a dishtowel.

"Ok, his job put a strain on the marriage. I get that, but you guys were magical together when you worked as a team. You clicked on the same wavelength, like perfect partners. You focused on building a family together and making us happy. When you find that kind of love in life, you have to do whatever it takes to hang on to it and make it work."

Doina put away her dishrag and stood still in the middle of the kitchen floor staring at her son. The glisten of emotion gleamed in her blue eyes.

"I know you want him to think of it on his own." Colt read the last line of the email from Kildeer, which read; '*see you tomorrow night*'. "Tell him what you need from him. If you want him to stop going away every summer to camp, tell him. If you want him to cut back on his recruiting trips, tell him."

"It's useless." Doina shrugged, a red curl slipping from her pinned bun. "We're in our sixties. I need a full-time husband."

"It's not useless," Colt replied. "If it's worth saving, then do what you have to in order to save it, even if you have to give him the answer. He can get inside the head of a pitcher or help a batter out of a slump. But when it comes to people in real life, he's a little clueless. You always bunted him along in the right direction. Maybe, it's time for you to swing away."

"Swing away?"

"Swing for the fence," Colt explained, as images of Ellie's smile popped into his mind. "Take your best shot and go for the home run. If you love someone, sometimes you have to fight for them, even if it means going past halfway to prove how much you want it to work out."

"Well, I, uh, guess..."

"Listen, mom. How often in life do you find your true love—your soulmate—that partner that just fits perfectly?"

Doina stepped closer to Colt. A tear filled her left eye, followed by a hint of a second in her right. She drew him into a tight hug. "When did you become so smart when it comes to love and relationships?"

"I don't know, Ma," he replied. "I just... I think I've figured something out for myself... I gotta go. I've got a couple errands to run."

As he grabbed his coat and keys, his mother moved a strand of his hair out of his eyes and kissed him on the forehead.

"If there's someone out there like that for you," she said with a twinkle in her eye. "Do yourself and favor and consider your own advice."

Colt hugged her around the back of her neck and patted her shoulder like a ballplayer.

"Maybe I will," he replied.

29

THE TIP

Ellie kissed Braden goodbye as he jumped into the car with Laura and Lainey, Ronnie, Mikey, and Stevie for an overnight baseball camp at East Stroudsburg University. Hiro Yu tossed Braden's oversized duffel bag and baseball backpack into their rack atop the vehicle while Braden clutched his mother in a tight hug.

"Thanks again for letting me go with them," he said. "You're the best mom ever."

Ellie stroked her son's hair with one hand and cleared the tears from her eyes with the other. "Love you."

"I love you too, Mama."

As the suburban cleared the bayberry bush, Ellie read through the pre-workout objectives that her new trainer emailed her. She stood in front of the barn where Braden threw the ball and extended her arms. Rotating them in small circles, she expanded to wider ovals and then reversed direction.

A yellow jeep pulled into her driveway. A tall, muscular man in a tight t-shirt that barely covered his bulging chest stepped down from the runner with a bag slung over his shoulder.

"Eleanor Shaw?" he asked her.

"That's me. Phil Jones? Nice to meet you. Or, well, nice to see you again, anyway."

"Right, there was that one time," Phil said, shaking her hand. "Right here in your driveway."

"It was dark, so..."

"Yes, I wasn't sure I'd find this place again," Phil said. "I see you're doing the stretching exercises I emailed you. Are you ready to get started?"

Ellie nodded as he opened his bag and took out a series of rubber bands and plastic tubes. The last time she saw him, during the past baseball season, he'd had a bit of a beer gut with mangy hair and three-day stubble. But this more well-groomed version of Colt's former roommate impressed her with his trim physique, bulging arms, and professional demeanor.

Maybe even immature frat boys and jocks can change.

Phil pulled out a leather notebook and read through his workout plan with her. He handed her a printed sheet with diagrams and descriptions of each exercise.

"You played ball with Colt?" she asked.

"Sure did."

"What was he like in college?"

"Best guy you'll ever meet."

The word 'cheater' sprung to her mind.

"He'd give you the shirt off his back," Phil added.

The memory of Colt mowing the lawn, with his bare chest coated in sweat and dust, popped into her mind, along with the image of Braden peeling off his own shirt and imitating his coach in the golden afternoon sun.

"It was a shame how they treated him over at Lehigh," Phil continued.

"What do you mean?"

"I don't know all the details. But if you ask me, I think they screwed him. He couldn't tell me anything," Phil said. "I'm pretty sure his dad could have stood up for him better than he did."

Colt decelerated into the sharp curve as he exited Route 70 and made his way past Hellertown toward Springtown. He flashed back to the first time he arrived in the tiny hamlet with all his belongings strapped into the back of his pickup truck and his L-screen protruding into the wind from the drag of the cab.

His one-sided conversation with Ellie, from two weeks earlier in her driveway, echoed through his mind.

"How are we going to explain this to the kids?" she shrieked before launching a breathless tirade that pierced him like a thousand darts in the face. "How am I going to explain this to Braden? They're going to kick you off the board. They'll fire you in shame. It'll be all over town; all over the school. Everyone'll know. I'm not sure you'll even be able to keep your teaching job. Don't you think these kids have been through enough? Now, their coach turns out to be a cheater? Fired from his job for breaking NCAA rules. Did you think we wouldn't find out? Did you think I'm stupid?"

Colt stood helplessly, searching for words that he couldn't formulate fast enough in his brain.

"I told you I hate cheaters and cheating," she continued. "There's nothing worse. God, I can't believe we almost ... I almost ... oh, I feel sick. I never should have ... What's wrong with you. What the hell's wrong with me? How could you? ... Ugh, you make me sick."

The words reverberated in his mind. The darkness of her brown eyes shaded black, and her smile faded to an expressionless purse.

Colt turned the corner onto Main Street and accelerated toward Springtown. As he pictured Ellie's ashen, stone face, pale from the glow of the moonlight and yet shadowed from the eaves of her Victorian farmhouse, he closed his eyes.

"Get out," she spit the words at him as she turned her back and retreated to her house. "Just go."

"*Just go*," the words repeated in a loop in his mind.

For a split second as he dove down Main Street, an impulse to keep his eyes closed and careen into a ditch overwhelmed him. Being fired from the coaching job at Lehigh once represented rock bottom for him. But losing Ellie and Braden, the Bees and possibly his gig as an Art teacher cast him into an even deeper emotional abyss. He recalled his despair prior to that fateful day when he first pulled into Ellie's gravel driveway. He never thought his life could unravel even worse. And yet it had.

They'd all know. They'd all look at him differently. He dreaded showing his face in the town that had accepted him, appreciated him, and given him the chance at redemption that his university and his own father had denied him.

Like any of it mattered now. And, yet it did matter to him. He'd never be the hero he wanted to be. But he could at least salvage the situation before moving on and finding his next destination in life.

He arrived at the Springtown Diner after the lunch crowd. He parked his truck out of sight behind the back of the building and entered the side entrance. Without taking a seat, he wandered about the restaurant looking for Andrea Pawlecki. The manager asked him to seat himself, and he selected the same both he occupied the first time he came to the diner—by the pictures of the Springtown All-Star teams from the late seventies.

Andrea emerged from the kitchen and spotted him right away. Instead of walking over to him, she called through the kitchen to speak with the head fry cook before ambling past a row of round tables to wait on him.

"I thought you left town," she said, as she stood over him.

"I'm not here to eat."

"You're at a diner, Hon. We don't sing or dance."

"Good one."

"It's why they call it a 'diner'," Andrea drawled the word *diner*. "You dine here."

"I wanted to talk to you."

"Oh, do you now?" She motioned back to the empty tables and booths behind her. "Well, as you can see, I've got a busy workload, so I'm not sure I can sit around and chit chat."

Colt had his work cut out with Ellie's acerbic best friend. He looked past her shoulder and straight into the kitchen where the fry cook flipped a set of pancakes causing the grill to hiss. "Fair enough. Can I just have a minute of your time?"

"You got an order for me?" She tapped a pen against a blank pad. "I can't just stand here shooting the breeze."

"I know Ellie's pissed at me."

"You had to be a cheater." She shook her head. "You could have been an embezzler, an arsonist, maybe even a carjacker."

"I'm not..."

"But, a cheater," she ignored his rebuttal. "It would have been better if you were an axe murderer—as long as you were honest with her about it."

"There's a lot more to it than that," Colt said. "I..."

A bell dinged across the diner and captured Andrea's attention. She flipped her index finger into the air, putting him on pause, and walked away. Colt slumped in the booth and sipped his water glass. Andrea returned with a plate full of buttermilk pancakes. She balanced that with another plate containing a side of home fries on her bicep. Like a circus juggler, with her other hand, she slid in front of him a tall, thin sculpted glass filled with a creamy milkshake and topped with whipped cream.

"The taters are crisped up extra." She clanked the plate across the smooth laminate and stuck a straw into the milkshake. "You like it malted."

"I didn't... I'm not hungry... I just—"

"You are hungry, hon," Andrea contradicted him.

"How did you know what I..."

"Like I said. A woman always knows." Andrea glanced over her shoulder, brushed off her apron, and sat across from him in the booth. She exhaled with a huff and stole a chunk of potato from his plate. "But I did misjudge you. And Ellie did too. We all did."

Her words stung him and robbed him of his appetite for the late lunch Andrea laid before him.

"Why are you even here?" she asked. "I figured you'd be long gone by now."

"I don't expect anyone to welcome me back with open arms," he replied. "It's over. I get it. I'm just here to stand up for the Bees and make sure they're set up for a successful season next year. I owe them that much. Then, I'm out of here; out of everyone's hair. I swear."

Andrea stared at him, nodding her head, as if studying him, analyzing him, and sizing him up. Did she believe him? Did his words have any credence with her?

"You know," she said. "Ellie tried to sign up as the coach next year, but they're probably just going to disband the team.

A pit of sadness washed over him; his worst fears had come to fruition—he'd let her down. He'd always known in the back of his mind that kissing her would be like playing with fire. The stakes were too high. He was just a simple immature jock—unworthy of her.

"You're the last person that can fix our screwed-up baseball league," Andrea added. "Nobody can beat Kildeer and Smalley at their game. It's hopeless."

"I have an idea." Colt ignored her negative sentiment. "But I need your help."

Andrea clanked her fork along the plate, dipping a double-sized chunk of pancake across the puddle of maple syrup that she'd poured. "What do you need from me?" she asked with a sigh.

"What's this agenda item in Kildeer's email about?" he asked her and showed her his phone. "Reassessing the constitution of the board? Collapsing the B-team? What's going on?"

"Ellie says they're going to make a big production out of your cheating scandal," Andrea replied. "They're going to vote you out. And, rather than let Ellie back in as coach of the Bees, they're going to take Tonio and Stevie and make the rest of the players subs that they only call if they're short players for a game."

"God, that's terrible," Colt said, his stomach turning at his unfortunate role in dashing Braden's opportunity to play ball. "Didn't they just have a board meeting?"

"One of their better players moved out of town and they decided they needed our players to fill out their roster. So, they want to gut us to give themselves a few extra subs."

Colt rubbed his forehead and eyed his fork in Andrea's hand.

"To be honest," Andrea sighed, waving a triangular sliver of his pancake in the air. "Ronnie's not even sure he wants to play next season."

"Aw come on." Colt looked her in the eyes. "He's got to play. He's really good."

"It may not matter. He might not get the chance anyway."

Colt noticed a splotch of red lipstick on the straw to his milkshake as he changed the subject. "What do you know about Oscar Schneider?"

"Mr. Schneider?" she repeated. "She slid the plate of pancakes across the table and motioned for Colt to pass her the knife. "I haven't thought of that name in a while. It must be almost a year now since he left town. Well, half-a-year anyway. He left a few months before you showed up."

"Do you know where he is?"

"No clue." She finished off his pancakes and set to work on his potatoes. "Retirement home somewhere, I think."

"Should I order a dessert with that?" he quipped.

"I think you've had enough. You'll spoil your dinner."

Andrea stood to greet a group of teenagers who entered the

front door. They lingered by the reception area waiting to be seated. The manager gave her a sharp look to get back to work. Before leaving his booth, she tapped him on the shoulder as he flipped a twenty-dollar bill on the table.

"I don't know where Mr. Schneider lives now," she told him. "But Mr. Harley at the convenience store would. They're about the same age."

Colt left his truck behind at the diner and walked across the empty lot to the intersection where the convenience store faced the blinking light between Main Street and Elm. The bells jangled as he entered the small market. He walked straight to the counter.

Mr. Harley stood on a step stool restocking the cigarette rack.

"Hey, Mr. Harley," Colt said. "You know where I could find Mr. Schneider?"

Harley descended the ladder with a harsh frown directed at Colt. "How long you lived here? No 'Hey Mr. Harley', 'How's it going Mr. Harley', 'Nice to see you Mr. Harley'. Is the delicate art of small talk just dead?"

"I thought your motto was 'small talk, small people?'"

"You sassing me?" Vern Harley asked him with his finger wagging across the air. "Small talk, small town. That's what I say. It's what differentiates us from the zombies in our big cities."

"Okay, okay, fine. I got it." Colt squinted. "How are you, Mr. Harley?"

"Never mind the idle chit chat," he snapped. "What do you need Schneider for?"

Colt sighed in exasperation but reminded himself that he needed help from the temperamental shopkeeper. "I was hoping you could give me a quick tip. Do you know where he's living now?"

"I told you to take care of the Shaw girl," Vern changed the subject. "What'd you do to her?"

"Nothing, I didn't..."

"She come in here looking all chipper and happy 'til a couple weeks ago. Now, she don't look too happy. You get with her and then take off on her?"

"No, Jesus, no." Colt stepped back from the counter. "I want to help her and her kid."

"That's a damn good kid she's got there."

"The best," Colt said, grabbing a beef jerky and a bottle of Mountain Dew and placing them on the counter with a twenty-dollar bill. "He's talented and sweet. A nice kid all around. And funny. He cracks me up when he gets so excited about baseball or these funny little drills we do together. And smart..."

"You know he ain't your kid," Mr. Harley interrupted him. "Right?"

"Yes, of course," Colt collected himself. "I just need to speak with Mr. Schneider. I'm hoping he can help me figure out how to help Ellie... and Braden."

Vern took the cash and placed it into the register. He slid the beef jerky and soda across the counter. "Sycamore Hills Convalescent Home in Hellertown, next to the town pool. Take Main Street all the way out there. Can't miss it."

"Sycamore Hills," Colt repeated to himself.

"Better fly in his kids from California, maybe find one of his long-lost cousins or dig up his dead wife," Vern said. "They won't let you see him if you're not a relative."

"A relative," Colt repeated. "Got it."

Colt gathered his items and awaited his change from the $20 that Vern slipped into his cash drawer. The elder shopkeeper gave him a wink and a nod before he collapsed his ladder and tucked it into the tiny bathroom adjacent to the main counter.

"Good luck, Son," he said with a wave and a mischievous smile. "And thanks for the generous tip."

30

THE BOARD MEMBER

The Sycamore Hills Convalescent Home wasn't just next to the Hellertown municipal pool, it was in the same complex. The non-descript brick building shared a parking lot and well-cared for landscaped property with the family entertainment center. The main entrance to the two-story facility sat on ground slightly higher than the fenced pool. The sun blared across the bright white cement sitting area. Young children scurried up the ladder to two fiberglass diving boards and plummeted into what looked to Colt like a giant vat of bright blue Windex.

The unmistakable smell of chlorine and the spray of the splashing water misted his skin as he entered the facility through the automatic sliding doors. The waft of pool chemicals dissipated as the combined stench of industrial-strength laundry detergent, human body odor, and day-old chicken noodle soup triggered an instant headache.

"I'm here to see Mr. Schneider," he told the attendant at the front desk.

"Are you a relative?" she asked.

"A relative?"

The woman glared at him from behind her cat's eye librarian glasses and her ash, grey bouffant hair.

"No, well, yes, son, his son..." he started. "... uh, in-law on the Smith side. The Smiths and the Joneses... And the Johnsons."

"You're related by marriage?" she clarified.

"My mother was a Johnson and a Jones," he babbled. *Why hadn't he formulated a better plan or cover story in advance?* "We're once removed."

"Does he know to expect you, Mr. uh, Jones? Or, is it Mr. Smith?"

"Kildeer," Colt said, his plan formulating in his head as he spoke. "My dad was a Smith. Smith-Kildeer. We're big down in the Springtown area. Mention that I'm a Kildeer."

The attendant looked at him, bewildered.

"I know. It's spelled just as horrible as it sounds." Colt leaned on the front desk then thought better of it when the attendant glared at him again. "He'll confirm our connection."

"Ok, Mr. Kildeer." She jotted his name on a visitor entry sheet. "Is that one 'L' or two?"

"Go ahead and make it two."

"I'll let your, uh, father-in-law know you're here," she said with a strained smile and turned to leave.

"It's regarding the GPYBA," Colt called to her as she pushed through the double doors into the hallway beyond the lobby. "It's a baseball league. Make sure you tell him that. The G-P-Y-B-A. He'll understand."

Colt took a seat facing a wide bay window overlooking the pool area. After a few minutes a tall, lean, and slightly hunched elderly man shuffled across the carpet toward him. He wore dark brown gaberdine and rayon trousers with a flimsy beige button-down shirt over a white V-neck t-shirt. His thin white hair matched the stubbly whiskers that protruded from his chin and cheeks. He ran his hand through his thin, wispy hair, causing several clumps to stick up into the air.

"Kildeer?" the man called, looking side-to-side. "Little punk. Where are you?"

The receptionist glanced nervously at Colt.

"Mr. Schneider," he said with a wave and a cheerful smile. "Over here. It's me."

"You're not Garrett Kildeer," the older gentleman said, prompting the receptionist to perk up from her desk like a prairie dog.

"No, no," he replied. "I'm Colt. Remember me?"

Schneider stopped and looked at him, perplexed. Colt could feel the receptionist's eyes watching.

"I'm one of the Smiths," Colt said, as Schneider ambled his way forward. "You know on the Johnson side. I'm Mary Jones', uh, you know, I'm with the Wilsons."

"You mean the Watsons?" he muttered as he took a seat across from him by the bay window.

"Right, right, of course." Colt widened his smile and put on a show for the receptionist. "They all miss you and give you their love."

"All thugs and pains in the ass the whole lot of them."

The attendant, satisfied with the interaction, went back to typing her memo with her head bowed into her computer monitor.

"How do you like this?" Schneider asked as he looked out the bay window. "All the rooms face the same view. We get to sit and watch the youngsters having fun in the pool all day."

"At least it's a nice view."

"Who are you again?" Schneider asked. "How do you know that coconut, Kildeer, and why are you here asking me about the GPYBA?"

"My name's Colt Gibson." He leaned in and softened his voice. "I'm on the Springtown Board of Directors for the youth baseball program."

"Colt?" he repeated. "Like a horse?"

"Something like that."

"Gibson?" Schneider perked, his demeanor spryer and more alert. "Related to Butch Gibson?"

"That's my dad."

"Then you're Colt Gibson."

"That's what I said."

"You took that charge in the Four-A Championship game."

"You remember that?"

"Took out their best player," Schneider replied. "I don't think you would have won if you didn't foul out their big gun like that."

Colt smiled at the recognition. The memory of closing his eyes, lowering his hands across his chest in a screen, and letting Derek Williamson slam his massive body against his face and drop him to the gymnasium floor like a load of bricks flooded his mind.

"You're related to Kildeer too?" Schneider asked.

"Huh, oh, no," Colt said, the memory dissipating as quickly as it formed. "They wouldn't let me speak with you unless they thought I was a relative."

"And you're on the board in Springtown?" Schneider mused. "I used to be on that board as well."

"Apparently, you still are."

The receptionist walked over to the pair and placed her hand on Schneider's shoulder. "Is everything alright, Mr. Schneider?"

"I'm one of the Wilsons," Colt said.

"Watsons," Schneider interjected. "I'm just speaking with my uh, my nephew here. He's one of the Watson boys. So wonderful to reconnect. He wants to take me out for a walk around the pool."

"I thought he was your son-in-law?" she asked.

"Yes, that too," Schneider raised his voice. "Married my beautiful daughter Belinda."

The receptionist raised her eyebrow and eyed Colt suspiciously.

"We're from Springtown, don't judge us," Schneider snapped.

"Love is love," Colt added.

The receptionist shook her head and continued across the room to check on another elderly woman sitting by a fireplace in the back of the common area. Schneider watched in silence as she moved out of earshot.

"You know, Son, I would have been the President of the Board," Schneider continued. "When Lester Springman retired, he told me I'd be his replacement."

"Springman?" Colt asked.

"The family dates all the way back to the incorporation of the town in 1895," Schneider explained. "The Funks and the Springmans built the old mill next to the creek and employed pretty much everyone in town for the next fifty years."

Colt leaned in to hear Schneider's raspy voice more clearly. "Now, about the baseball program…"

"Of course, they settled the place in the seventeen-hundreds," Schneider continued. "Built the Methodist Church in 1842. Then they built the Lutheran Church in 1872 and the Grace Church in eighty-eight, or maybe eighty-nine. No, I'm pretty sure it was 1888."

"That's all great," Colt prompted Mr. Schneider. "Believe me, I really love the town. Now, about the baseball program."

"You're related to Kildeer?" Schneider asked again.

"Well, not exactly."

"Goes around like he's God's gift to baseball, that guy," Schneider said, puffing his chest and pounding it like a gorilla. "He was pretty good as a kid. I'll give you that. I coached him from the Peewee league to the Midgets. Had his best year as a Shrimp."

"Yes, he's the President of the Board, now and—"

"Did he tell you all about how he played in college?"

"Alleghany State, I think he said it was."

"Benchwarmer," Schneider spat the words. "A scrub. He sat his freshman year and quit after that. I'm not sure he even graduated."

"Well, you may know that he runs the league in town now."

"Oh, right." Schneider picked up on his unfinished thought from a few minutes earlier. "Springman told me I'd be the next President of the league after he quit. Poor old bastard was suffering from gout or cancer or something."

"What happened?" Colt asked, surprised at his own interest in the rambling, disconnected narrative.

"They put him on some medication that caused him to break out in a rash."

"No," Colt interrupted. "With the board?"

"Right, Kildeer screwed me over, that's what." Schneider leaned back, his facial features hardened, and his eyes fixed on the wall behind Colt. "Just before the annual board meeting, Springman tells me I'm in. But you know as you get older, it sucks how when you gotta go, you gotta go."

"Uh, okay, right." Colt nodded along.

"I mean, I just went before you showed up," Schneider continued. "And I could totally go again."

"I could see how that would be a challenge."

"Sometimes I go three or four times a night..."

"The board meeting?" Colt interrupted.

"Right," Schneider snapped back into his story. "We start the meeting. That's back when we had five or six board members. We're talking about renaming Mucky Gulch Field to something a little jazzier like Happy Park or something nice like that when I gotta go. So, I excuse myself and visit the restroom. Granted, it takes some time for it all to come out and I gotta wiggle for a good couple minutes to stop all the dripping and dribbling from getting all over my trousers."

"Yes, okay, I got that part," Colt interjected.

"By the time I get back, they already picked out the new stadium name and Kildeer's somehow voted in as the next President."

"I bet you're pretty pissed off about that?"

"It was a hundred years ago," Schneider mused. "The guy's a dipstick, but there's nothing I can do about it now."

"Actually, maybe there is, Mr. Schneider," said Colt, eyeing the reception desk. "Or should I call you 'Uncle Oscar'?"

31

THE MEETING

Ellie brushed her hair with urgency. She fanned the hot air from her blow-dryer across her wavy locks. Then she applied lipstick and blush. She called Braden on her cell phone to confirm that he'd be back from baseball camp with his fellow Bees teammates later that evening and that he'd be alone at home for about an hour until she returned.

"Make sure you thank Mr. Yu for the ride and for dinner," she instructed him. "I'll see you when I get back from the meeting."

She scrolled through her emails muttering to herself. "Come on, come on."

Downstairs Andrea clanked plates in the kitchen. Ellie straightened her blouse and brushed a wisp of hair out of her eyes. Satisfied with her appearance, she exhaled the nerves from her chest and clomped down the stairs to find her purse.

"Did he call?" Andrea asked. "Is he coming?"

"I don't know," Ellie replied.

"It's simple," Andrea shot back. "Just scroll through your incoming messages to see if he called you."

"No, he didn't call," Ellie snapped. "And I don't want to talk to him, he's a cheater."

"Did you really have to tell him to leave?"

"I didn't."

"*'Get out'* sounds definitive to me."

"Of my house," Ellie snapped. "He's still paying rent, so I didn't kick him out."

"He wasn't in your house," Andrea reasoned. "I thought you were on the patio."

"Same difference," Ellie said, waving away her friend's comment. "And then he just packed up and left. Ran away. Ditched me like the immature frat boy I always knew he was. He left me flat when I needed him just like the other cheater in my life, Jeffrey."

"He's hardly anything like Jeffrey." Andrea raised her hand as if Ellie had crossed some egregious line in her frustration.

"Once a cheater, always a cheater," Ellie shot back. "I don't need that in my life."

"He seemed earnest to me."

"Frat boys always seem that way," Ellie raised her voice. "They all major in How to Fool Women. The classes consist of Lying 101, Deception 201, and Advanced Cheating Thesis 301. They're all the same."

"You really think Colt's in that class?"

"It's not even about me," Ellie huffed, grabbing her keys, and heading out the back door. "He got so close to Braden. And I let him. And I knew I shouldn't. I told you that the first day he showed up."

"You couldn't have known…"

"It's my job to know." Ellie's face flushed and the veins in her neck bulged. She cast the memory of Colt Gibson's blue eyes and broad smile out of her mind. "Come on. We have to fight for their opportunity to play ball now, after he created this mess for us. I'm pretty sure there's nothing we can do about it. It's kind of pointless to even go to the meeting."

Andrea followed Ellie out the screen door to the patio and across the driveway to her car.

"They're going to outvote him two-to-one. That's if he even shows up at all. They can do whatever they want. We lose either way."

"There's got to be something we can do? Why else would Colt show up at the diner?"

"It doesn't matter anyhow," Ellie continued. "I don't know what he was doing there or why he's asking about Mr. Schneider. What can Schneider tell him that could in any way be useful? The guy's in a convalescent home."

"He was such a nice man," Andrea remarked as they backed out the driveway and passed the bayberry bush onto Main Street. "After his wife died, those kids of his just took off to the west coast."

Ellie didn't respond, lost and wallowing in her frustration.

"Such a shame his kids stopped paying his rent," Andrea continued. "The sons sold his car and furniture. His witch-of-a-stepdaughter, Belinda Smith-Watson, got married for like the third time and took ownership of his house so the state couldn't take it. And as soon as she hit the five-year mark, she dumped him in that terrible place on the state's dime."

"Shameful," Ellie agreed with a sigh.

Anger at Colt blurred in her mind. How could he have cheated like that? And worse, he never told them. Why didn't he trust her? Maybe he just screwed up and regretted it. Or from what Phil implied, it might not have been all his fault. Why couldn't he have told her? Had he just come clean, they might have gotten past it. But she had to hear it from Kildeer, the snake who wanted to cut her son from the town baseball program.

"Mr. Schneider was a great tenant, and he loved living in your garage," Andrea continued. "I always enjoyed chit-chatting with him."

Ellie tried again to wash Colt's image from her mind.

"Doesn't matter," Ellie cut her off. "He's gone. Colt's gone. They're gonna disband Braden's team and take away his favorite activity."

Ellie and Andrea arrived at the school cafeteria, which also served as a gymnasium. The dark, windowless room contained nearly every A-team parent and a few from the B-team. Kildeer and Smalley served pizza and buffalo chicken wings as a thank you to them. The buzzing of voices swirled around Ellie's head. Gossipy whispers assaulted her ears and gave her a mild headache. She surveyed the room and saw very few friendly faces.

She found Laura Yu and Joe Dalton at a round table near the front of the room. The B-team attendance was sparse. Hito Yu was busy driving Mikey, Ronnie, Braden, Stevie, Lainey, and Lilly home from baseball camp. Several other parents had to stay home to watch their younger children. Just before the meeting started, Mara Wiltshire entered the cafeteria and joined them as Kildeer and Smalley took their places at the head of the room.

The image of Kildeer and Smalley at the main table, with Colt's seat empty, triggered a gasp of realization in Ellie. She nearly jumped out of her seat as her heart filled with excitement.

"What the heck?" Andrea asked.

"Colt's not here," she beamed.

"I know, but why are you happy about that?"

"They don't have a quorum."

"Okay, so..."

"So, they can't vote as a board. They'll have to open the votes to the floor."

Andrea looked over her shoulder at the twenty A-team parents and back to the handful of B-team parents. "Dina Maletti and Bob Biegacki are over there with the A-team crowd. You think they'll vote to save the Bees?"

Ellie made eye contact with Dina, but Dina averted her gaze.

"I don't think so," she whispered, as Kildeer motioned for the crowd to hush so he could start the meeting. "At least without Colt, we have a chance. If he were here, they'd have total control."

As the room silenced and the crowd focused forward, the clanking of the double doors to the entry area adjacent to the cafeteria echoed. Ellie whirled to catch a faint glimpse of Colt's shoulders moving past the opening into the dark hallway.

COLT STOOD on the other side of the wall from the cafeteria just out of sight from the crowd. He had peered into the room—and realized that the meeting was about to start. But he dipped out of sight when he saw Ellie's head spin in his direction. He watched the door to the bathroom close and heard the latch clip into place.

"Seriously?" Colt wheezed. "You just went back at the gas station along the way. You really have to go again? Now?"

Colt heard Kildeer call the meeting to order. He asked Smalley to note the attending board members. Colt swore to himself and trotted through the entrance to the cafeteria.

"Wait," his voice bounded across the polished linoleum tiled floor. "I'm here. We have full attendance tonight."

Kildeer and Smalley looked at each other in surprise. They glared at him with sly grins and invited him to come take his seat.

"We have an important agenda tonight," Kildeer said, motioning toward the crowd. "That's why we have such a full house."

Colt slowed his pace toward the head table to buy time. He caught Schneider's faint hum from the bathroom around the corner from the cafeteria. Ellie sat at a table in his peripheral vision. He caught a glimpse of an eyeroll just before Andrea nudged her to stop.

Colt took his seat. His gaze connected with Ellie's for a split second before they both broke contact and looked away. Despite recognizing most of the faces in the room, Ellie's stern expression and the way she avoided looking directly at him left him lonely and feeling like an outsider.

Why did I even come here? How am I going to fix this?

"I'm surprised you showed up," Smalley taunted Colt.

"I'm on the board, aren't I?"

"For the time being," Smalley sneered with a coy smile. "You have to know by now that your secret's out."

Kildeer stood and walked toward an aisle between the A-team tables on the right and the B-team table on the left.

"I'm not sure who's heard what," he started. "I want to set the record straight and be transparent to all our wonderful parents who make this program as great as it is."

Colt watched Ellie scroll through her emails. She waved her phone in the air as if trying to find a stronger signal. She held it out from her body and then tapped the side of it.

"I don't think WiFi works that way," Colt heard Andrea whisper to her. "It's not a transistor radio."

Kildeer's voice droned like a teacher in school who only resonates with the one or two interested students in the room. "Integrity and the best interests of all the children in our program are of the utmost importance to us. That's why I feel compelled to share with you some unfortunate details about something we've learned about Mr. Gibson, who has served on our board for the past several months, and who coached our B-team last season."

Colt looked past Kildeer to the doorway from the foyer. His laser focus resembled a cat awaiting his dinner bowl to be filled with catnip.

"We have a code of conduct that our board members sign. It strictly and explicitly forbids improprieties such as harming the children in any way, violence, use of profanity, and any form of cheating whatsoever."

"Jesus," Ellie muttered to Andrea and a few others in her immediate vicinity, even Colt overheard. "Get to the point."

"It's come to our attention that while serving as an assistant coach at the Lehigh Men's baseball program," Kildeer paused for dramatic effect. "Colt Gibson was fired for breaking multiple NCAA rules and regulations. He was let go for cheating."

As a few parents in the crowd gasped and others whispered into each other's ears, Colt scanned the entry to the cafeteria. He heard the toilet flush and the water from the sink hiss.

"Because we have a no tolerance policy for cheating and cheaters," Kildeer continued. "I motion that we remove Colt from our board and bar him for life from coaching in our program."

As Kildeer monopolized the attention of the parents, Colt pulled out his phone and sent a text. He watched helplessly as his phone struggled to generate enough reception to send it to the intended recipient. He had one chance to salvage the Springtown Bees. A bad internet connection would completely derail his plan.

32

THE VIDEO

Ellie didn't know what to expect at the meeting. She hadn't seen Colt in a couple weeks since he'd vacated her apartment. Maybe her disdain for cheaters caused her to overreact in the moment. She didn't trust Kildeer for a second. But Colt's evasive reaction to the accusations, and his hasty flight from Springtown the next morning provided the disappointing confirmation in Ellie's mind to the allegations against him. He loaded his truck early and left the apartment without an explanation or even goodbye.

If only he had told her soon after they first met.

During the week leading up to the board meeting, she poured through her interactions with Colt and how she let him into her life. She couldn't be that bad a judge of character, could she? With his positive, uplifting coaching style he brought to the Bees, and his gentle approach to mentoring Braden, she couldn't imagine him willingly violating NCAA rules. Despite his guilty eyes, as she lectured him that night, there had to be an explanation. She spent the week trying in vain to uncover it.

After her first session with Phil, she'd fired e-mails to various athletic and administration departments at Lehigh. She contacted the Athletic Director to inquire about the details surrounding Colt's dismissal. She made a few calls to track down Butch's official Lehigh e-mail address. She even Googled to find a personal e-mail address for him, consisting of the handle *bndgibson* with a string of numbers and an *aol.com* ending.

"AOL," she scoffed. "Figures."

She wrote Coach Butch a long, rambling note about how Colt had managed the Bees to an unexpected successful season, and how he'd helped her son and so many other kids in the community gain skills and confidence. She detailed the politics of the town program and how Colt had tried to stand up for her, her son, and his team. She copied both his professional and personal e-mail addresses, hoping for any possible mitigating explanation regarding Colt's mysterious termination or why he might have cheated.

She realized she might learn nothing. Or she might uncover an even uglier side of Braden's coach and mentor she didn't want to see. If Phil was right and the father could've done something, she might not hear anything at all. But she wanted a reply to shed light on the situation. Maybe she just needed closure to the whole experience with Colt.

She had hoped to receive a response from anyone before the meeting ended. Soon, the board would disband the Bees. Braden would be left in the cold as some sort of alternate, sub or practice player. And thoughts of Colt would disappear from their lives for good.

Smalley seconded the motion to oust Colt from the board.

Ellie's phone buzzed in her pocket. She expected an e-mail—maybe from the Athletic Director, maybe from Coach Butch himself. Instead, she had a text, from Braden. She tried to open it, but with the poor cell reception in the drab concrete cafeteria, the message would not load.

Ellie stood with her phone in the air and walked toward the

back of the room. She waved it about searching for Wi-Fi reception. As she focused on retrieving the text from her son, Colt's voice bounced off the back wall.

"Hold on," he said, his voice amplified by the four glazed cinderblock walls. "Let me just say a few words."

"It's too late," Smalley snapped.

Joe, Laura, and Mara all called out to let him speak.

"Fine," Kildeer gave in once Dina and Robert joined the chorus of voices from the A-team table.

"It won't make a difference," Smalley chimed in. "But say what you need to say so we can get this over with."

Ellie looked up from her phone as she waited for the message from Braden to materialize in her text window. Colt looked neat and trim in beige cargo shorts and a crisp, blue and white striped button-down shirt which caught the light in his eyes. He didn't look at her as he spoke, and for a moment, she wished that he would.

"I never came here to coach youth sports," Colt said, standing at the head table between Kildeer and Smalley. "I was just looking for a nice, quiet place to hide out for a couple months, while I sorted what I wanted to do with my life. I didn't ask to coach the Athletics or the Bees. I certainly never expected to end up teaching art to your children."

Ellie leaned against the back wall and listened to him speak. As she did, Braden's text appeared.

> Braden: Home now. Some lady from Lehigh left a message. She said she tried to call your cell phone, but it didn't go through.

Ellie stared at the message in surprise. The Lehigh Athletic Director and the entire baseball staff were all men. She paused to listen to the rest of Colt's speech.

"But you were all so welcoming, and so nice to me. Mr. Dalton gave me a job. The school board gave me a chance to teach. And, I had the great honor of coaching your amazing kids to the best of my ability. I thought after leaving college that I'd never feel a part of a bigger team again. But you've showed me what it's like to be a part of a community. And this is a wonderful little town, full of great people. That's why it's so heartbreaking to lose your trust."

Ellie tried to anticipate Colt's point. She couldn't decide whether to call Braden or hear out the rest of Colt's sentiment.

"I wish I could say something to ease your concerns," he continued. "I know many of you are confused, disappointed, even angry at me. I wish I could say something more about this. But, you see, I signed a Non-Disclosure Agreement with the university, which bars me from discussing any of the details about what happened. I gave my word and, I have to honor that agreement."

Ellie's phone suddenly gained solid connectivity to the cell network. It dinged several times as pent-up e-mails and texts flooded her in-box. She saw an e-mail from the Lehigh Athletic Department. As Colt spoke, Smalley and Kildeer stood. They exchanged glances and motioned to each other that they should cut him off.

"I only hope you can trust that I've always had only the best intentions for all your kids. And, I hope that you'll forgive me for this cloud that hangs over my head."

Smalley nudged his shoulder in front of Colt's and raised a hand to divert attention in the room to him.

"Well, I think that's enough from you," he interrupted.

"Last point." Colt ignored Smalley's intrusion. "There's no reason to disband the Bees. Ellie Shaw is willing to coach. She's got a heart of gold and she'd do as well or better than me in a heartbeat."

Ellie looked up from her phone at mention of her name. Her eyes connected with Colt's blue irises for a moment before she looked away to review the e-mail.

"Don't let these guys take baseball away from your children," he quickened the pace of his voice. "They're little kids who just want to play and learn and have fun. They don't care if they're an A-team or a B-team or a Q-team or a Z-team. They'll win. They'll lose. And when they're done, they'll have ice cream, run around the yard until they're tired, and play video games on their phones at night. It'll get plenty more competitive in middle school and high school. But for now, at this age, they should just let everyone play."

Smalley stepped in front of Colt and extended his arm across his chest. "Have a seat," he snarled. "It's time for us to conclude our meeting."

Joe Dalton stood and shouted, "Let them play."

Mara Wiltshire and Laura Yu joined him. Dina and Robert added their voices.

Ellie watched Kildeer and Smalley struggle to quiet the crowd. She looked back at her phone to read the message from the Lehigh Athletic Department, hoping it would shed some light or even exonerate Colt from wrongdoing.

We hold the status and internal interactions of our coaches and staff confidential. The matter in question is between the university and a private former employee, who is bound by a Non-Disclosure Agreement. We are unable to provide any further information at this time.

Ellie hunched her shoulders and tucked her phone into the back pocket of her jeans.

Game over.

The clamor in the room rose to a level where Kildeer had to raise his voice to maintain minimal order.

"We have a motion for Colt's dismissal as a board member and a second," he announced over the voices of the disgruntled parents in the crowd. "All in favor?"

Ellie shot one last look at Colt, alone on the stage, looking agitated and helpless. He gazed past the crowd, out the back of the gym, as if already planning his next escape.

Ellie's phone beeped again. The vibration against the small of her lower back startled her. A new reply sat atop her e-mail inbox. She recognized the AOL address as belonging to Butch Gibson. She scanned the short note responding to her inquiry. She stared with confusion at the signer of the e-mail: Doina Gibson.

Colt's mother?

THANK you for reaching out to me. Your cell phone went to voicemail, so I called the home number and spoke to your son. There is more to this than you know. I tried to reach my husband to clear this up with you, but he is currently on the field coaching at a camp. It's gotten too far out of hand. I never should have let it come to this. And it's way past time to come clean. So, I drove to Altoona this afternoon to address it with my husband directly. Attached is a video explanation that will hopefully help in your meeting. If I get my way, he'll release it to the press within the hour.

THE E-MAIL CONTAINED a blue hyperlink below Doina's name. Ellie felt every nerve in her body illuminate like the grand finale of a fireworks show.

"Stop," she screeched.

Neither Kildeer, nor Smalley spoke. All the heads in the room turned toward her. Blood rushed to her cheeks.

The phrase *"within the hour"* echoed in her mind. Would the video exonerate Colt? Would it make matters worse?

"I have an email." Ellie held her phone in the air for all to see. Her stomach churned with nerves at the thought of playing it sight-unseen for the entire room to hear.

Ellie watched Colt's eyes flinch. He rotated his gaze from the phone in her hand to the dark void outside the cafeteria door. From her unique vantage point at the back of the room, she caught a glimpse of movement in the shadows of the hallway by the bathrooms.

An elderly man appeared like a ghost in the dark. Fixated on Ellie and her phone, nobody in the meeting room noticed, except Colt, by the look of his exasperated expression. The old man scuffled aimlessly across the foyer with his back to the cafeteria. Confused, he looked side-to-side and wandered in the wrong direction, away from the bright, people-filled room.

Ellie watched Colt stand to chase him, but she froze him with her eyes.

"I have an email that might exonerate Colt from blame in the scandal that resulted in his firing," she announced.

The crowd again erupted in crosstalk. Colt looked at her in disbelief.

"What are you talking about?" he called to her.

The volume in the room escalated as the parents buzzed. The murmur filled the shoddy drop ceiling overhead.

"What is this video?" Kildeer asked. "Who sent it?"

"It was sent to me by..." To Ellie, the phrase 'Colt's Mom' didn't sound like a compelling talking point. "It doesn't matter."

Colt looked completely confused.

"Have you seen this e-mail?" Kildeer asked Ellie.

"Yes," she answered. "Well, no."

Several members of the crowd laughed at her flip-flopped answer.

"I know what's in it," she stumbled to find the right words. "Or, I've been told what it's about."

Kildeer and Smalley trained their beady eyes on her like wild animals stalking prey.

"This is ridiculous," Smalley shouted over the uproar of the crowd. "I vote we oust the bastard and get this over with."

The crowd continued to grumble. B-team parents yelled for Kildeer to allow her to play the video. A-team parents expressed anger at the disruption and questioned what was going on. During the confusion, Ellie found the invite to the meeting and hit "Reply to All".

"I'm emailing this to the board members and copying every parent in the league," she said as she typed on her phone with blazing dexterity. "It includes a video where Coach Butch Gibson provides the real story of what happened with Colt and his job as a coach of the Lehigh baseball team."

Or at least, I hope...

Ellie pressed play on the video and turned up her volume as high as it would go. The audio barely filled the room enough for the nearest table to hear. At the same time, several other parents played the clip on their phones from her e-mail. The confluence of mistimed streams caused a confusing overlap of repeating voices like an orchestra warming up before a performance.

As the chaos broke out, Colt stood on his toes and looked into the darkened hallway. What was he looking for? She could only make out bits of phrases and disconnected statements from Butch's announcement.

"... take full responsibility," Butch's voice echoed from her phone. "... willingly confirm that I am the sole perpetrator of these violations and no other coaches are to blame but me."

Ellie strained to pick out other comments out of the air as the playbacks from different phones competed with each other. Joe Dalton stood with his phone in the air.

"It's on ESPN right now," he shouted.

More phones played conflicting audio. The room filled with garbled echoes and white noise.

"... decided to retire to focus on my family," Butch announced in his video from the side of a bright green and brown baseball field. "... regret that I allowed assistant coaches to cover for me, when I was to blame, and they were not. I only hope I can be forgiven for my selfishness and my mistakes."

Kildeer raised his hands, like a quarterback trying to quiet a loud home crowd. "I have to remind everyone, we have a motion and a pending vote." He raised his voice above the rumble of the parents and the buzz of the video playbacks.

"You can't vote him out now." Andrea stood and faced the parents. "You all saw the video. He's innocent. He didn't cheat. His father did."

"He was still part of it," Smalley snapped.

"This isn't fair," Mara stood shoulder to shoulder with Andrea. "I know many of you have seen Colt in action. He's the best coach Mikey's ever had. And he's a hell of an amazing guy."

"He's given my son so much confidence in himself," Andrea added. "He's made a huge impact on all these kids."

From across the room, Colt waved at Ellie and pointed at his phone. Ellie shook her head at him in confusion.

The hell is he trying to tell me?

Seconds later, her phone buzzed. A text from him popped onto her home screen.

> Colt: Can u fund shindig down in hell?

What shindig? In hell? She watched him type a second message.

> Colt: Can u find schneider down the hall?

> Ellie: Schneider who?

Then, the connection between the creaky old man in the hallway and Colt's message flashed in her mind.

> Ellie: Mr. Schneider? From the apartment?

> Colt: I'll explain later. Hurry.

She flashed him a thumbs up and bolted out of the cafeteria to catch up with Mr. Schneider. The meeting echoed through the halls as she searched for the missing old man.

"All in favor," Kildeer said, loudly enough to compensate for the chatter of the parents.

"Wait," Colt shouted, his booming voice bouncing down the hallway.

Ellie ran around the corner past the bathrooms and the administrative office. The light from the cafeteria faded as she rounded a curved hallway past the library. Hallways diverged to the left and right. She listened for footsteps, trying to decide which way the codger may have wandered. Though she could still hear the muffled voices in the cafeteria, she also could understand how the dark, non-descript hallways might be confusing to the elderly man.

Ellie's phone buzzed again in her pocket.

> Andrea: "Where r u?"

> Ellie: The library. Need your help.

> Andrea: The library? All hell's breaking loose in the cafeteria.

> Ellie: Need you now. HURRY!

Ellie called to Mr. Schneider. Both hallways extended into the darkness. Which way to turn? She heard footsteps behind her.

"What's going on?" Andrea asked. "You need to get in there now."

"I need to find Schneider."

"Mr. Schneider? Here? Why?"

"No clue," Ellie replied. "You go one way; I'll go the other."

Andrea grabbed Ellie by the shoulders and peered into her eyes. "He's fighting for our kids. I'll find Mr. Schneider. You get in there and support him."

33

THE ASSAULT

Ellie reappeared in the entryway to the cafeteria, but without Mr. Schneider at her side. She took her seat next to Joe and nodded at him. Colt raised his voice and projected it across the room.

"Since this vote has to do with my status as a board member," Colt spoke over Kildeer as he tried to call for the final vote. "Obviously, I should recuse myself from taking part as a voting board member. So uh, therefore, by the rules that Ms. Shaw pointed out at that first board meeting, we don't have a quorum."

Colt noticed Ellie smile, then cover her mouth to stifle a laugh.

"And, if I understand correctly," he continued. "When that happens, we have to rely on the consensus of the parent vote to pass the motion."

Kildeer's eyes flared in realization. Smalley sighed loudly. He stood and walked out from behind the head table, squared his shoulders to Colt, and gave him a menacing glare.

"We all know his daddy's just protecting him," Smalley announced to the crowd. "This guy's a scumbag and we don't need his kind on our board or in our program."

The parents continued to murmur and debate among themselves. Kildeer and Smalley conferred by whispering back and forth as the structure and organization of the meeting fell apart. The volume of the parent's side conversations and grumbling rose to a jumble of incomprehensible voices.

"As long as we're talking about cheaters," Mara raised her voice above the din and moved toward the A-team crowd. "How about Timmy Crowley?"

The room silenced as if air leaking from a set of tires. Smalley and Kildeer froze.

"That's right." Mara glared at Dina, Robert, and several other parents at their table.

Smalley and Kildeer exchanged nervous glances, the first moment of the evening where they looked vulnerable.

"Come on," Mara continued, the hint of a laugh in her voice. "I was an A-team parent, remember? We all knew it. And you all know it right now. If we're talking about league rules, the kid's twice the size of anyone else. He hits home runs every game. And he doesn't even go to Springtown Elementary."

Kildeer stepped toward Mara with his arms out as if corralling a loose sheep.

"He's an illegal player," she continued. "He doesn't live in town. He's from Applebachsville. You don't think the kids talk to each other on the bench and then spill to their parents?"

"Now, Mrs. Wiltshire," Kildeer moved into damage control mode. "You don't know..."

"And he's eleven." She refused to yield the floor. "But, as long as he helps win games, I guess cheating is just fine with Mr. Kildeer and Mr. Smalley."

Kildeer and Smalley closed ranks. Smalley nudged past Colt and whispered in Kildeer's ear.

"The Crowley's are looking at homes in town," Kildeer said, also raising his voice to regain order and attention. "We'll look into his age. We have all the birth certificates on file. If there's an anomaly, of course, we'll correct it."

As Kildeer addressed the crowd, playing defense for the first time in the evening, Colt rattled another text to Ellie.

> Colt: Where is he?

Ellie looked over her shoulder, shrugged, and checked her phone.

Kildeer, Smalley, and Colt stared at each other as if locked in a dual, waiting for someone to draw first. Kildeer made a motion to drop the vote regarding Colt's status on the board in light of the new information about the Lehigh baseball cheating scandal that Ellie surfaced. Colt nodded in agreement.

Some members of the crowd cheered. The positive vote settled the side voices and gave Kildeer better control of the meeting.

"That still brings up our second agenda item regarding the consolidation of the A and B teams," Kildeer continued. "We've already absorbed Tonio Maletti and Willie Biegacki. And until the Crowley's officially move to town, we'll likely make him ineligible to play—just to be sure that we remain above board. That means we'll need to promote another player from the B-team, probably the Yu girl."

"Which one," Andrea asked. "They're twins."

"The bigger one," Smalley responded. "The one that can hit."

At Smalley's comment, Laura Yu gasped.

"You're going to separate the twins?" Mara looked across the crowd of parents in disbelief. "You'll take one and cut the other?"

"Regardless," Kildeer cleared his throat and raised his voice to maintain the control he'd just regained. "That leaves the B-team with only nine players. And we can't, in good conscience, support a team that has the minimum number of players with no subs."

"We'll recruit," Colt argued. "We'll figure it out. To be honest, I don't know if there's a player on our team that would be willing to play for you."

"We'll take who we need from the B-team," Smalley blurted, jutting his chin out at Colt.

The murmur from the crowd grew again as Smalley puffed his chest and arched his back to measure as tall as his adversary. "Mikey'll also have to join us, of course, if he wants to keep playing. They won't have a choice; none of them. What's important here is that the A-team remains strong and viable."

"I hate to say it." Kildeer made more of an attempt to express a hint of empathy. "With Tommy Tremblay quitting, you can't even field a full nine-man starting line-up."

"They're not men," Laura stood up and corrected him. "They're boys and girls. You always forget about the girls."

"It wouldn't be fair for us to take a registration fee and forfeit all the games when you can't field a full team," Kildeer spoke over her interjection.

The A-team parents whispered and nodded in agreement. Ellie's face flushed. She gazed at her phone looking for a response from Andrea. She locked eyes with Colt. They both knew he didn't have the votes if he recused himself again. But it would be an automatic two-to-one loss if he didn't.

"I motion to eliminate the B-team and absorb the two or three travel-worthy players to the A-team," Smalley projected his voice to the back wall.

"This is exactly what I warned you about," Colt shouted to the crowd.

"Second," Kildeer said.

"Wait," Colt interrupted, again processing as fast as possible to invent additional stall tactics. "Between the second and the vote, board members get to make their arguments to impact the decision."

"It's useless," Smalley leaned over and whispered in his ear.

"Unfortunately," Kildeer added. "You already spoke on this topic. It's getting late. We just need to vote and move on."

"It's over," Smalley leaned over and whispered in his ear. "You're through."

Colt watched Smalley's shifty eyes. Having spent most of his life studying the faces of opposing pitchers for the slightest of tells, Colt knew the look. He recognized the egotistical stare down, the forced confidence of an adversary, both pumping themselves up for the battle and deathly afraid of giving up the big hit to lose the game.

"You know what I think?" Colt pasted a playful smile across his face and turned to address the crowd. "I think Mr. Mini-Kildeer here is afraid. He's afraid that our mighty little Bee team has gotten too good."

Smalley scoffed and glared at Colt.

"He's afraid," Colt continued. "He's fearful that he's just not good enough; that his style of coaching—yelling and screaming at your kids—is inadequate in this day and age. Isn't that right?"

Colt watched Smalley's face shade red. He continued his full court press.

"What do you all think?" he asked the crowd. Many of them nodded their heads and made eye contact with him. "Is this the type of coach you want in charge of your kids?"

The jarring clank of the double doors rattled across the hall. Colt looked up, expecting to see Mr. Schneider finally finding his way to the meeting. Instead, Darius Wiltshire entered the room. Borrowing time against his shift, he donned his full olive-green sheriff uniform from his tall round-brimmed hat to his black polished boots. His large, imposing frame strode down the aisle and took the seat next to his wife, Mara. She clasped his hand, kissed him, and whispered something in his ear that made him smile.

"Our team is more fun than his team," Colt continued to stall. "We've already beaten teams that his team lost to."

Smalley stepped closer to Colt and stammered about missing

players and bad weather. Colt ignored him and continued. As he did, he stole a quick look at his phone and saw a new text from Ellie.

> Ellie: Andrea found him. He has to go to the bathroom again.

Colt concocted a new line of dialog to keep his monologue going.

"How many of his players did he call fat or slow?" Colt addressed the crowd and walked around the A-team table. "How many of your kids did he insult, demean, and harass in this unacceptable way? How many of you traveled, two, three, four hours to tournaments, only to see your kids sit the bench every game? Is this really the experience you want for them?"

Kildeer gave Smalley a panicked look as the crowd murmured in support of Colt's impactful soliloquy.

"That's enough," Kildeer interrupted.

Smalley's face burned red with anger.

"The motion is seconded," Kildeer announced. "All in favor?"

Colt faced Smalley like a western gunfighter. Their eyes locked. Smalley projected his chin forward. Colt noticed his fingers twitch.

"I thought we had a policy against profanity," Colt continued to rail as if Kildeer didn't exist. "How many of your kids did he yell at. How many did he berate or swear at?"

Out of the corner of his peripheral vision, he watched Smalley's eyes bulge. His face brightened even redder. Andrea still hadn't arrived with Schneider. He read panic in Ellie's eyes. He had little leeway left to stall. He had one last risky chance to derail the meeting, if he could make it happen.

"Maybe we should vote *him* off the board," Colt shouted with an accusatory finger pointed into Smalley's personal space.

Colt's last comment set Smalley over the edge. In the background, Colt saw Andrea scurry Schneider into the back of the room. Ellie stood to wave them forward. Colt knew the parents couldn't see his face as he turned his back to them and faced Smalley.

He had gotten into pitchers' heads this way several times during his playing career. When he needed to get on base, it almost always worked. With a wink, and the smuggest smile he could muster, he puckered his lips and blew the man a taunting kiss for only him to see.

In the foreground, as Smalley loomed forward and cocked his fist, Colt dropped his hands in front of his chest. *A sacrifice—for the Bees... for Ellie.* He closed his eyes and braced for the impact.

Smalley's knuckles collided with the groove of Colt's eye socket. He fell straight back. The B-team table—specifically Mara Wiltshire's lap—broke his fall and stopped him from cracking his skull on the floor.

Ellie yelped and ran to his side. Other parents stood, gasped, and buzzed with shock. Darius sprang into action, tending to Colt, who rolled around semi-coherently on the ground. Smalley stood over his fallen adversary at first, but then cowered to his seat upon recognizing the gravity of his action.

Colt fought through the fog in his head. Darius, Ellie, Andrea, and Garrett all helped him to his feet and maneuvered him to the chair opposite Smalley at the head table. The voices sounded distant. Colt heard the rattle of the ice from the machine in the kitchen. He watched all the parents stand and stare. The skin around his left eye swelled closed. Someone pressed a gallon-sized plastic bag full of searing cold ice against his puffy, swollen mound of bloody flesh.

Ellie sat close to him. She rubbed his back and whispered to him. In the commotion, he watched Darius escort Jay Smalley down the aisle, past Oscar Schneider, still standing at the back of the room next to a shellshocked Andrea. With a clank of the double doors beyond the foyer, Darius maneuvered him out of the building in handcuffs and into the parking lot.

Shaking his head, Colt cleared the cobwebs from his mind. He braced himself on the table and stood.

"I vote 'No'," he said.

Kildeer scoffed and scanned the crowd. "I hardly think ..."

"I vote 'No' also," echoed the thin, scratchy voice of Oscar Schneider from the back of the room. "That's two votes by valid, active board members to one. The motion fails."

As Schneider walked by Ellie, he leaned into her and muttered, "Sonofabitch, Gibson takes the charge again."

EPILOGUE

THE DIAMOND

Braden had grown two inches taller and twenty pounds heavier since the wild emergency board meeting a year earlier. Since then, during his successful 11-U season, the Springtown Bees finished one game above .500 and solidly in sixth place out of twelve.

On the same night that Jay Smalley punched Colt in the face at the now legendary meeting, Colt and Oscar Schneider orchestrated a motion to incorporate Springtown Valley as a full-fledged team in the GPYBA, as opposed to an exhibition squad. Unencumbered by a contrarian majority vote, with Jay Smalley removed from the room by Officer Wiltshire, they had free reign over Garrett Kildeer. The President of the Board couldn't even get a procedural motion to close the meeting to pass without both Oscar and Colt agreeing. And of course, they both refused to even second his motion to adjourn until they had unveiled their entire agenda.

Establishing the Bees as a legitimate competitor in the league extended full liability insurance coverage to Ellie's well-groomed private field. Their ensuing spring season culminated in their appearance in the championship game.

Colt and Braden stood by the car waiting for Ellie. Braden's white and royal blue uniform with the word BEES across the chest matched the hue of Ellie's Ford. Colt lifted his royal blue cap, with a big letter "B" in the center of it and scratched his head in the early summer heat.

"Come on Ellie," he called to her. "We've gotta go."

"Come on, Mom," Braden echoed Colt's exasperation.

From the balcony of the garage apartment, the front door to Colt's former place of residence opened. Oscar Schneider stepped out and took a deep breath of the morning air. He peered down the stairs, straining to watch Ellie face off against the broad side of the barn.

"That you making all that noise again, Missy?" he called to her.

Thwack, thwack, thwack.

"Three more," Ellie called to Colt and Braden. "Then we can leave for the game."

"Come on," Colt urged her, the keys to his truck rattling in his hand. "Last game of the season. Championship game. I can finally quit the board and name Oscar or Darius the next president."

"It's not the last game," Braden reminded him. "If we win, we move on to the states at Hershey Park."

After her final hard warm-up throw against the battle-worn wood of the garage, she turned and fired a hundred-fifty-foot strike to Braden who snatched the baseball out of the air and tucked it into his baseball bag.

Colt secured his L-screen in the back of his truck and opened the door to his cab.

"If I'm going to throw an effective batting practice, I want to make sure I'm properly warmed up," Ellie explained, readjusting her hair beneath her royal blue baseball cap, and walking toward Braden and her Ford. "Let's go show that group of big A's what we Bees are made of."

Braden lugged his baseball bag and ducked his head into the Ford with Ellie, while Colt started up his truck.

"Good luck today," Schneider called down to the trio. "Give my love to Kildeer and congratulate him in advance for finishing as the runner up in today's championship game to you guys."

The A's had finished the GPYBA regular season in third place, posting a 4-3 win in the semifinals to reach the championship game. The Bees battled their way to fourth place, upsetting the undefeated first-seeded Allentown A's in the semi-finals.

At one point, by the end of the fourth inning, the Allentown coach flagged Colt and demanded to see his roster and book of birth certificates as he couldn't believe they were all the same players from the past season.

The win against Allentown set up the cross-town showdown between the two Springtown squads at Victory Field.

As co-coach of the Bees, Ellie worked with the batters and threw most of the batting practice. A year's worth of physical therapy and fitness coaching by Phil Jones strengthened her elbow and shoulder to the near potency of her college days. Colt worked on fielding and pitching. Tommy Tremblay rejoined the team, and Andy Tremblay returned as the official third base coach.

Butch latched onto a local minor league team as a part-time talent scout. With his extra free time, he accompanied Doina in attending the games to support Colt and cheer for the Bees. Colt noticed his parents standing, hand-in-hand by the third base fence next to Darius, with his arm slung affectionately around Mara's shoulder.

The parents all dressed in royal blue Bee's t-shirts, matching the stylish golf shirts worn by the coaches and the new uniforms donated to the players by Dalton Industries. In return, Ellie draped a vinyl advertisement over the centerfield fence for Dalton's business. She added a banner for the diner in left field and Harley's Market in right.

Colt built wooden bleachers one weekend while Ellie left town to visit her aunt Gertrude's sister. Like he had with the fencing, he aimed to surprise her. But in her hectic tax-season frenzy with her three different jobs and Braden's demanding middle school homework schedule, she never noticed them until he walked her to the field one night and pointed out the new enhancement.

The sun shined brightly in the sky for the GPYBA championship game at Springtown's Victory Field. The players lined the basepaths as the Springtown Elementary Choir warbled their way through the national anthem. Braden held his hat over his heart and mumbled the words to the song. He smiled at Mikey Wiltshire's little sister, who sang in the group. He also turned to wave to Ellie as the song reached the last line *"... and the home of the brave."*

The head umpire dusted the dirt from the plate, hoisted his black chest pad into place and called "Play ball!"

By the third inning, none of the A-team players could figure out where Braden would throw the ball next. He located high and inside, followed by low and outside. When they expected a fastball, he fooled them with his changeup. When they thought he'd fire a strike, he tricked them into chasing out of the zone.

With the score tied at 0-0 in the last inning, Ronnie stepped to the plate. He faced his nemesis, Damien Smalley. With the count full, Damien hurled a hard sliding fastball. Ronnie connected and knocked the game winning hit over the fence.

After the game, Colt posed for the team picture with Ellie and the overjoyed members of the Mighty Bees. They took a second photo with the parents included.

Even at ten and eleven, the players ran to the playground like wild animals. Colt watched them through the woods. They hung from the monkey bars, leapt off the swings, and took turns down the slide. While much bigger now, they looked no different to him, than that first day when he pulled into Ellie's driveway for the first time and met little Braden at what eventually became Shaw Field.

"Both Mikey and I'll be fresh and rested up to pitch next week in the states at Hershey Park," Braden declared to Colt, before chasing Lilly around the outfield and through the woods to meet up with the rest of the players.

Colt hobknobbed with Ellie and the parents for a few minutes, giving multiple rounds of hugs and posing for additional selfies. Andrea invited the entire team to the diner. Colt declined. Instead, he raced back to the house in the pick-up truck ahead of Ellie and Braden, while they joined the team for celebratory pancakes and milkshakes.

As he pulled into the driveway, he inspected the new roof on the old farmhouse and the fresh paint job. His shoulders still ached from spending most of his spring break sprucing up the place and propping the front porch.

Probably the worst Art teacher in the history of secondary education. But I can paint alright.

He took a moment to marvel at how fresh, young, and happy the house looked. It reminded him of that first photograph he saw of the place in the Lehigh University housing office catalog.

He darted through the screen door to the kitchen and up the creaky wood stairs. He scrambled into the bedroom and fished through his underwear and sock drawer for the four little boxes he had hidden.

He ran out to Shaw Field, passed through the gate next to the twenty-foot backstop and paced down the line to first base where he placed one of the boxes right in the middle of the bag. Likewise, he left a box on second base, third, and home.

The hum of Ellie's Ford filled his ears as it glided over the freshly paved driveway. He had installed it a few weeks earlier and now missed the gravelly sound of the tires rolling over the dirt and pebbles. He trotted over to hug Braden as he emerged from the car, dirty from the game and sticky from the maple syrup.

"Mrs. Pawlecki showed us where they're going to hang our picture in the diner." Braden couldn't wait to tell Colt. "It's going to be right next to the booth we always sit in. We'll be able to look at it forever."

"We should use the one with all the parents," Colt said.

"Mom already suggested that," Braden acknowledged.

Colt gave Braden a high five and helped him with the baseball bag. Before he could address Ellie, she zipped into the screen door and disappeared into the kitchen.

"What's with your mother? Isn't she happy about the game."

"She is. She talked to me in the car about your present for your anniversary of dating."

"She did?" Colt mused. "What'd she say? Did she tell you what she got me?"

"Sort of," Braden replied with a wide grin. "It's a surprise."

Ellie returned from the kitchen. The screen door slapped the frame. She held a small square box with a gold ribbon wrapped around it.

"I'll be in my room," Braden giggled, running back into the house.

Colt eyed the present Ellie held in her hand. "I have something for you too."

"I don't see anything, Lehigh," she sassed him.

"You first."

"Because you've got nothing for me," Ellie continued to haze him. "You probably totally forgot, Frat Boy, didn't you?"

"You just have that one little box?"

"That's one hundred percent better than you did."

"Is it now?" he teased her. "Follow me."

Colt motioned to her, maneuvering toward the field. Ellie spotted the box with light blue ribbon sitting on top of the first base bag and walked over to it. She carefully unwrapped it and pulled out a bracelet with a little charm.

"A baseball bat," she exclaimed. "It's beautiful."

Colt stood and waited.

"Why'd you put it on first base?" she asked. "Think I'm going to kiss you now?"

Colt didn't reply. He stood on the mound looking at her. Ellie returned his gaze, confused, until he glanced over his shoulder at the present wrapped with a little red ribbon sitting on second base. Ellie looked around the basepaths and saw the three presents on each of the remaining bases.

"Oh, I get it," she nodded in belated understanding. "You want to get me to second base now?"

"Lafayette at its finest," Colt quipped.

Ellie opened the second present and pulled out a set of dangling earrings with little round balls at the end of two short chains. "Ah, they're baseballs. So, it's a baseball theme?"

"Just keep going," Colt smirked.

Ellie returned his smug expression and shook her head. "Little jewelry is nice. But it'll never beat what I got in my box for you."

"Keep going, Coach. I dare you to go for third."

Ellie trotted to the next base and opened the box with the purple wrapping. Standing on third base, she pulled out a necklace and smiled. "And this one has a little baseball glove on it. I've never gotten four whole presents after just one year of dating."

"I've never dated anyone for one whole year," Colt sparred with her.

Ellie sauntered down the third base line toward home plate. "Should I slide?" she joked.

She slipped the little gold ribbon off the plain white box. A velvet black box hugged the inside of the cardboard container. Nerves visibly washed across her face, draining the blood from her cheeks as she opened it to reveal a diamond ring. It protruded from its velvety bed and twinkled in the mid-day sunlight.

She caught Braden behind her filming the scene on his phone. She turned to the mound to find Colt in front of his L-screen on one knee.

"Oh my God," she yelped. "Seriously?"

"Well," Colt started to respond. "Will you..."

"Yes," she squealed and ran to the mound to hug him.

They embraced for a minute or two kissing. Once he placed the ring on her finger, he motioned for Braden to join them.

"Did you tell him, Mom?" Braden asked.

"No, Honey," she replied. "Why don't you, uh, keep filming."

She handed Colt her present, a similarly sized white box with gold ribbon. Colt looked at it, dubious, but glad that he made her open his white box with gold ribbon first.

"You can't possibly compete with my anniversary extravaganza," he said to her. "Lehigh always beats Lafayette."

"Just open it, Cowboy."

Colt removed the ribbon. He slid the top of the box away from the bottom. He fished through the blue and pink tissue paper and pulled out a grainy black and white photo. His mind struggled to comprehend.

"It's some sort of x-ray or something." Realization dawned slowly across his mind.

"It's actually called an ultrasound," Ellie replied.

"An ultrasound?" Colt asked as the wheels in his mind ground against each other.

"Yes, Lehigh. Do you know what that is?"

"It's... it's..." Colt struggled to formulate the words 'pregnant' or 'baby'.

"Oh, and by the way, Mr. Springtown Baseball Board President," Ellie smirked as she ribbed her newly established fiancé. "You're gonna need to stay on that board for at least another ten years."

ACKNOWLEDGMENTS

To my parents Greg and Jane McLaughlin for convincing me that I could accomplish anything with the right drive, ambition, and enthusiasm.

To my siblings and best friends, John McLaughlin and Sarah Campagnone for all their engagement and input into my storytelling and for sharing the creative process with me.

To my wife, Alicia and our two boys, Casey and Shane McLaughlin, for all their love and support in enabling me to focus on my writing ambitions.

To my Avon High English Teachers, Janet Singer Schwartz and Ken Lukasiewicz, who each inspired me to love crafting words and ideas into stories.

To my group of online writing friends and confidants for their guidance and encouragement, including: Dominic Breiter, H.R. Kemp, Rich Shifman, Barry Litherland, and Peter Marzano.

To my publisher, Michael Dolan, and editor, Vanessa Lanang, for their partnership, expert advice, and faith in giving me the opportunity to bring my story to the marketplace.

MEET THE AUTHOR

Greg McLaughlin lives in Greenwich, CT with his wife, Alicia. He has two adult sons, Casey and Shane. He graduated in 1991 with a degree in English, Creative Writing and a minor in Film Studies from Rhode Island College in Providence, RI.

He's written and self-published more than a dozen fictional novels and screenplays for the past twenty years. *Heading for Home*, about the struggles of a single mother, her young son and the former college ballplayer that tries to help them battle small-town youth sports politics, represents Greg's first novel published by Winding Road Stories.

Printed in the USA
CPSIA information can be obtained
at www.ICGtesting.com
CBHW010855051024
15376CB00009B/352